THE PAPER GIRL OF PARIS

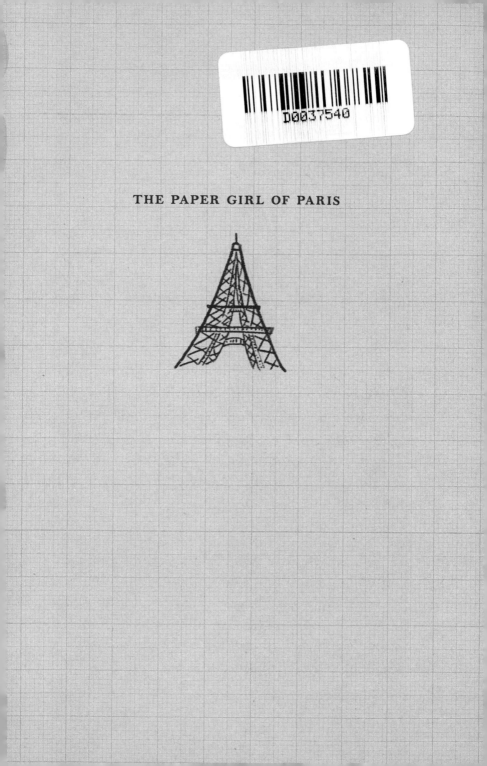

the
PAPER
girl of
PARIS

JORDYN TAYLOR

HARPER TEEN
An Imprint of HarperCollinsPublishers

HarperTeen is an imprint of HarperCollins Publishers.

The Paper Girl of Paris
Copyright © 2020 by HarperCollins Publishers
All rights reserved. Printed in the United States of America.
No part of this book may be used or reproduced in any manner whatsoever
without written permission except in the case of brief quotations embodied
in critical articles and reviews. For information address HarperCollins
Children's Books, a division of HarperCollins Publishers, 195 Broadway,
New York, NY 10007. www.harperteen.com
ISBN 978-0-06-293664-6
Typography by Jessie Gang
22 23 24 25 26 LBC 8 7 6 5 4
❖
First paperback edition, 2021

For Tim

CHAPTER 1

Alice

My family's first language is small talk. It's a fact I learned a long time ago, when I started going over to friends' houses by myself. At home, other people slip into banter like they're pulling on an old pair of sweatpants, but at the Prewitt residence, we make polite conversation like we're permanently trussed up in our Sunday best. In some ways, it's a blessing. It means we hardly ever fight, which isn't something most teenagers can say about their parents. But it can also be a curse—like right now, as we sit shoulder to shoulder in the back seat of this sweltering cab.

"So—what brings you to Paris?"

The taxi driver smiles at us in the rearview mirror. He must think we didn't hear him the first time around. But we heard him all right, loud and clear. This I know, because when he asked the question, I noticed all three of our bodies go rigid.

The ride was going well, though, given the circumstances. Dad and I listened like star pupils as the guy gave us a history lesson on Sacré-Coeur, the famous hilltop basilica off in the distance. We nodded our heads in all the right places and made empty promises to go up and watch the sunset when we could. The whole time, we kept our hands resting on Mom's legs, like she was a package meant to be handled with care.

The driver is still looking at us expectantly. He's probably wondering why the well-mannered family from New Jersey has gone silent all of a sudden. We're stuck in traffic on the boulevard Haussmann, where construction barriers are forcing all the cars into one lane. The light just doesn't want to change, so I make a point of staring down the intersection at the three white domes towering over Paris. The driver said there's only one point higher than Sacré-Coeur in the whole city, and it's the top of the Eiffel Tower. I'd give anything to be in either place right now—or really anywhere that isn't here, having to tell a stranger the bizarre reason why the three of us are in Paris for the summer.

Dad clears his throat.

"Family," he says quickly.

Mom shifts in her seat.

The light finally turns green, and we trundle on in silence. We turn off the sunny boulevard and begin weaving through shadowy streets that zigzag in unexpected directions. It seems absurd that none of us has any idea where we're headed, but then again, Gram always liked surprises and had a flare for the dramatic. She was the anomaly in our family. I reach into the pocket of my denim shorts and touch the strange brass key, wondering what in the world my grandmother was thinking before she died.

With every bump in the road, the questions rattle around my head like metal screws in a glass jar. After all these years, why did Gram still own an apartment in Paris? She left France to marry Gramps at the end of the Second World War, and she never went back. She never even talked about it. In the sixteen years I was lucky enough to have with her, I never once heard her mention her childhood. There were no old photographs in her condo, no keepsakes—nothing. Only after she died did I realize how strange it was, this massive gap in her history. Gram never held back in telling me about the times she cut work to join civil rights marches, or how she and Gramps once smoked weed on the roof of their apartment building, so it never occurred to me that she would be hiding something else. For some reason, my brain just accepted that Gram's life began when she first set foot on American soil.

We drive along a one-way street nestled between rows of uniform cream-colored apartment buildings with white shutters and tiny Juliet balconies. There are restaurants and coffee shops wedged beneath them at street level, full of people enjoying a peaceful Saturday morning. At a cross street, I spot the sign on the wall that says Rue de Marquis, 9^e Arr. Earlier in the ride, our driver explained that the "Arr" stood for "arrondissement," which is the name for the districts that divide Paris. There are twenty of them in total, and Gram's apartment is in the ninth. We're here. My heart pounds in my chest. If Mom and Dad see the street sign, they don't say anything.

The taxi driver makes the turn. We're at the mouth of a crescent-shaped street that twists sharply to the left, so you can't see where it ends. There are no shops here, only residential buildings with concave faces, keeping with the curve of the road. They aren't identical like the others we passed; there's a wide one with black shutters followed by a skinny one with no shutters at all. Finally, the driver comes to a stop in front of an ancient-looking building with a yellowing façade, stuffed between its neighbors like a snaggletooth.

"Numéro trente-six," he says.

Dad pays the fare with the euros he got from the bank, and the three of us climb out onto the sidewalk in front of number thirty-six. Surveying the building through my round tortoiseshell glasses, I note that it looks like the oldest on the block. There are cracks in the plaster and chips of paint missing from the emerald-green double doors. Dad goes to inspect the electronic keypad next to the entrance, while I hang back at the curb next to Mom. I wrap my arm around her shoulders and notice how bony they feel under her baggy gray cardigan, which she's somehow wearing despite the heat. She'd normally be in a sundress, something showing off the legs toned from hiking in the hills behind our house, but then again, she hasn't done *that* in a while either.

"You never know, Mom. This might be kind of fun."

She wraps her sweater tighter around her body and gazes up at an unspecific spot on the building. She could be smiling or wincing. It's tough to tell.

"We'll see, Alice."

Poor Mom. First she lost Gram, which was hard enough on its own, but then we read the will, and Mom learned there were things she never knew about her own mother. *Big* things. Mom has been a mess for the past two months, barely able to pull herself out of bed and get dressed for work. Dad had to remind her the fifth graders wouldn't have an English teacher if she didn't get moving. I always did what I could to make her happy when we both got home from our respective schools, like baking cookies or finding something stupid to watch on Netflix—anything to take her mind off Gram. None of it seemed to have much of an effect . . . but I'm going to keep on trying. It seems like the least I can do, given that I'm the one who ended up with this apartment.

"We're in," Dad says triumphantly, holding open the door.

It's a good thing Gram's lawyer left a note about the code in the will.

The lobby looks as old as the outside of the building, with peeling wallpaper, a dusty chandelier, and a tile floor that might have been white once, decades ago. It's mostly quiet, save for the faint sounds of footsteps coming from the floors above. Any minute now, I feel like Gram is going to jump out and yell, "Surprise!"

"Who remembers which apartment we're going to?" Dad asks. He's using the upbeat voice he typically reserves for prospective home buyers. I guess we both have our own ways of trying to cheer Mom up.

"It's number five," I volunteer.

The wooden stairs creak and groan under our feet. Mom doesn't respond to any of Dad's cheerful observations about the banisters and the crown moldings, and I wonder if he's having second guesses about relocating us to Paris for the next six weeks.

The trip was supposed to help us unwind after a difficult few months. "You two are off for the summer, and Todd's practically forcing me to take a good, long vacation now that the Willow Street mansion is out of the way," Dad said over dinner one night. (This was after we read the will.) "We can all go check out the apartment, and I'll work on settling Gram's estate while you gals explore a new city. What do you say?"

My heart thumps harder the higher we climb, until I'm sure everyone can hear it reverberating off the walls. I'm still in shock that Gram left the apartment to me instead of Mom, although it's true that we *were* very close, and I saw her a lot more than Mom did, because her condo was close to the high school; I could see it from the windows in the third-floor science lab. I would stop in to visit her all the time on my walk home; she would put out coffee and banana bread and we'd talk about whatever was on our minds, from my nonexistent love life to the latest drama in her Saturday-afternoon bridge club. And then, of course, there was that stretch of time in the first grade, back when Mom had all those doctor's appointments, that Gram would pick me up from school and make me dinner every night. We had a special bond from the start.

I remember a cold, rainy day back in February, when I was sitting at her dining room table and tracing my finger around the rim of the polka-dot coffee mug she always reserved for me. "Gram," I asked sullenly, "what does it mean if I still don't have a date for the spring semiformal?"

Gram raised one of her wispy white eyebrows. "What does it *mean?*"

"Yeah."

She snorted. "It means you haven't gotten around to asking anybody yet."

My neck and forehead are damp by the time we reach the

door with the rusty number five on it. There doesn't seem to be any air-conditioning in the building, and it's late June. Dad comes up next, with Mom bringing up the rear. We all take a moment to catch our breath. And then it's time.

"Do you want to do it?" I offer to Mom. I want her to feel like the apartment belongs to both of us.

"No thanks," she says. "You go ahead."

With trembling fingers, I take out the key. It fits into the hole and turns with a satisfying click, and I gently push open the door.

My first impression is that it smells like an old book: moldy and musty but nevertheless inviting, like it's happy that someone has finally cracked its spine. We're standing on the threshold of a foyer with paneled walls and high ceilings, but it's too dark to get a sense of any of the rooms beyond.

"H-hello?"

I don't know why I just said that. It's clear that no one is here, and that no one *has been* here for quite some time. When I step into the room, the floor feels strangely soft underfoot, and I look down to find a thick layer of dust creeping up over the laces of the purple Converse sneakers I bought with my tutoring money. The dust is everywhere: on the wooden bench next to the door, on the coatrack in the corner, probably in the stale air I'm breathing.

Mom coughs into the sleeve of her cardigan.

"I think I'll stay outside, you guys."

"You don't want to explore just a little bit?" I gesture brightly into the shadows.

"We can stay here while you go look around," says Dad, taking Mom by the hand. Mom doesn't object to this plan, so the only thing left for me to do is press deeper into the darkness.

"It's hard to see where— Ow."

After feeling my way through an archway, I bang my knee into something sturdy. A table. Carefully, I feel my way around it, until a thin strip of light tells me I've made it to a window. The curtains are stiff, but with a little effort, I manage to pull them aside, and the bright summer sunlight floods into the apartment like a tidal wave. I hear Dad gasp, and not in a fake-enthusiastic Realtor way. I turn around, and my jaw drops.

"Oh . . . my . . . god."

There's only one way to put it: We've traveled back in time. We're standing in the middle of a fully furnished apartment that hasn't been touched in . . . in who knows how long. I'm in the dining room, staring down the length of an elegant wooden table. To my right, there's a buffet with silver candlesticks and serving ware on top. Large paintings in ornate gilded frames cover the walls from end to end. The place reminds me of a movie set, only it's real—and it must have been pretty fancy back in its day, which makes me wonder how Gram could have ever lived here. She always said she was penniless when she arrived in America with Gramps, the two of them making do on one square meal a day.

Over at the door, Dad convinces Mom to venture into the apartment. On her first step, she slips on the dust and nearly falls over, but Dad steadies her just in time.

"Look at the dining room, Diane!"

"I see it, Mark."

"This isn't so bad, right?"

"Speak for yourself."

I wish there were something I could say to make it better, but I know there isn't, so I open a set of double doors and walk through to another darkened room. I follow a second strip of light to a set of curtains, drag them open, and take in the sight of a lavish living room. There's even more expensive-looking artwork in here, and an upright wooden piano that must be extremely out of key by now. I take a lap of the room, marveling at the massive fireplace and the mirror resting on the mantel. I poke one of the upholstered armchairs by the window, and a cloud of dust dances into the air. The apartment is definitely pleased to see me.

Careful not to disturb the carpet of dust on every surface, I tiptoe from room to room, wishing my eyes could look in ten different directions at once. My parents are moving at a fraction of the pace, still peering around the foyer. I explore the kitchen and a small square room with a desk and floor-to-ceiling bookshelves. In the hallway branching off from the other side of the foyer, I open a closet door to find an eerie sight: a dozen coats still hanging neatly from the racks, like ghosts standing in single file. The back of my neck prickles. The apartment isn't just ancient furniture anymore; now there's something human about it. What would make a family abandon this luxurious apartment without taking any of their stuff? And could it really have been *Gram's* family?

"Hey, Alice, come take a look at this!" It's Dad.

They're still near the door, standing by a table against the wall. There are framed photos lined up all along it, and Dad is almost done using the bottom of his T-shirt to clean the dust off them. Mom stares at the ones he's cleaned already. Her face could be made of stone, if not for the muscle twitching in her jaw.

"D-did you guys find something cool?"

"I don't get it," Mom says.

The photos are all in black and white. The one farthest to the left shows a young girl sitting on a boardwalk. She's gripping the edge of the bench and twisting slightly in her seat, like she wants you to know she'd rather be on the sand than posing in a dress for the camera. She has shiny blond hair and freckles on her nose, and she looks incredibly familiar.

"Mom, is that you?"

But it can't be. This was taken decades before she was born. In the background of the photo, there are men in high-waisted swimsuits and women in structured one-pieces that look like dresses. People are carrying parasols, for god's sake. So that means—

"It's Gram," Dad says.

It hits me out of nowhere: the tightening in my throat, the tears welling in my eyes and fogging up my glasses. I busy myself with wiping them off so Mom doesn't see me like this. I want to be strong for her right now, but *I* miss Gram, too. I miss coffee and banana bread. I miss laughing at Gram's stories about Ethel from bridge club, who always fell asleep in the middle of the game. I miss showing Gram photos of my crushes on Instagram and having her rate them without mercy. But most of all, I miss having a family member I could open up to. I talk and laugh and get along with my parents, but I never talk about *feelings* with them. They're too reserved—I needed Gram for that. I swallow hard. I feel guilty every time I have those kinds of thoughts, because I know how much Mom is suffering, and I love her. I love Dad, too. By the time I put my glasses back on, the tears are gone.

I turn back to the photographs. Little Gram is in all of them. There she is sitting cross-legged in the grass beside a picnic spread, and there she is in knee socks and a tunic, posing in front of a school.

"So do you think this apartment is . . ."

The next photo answers my question. It's Gram again, sitting at what is unmistakably the long wooden table in the other room. I recognize the paintings on the wall behind her.

Gram lived here. This was her childhood home—her *very fancy* childhood home. I don't know what else I expected it to be, but the truth is so bizarre, I can hardly wrap my head around it. Maybe the family abandoned it to escape the war. But if that was the case, why didn't they ever come back? What happened to them?

I'm mulling over dozens of new questions when I notice the girl. In the photo from the picnic, she's lying on her stomach and flipping through a book. In the one by the school, she's posing next to Gram in a matching outfit. She doesn't look familiar to me, but she has dark eyes and dark curls just like mine, only she's much more beautiful. It's an objective fact. She looks like a movie star; I look like a dork who's *maybe* kind of cute, if you squint your eyes and tilt your head to the left.

"Mom," I ask gently, "did Gram ever say she had a sister?"

"No," she says. "Apparently there's a lot your grandmother never told me."

But there's no doubt about it. They have to be sisters. Farther on down the line, there's a professional portrait of Gram, the girl, and two people who must be their parents. The woman looks immaculate in diamond earrings and a necklace with a big gemstone hanging at the base of her neck. The man is rougher around the edges, his suit a few sizes too big for his thin frame, and I notice that he's missing the last three fingers on his left hand.

Dad squeezes Mom's shoulder. "Have you ever seen a photo of your grandparents?"

"No," she snaps, wriggling away from his touch. "All I knew is they died before I was born."

I have an idea. I find an opening in the top of the frame, slide out the photo, and flip it over. Sure enough, there's writing on the back: *Maman, Papa, Chloe, et Adalyn. 1938.* Chloe was Gram's name, which means her sister had to be . . . Adalyn.

I haven't heard that name before. In my grade at school, there are five Emilys, four Hannahs, three Ashleys, and three Samanthas, but nobody named Adalyn. I like it—more than I like Alice, which sounds so mousy and uptight. There's something about the dark-haired girl that makes it hard to look away, and it isn't just that she's prettier than any other human I've seen in my life. There's a strange sort of look in her eyes, like she's analyzing the person taking her picture.

"Her name was Adalyn," I tell Mom as I hand her the photograph. She slots it back into the picture frame without so much as a passing glance. Dad runs his palm over what's left of his thinning hair. He does it whenever he's in over his head and contemplating what to say next.

"Maybe we should go get some lunch," he suggests. "Diane, what do you think?"

"That's fine with me."

My heart sinks. I'm not ready to leave yet. I want to keep exploring—I haven't even seen any of the bedrooms yet. But at the same time, I know Dad is right. This is a lot for Mom to absorb all at once, and it's better for her if we don't stick around for too long. I don't want to be selfish. With one last sweeping look at the apartment, I make a silent promise to Gram that I'll be back as soon as I can. It's probably best that I come alone next time so I can stay for as long as I want.

I follow my parents into the stairwell and close the door behind us. I left the curtains open so the light will shine in.

Sunshine streams through the window above my bed in the rental apartment. It's eight o'clock in the morning and I'm wide-awake, buzzing with anticipation.

For three long days, my parents and I have been wandering around museums and other landmarks. We saw the Louvre, the Musée d'Orsay, the Eiffel Tower . . . and the whole time, nobody said a word about Gram or the apartment. Dad and I were Prewitt-ing even harder than usual, commenting on the *magnificent* paintings and the *stunning* architecture and desperately hoping that Mom wasn't too miserable. Finally, late last night, Dad got an email from the head of the cleaning crew saying they were done removing the dust and debris, and we were free to come back whenever we wanted. The guy said he'd never seen anything like

Gram's apartment—*une capsule temporelle*, he called it.

A time capsule.

I press my ear to the paper-thin wall between my room and my parents'. They must still be asleep. Quietly, I brush my teeth, change into shorts and a T-shirt, and put on my sneakers; they're the only shoes I brought with me, because I wear them with everything. As I slip out the door, I shoot my parents both a text so they don't freak out when they wake up. All things considered, it's probably a good thing I didn't come face-to-face with Mom this morning. I mean, she *did* say that I'm free to go back to the apartment whenever I want, as long as she doesn't have to come along, but it's hard to know what she's really thinking. I wish it were easier.

Part of me feels guilty for abandoning her today, but she does have Dad to keep her company, and after seventy-two hours away, the apartment at 36, rue de Marquis is pulling me back. As I make my way on foot up the rue de Richelieu, there's something about the world around me that seems inexplicably brighter, like somebody cranked up the sun. Walking past a tiny park, I notice a fountain that must be fifteen feet high, its jets of water arcing gracefully through the air. That's one of my favorite things about Paris so far—that everywhere you turn, there's something stunningly beautiful plopped in the middle of an ordinary city block. Our Airbnb is a cramped two-bedroom apartment over a cell phone repair shop, but across the street is a gorgeous church that was built in the seventeenth century. The city is full of surprises like that.

My first stop is a coffee shop I find along the way, a place so tiny and so aromatic, you could probably get your caffeine kick just by breathing in the air. Feeling bold when I step up to the counter, I use my so-so French to order a black coffee: *"Un café noir, s'il vous plaît."*

It's my go-to order, even though it's so bitter. Whenever we go to Starbucks, my friends Hannah and Camila order pumpkin spice lattes and mocha Frappuccinos with whipped cream on top. I'll admit they taste pretty good—okay, fine, they taste amazing—but Gram taught me to appreciate coffee that isn't pretending.

When the barista hands me my order, it isn't what I expected. The cup is three inches tall, smaller than kiddie size. The coffee is sludge-like, deep brown and opaque. There's barely any of it in here.

When I take a sip, I can see why. It's the strongest coffee I've ever had in my life. It tastes like a slap in the face. Is this a trick they play on Americans? Could she tell by my accent? But looking around me, I see other people drinking it, too, no problem. How are they doing it? I'm too embarrassed to ask for something else, so I take it with me in the hope that I'll get used to it, the same way I trained myself to tolerate cilantro. Every three blocks I take another sip, but somehow, I think it's only getting stronger. When I get to Gram's street, I force myself to down the last nose-wrinkling dregs before I toss the cup triumphantly into the trash.

I climb the stairs to apartment five, turn the key in the lock, and push open the door. Wow—the cleaners did an incredible job. I can see details that used to be hidden beneath the blankets of dust: the elaborate claw feet of the dining room table and chairs, the patterns on the oriental rugs in the drawing room, Gram's and Adalyn's smiling faces in the photographs next to the front door. It's like the whole apartment shifted into focus.

I still can't believe Gram left it to me.

I could go around studying every piece of furniture in the apartment, but what I really want to do is learn as much as I can about Gram and her family. Since we read the will I've been thinking about it constantly, shutting my eyes and replaying scenes in my mind, and now I'm certain Gram was intentionally keeping secrets. I remember a couple of times when her past *almost* came up in conversation, and she cleverly managed to steer things in another direction before I realized what she'd done.

Take last March, when I asked if she would look over my homework for European History, which was a detailed map of Germany's invasions in World War II. I thought she might actually be interested, since she was alive when it happened, but Gram scanned the page for no more than a second before setting it aside and asking, "Is this the class with the boy? Has he figured out how to properly kiss a woman?"

Yes, this was the class with *the boy*. After all my stress about not having a date, Nathan Pomorski ended up asking me to the spring semiformal. He kissed me in the middle of a slow song—or rather, he suctioned his lips onto the bottom half of my face, so that my whole entire mouth ended up *inside* his. It was horrible.

"Not that I'm aware of," I told Gram. "I already told him nicely that I don't want to hang out again, but I don't think he got the message. He keeps showing up at my locker to say hi."

Gram slammed her coffee mug onto the table with a *thunk*. "So tell him he kisses like a vacuum cleaner!"

At that point, we both dissolved into laughter, and the history homework lay forgotten.

I didn't get to see the bedrooms the other day, so that's where I go first. It isn't hard to find them. Farther down the hallway where I peeked inside the coat closet, I find two doors, each with a painted sign on it. One says "Chloe." The other says "Adalyn."

There's no question about it, I'm doing Gram's room first.

Gram's room—what a weird thought. I still can't process the fact that she lived here, that her hand turned this very same rickety brass doorknob. My heart beats wildly at the thought of finding some kind of clue about her past inside.

Oh, jeez. The room looks like a hurricane came through here. Gram's closet door is wide open, and clothes are strewn haphazardly across the bed. Random shoes and books lie open on the floor. I can't imagine what it looked like *before* the cleaners got to work. Is this how Gram packed to leave for America?

Two tiny objects on top of the dresser catch my eye, and the questions I was asking myself completely disappear as my throat tightens up again.

The tears come quickly, like there's a hand squeezing my neck and forcing my feelings to the surface. I wiped them away when it happened in front of Mom, but this time, I let them flow freely down my cheeks, hot and wet and salty—a real mess of emotion. I'm a wreck . . . and I'm immediately embarrassed about it. I usually don't cry in front of anybody, including myself. It was the needle and thread on the dresser that got me, a sliver of evidence that Gram, *my Gram*, once lived and breathed in this foreign room. She worked as a seamstress when she first moved to America, before she got her degree to become a teacher. She always loved to sew, though; she even made clothes for my stuffed animals when I was little. I pick up the needle and roll it between my fingers, and amazingly, like someone draping a blanket around my shoulders, the apartment starts to feel a little more like home.

I pull myself together and get back to looking around.

On top of the clothes pile, there's a long purple dress Gram apparently didn't want to take with her. Strangely, it has a yellow star sewn to the chest that looks like it was added later. The star says "zazou" in the middle. What does that mean? I know the Nazis made Jewish people wear stars on their clothing during World War II, but Gram was Christian.

I peruse the scattered clothes some more, caressing the fabric and wishing Gram were here to explain everything to me. Why was this place such a secret, and why did she leave it to me? Why not Mom? Was there something she wanted me to find? In search of clues, I move to the chest of drawers, finding only a few stray stockings inside. Argh. Give me a sign, Gram! Stupidly, I look over my shoulder to see if anything has magically revealed itself, but the room is the same as it was when I came in.

If it's mostly old clothes in here that Gram didn't want to take with her, maybe I should look in the room next door— the one that belonged to Adalyn, the mysterious great-aunt I never knew I had. I take one last lap of Gram's room and go back out into the hall.

Adalyn's door swings open with a long, low creak.

The first thing I see, in the mottled sunlight coming in from the courtyard, is a gorgeous canopy bed with carved wooden posts. I used to beg my parents for a bed like that *nonstop* when I was in the first grade, but then Mom went through that dark phase, and I learned pretty quickly how to censor my behavior. I guess I forgot about it by the time second grade rolled around, and I haven't really thought about it since.

I scan the room, wondering where to look first. If someone went into my room back home, where would they find my most personal belongings? No question, it would have to be my desk drawer. That's where I stash all my cringeworthy poems that will never *ever* see the light of day. It's also where I keep the address Nathan gave me for his summer camp in Canada; he asked me to write him letters because there isn't any cell service there, but I haven't gotten around to it yet.

I hurry over to the writing desk under Adalyn's bedroom window, but with my fingers on the knob of the drawer, I pause. I feel like a bit of a snoop, rummaging through her things. If Mom ever opened *my* desk drawer and saw the poems I wrote a few years ago, when she was in another one of her phases, I'd probably die on the spot. But all that being said, Adalyn hasn't lived here for years—decades, in fact. Wherever she is now, I doubt this stuff is particularly important to her.

Curiosity gets the better of me, and I pull.

Inside, there are pencils, blank stationary, and a few stray coins and bobby pins. There's also a leather-bound black notebook. I flip it open to the first page, and right away, I see paragraph after paragraph of tiny cursive handwriting.

There's a date in the top right corner: *30 mai 1940*—May 30th, 1940.

My heart skips a beat.

I think I just found Adalyn's diary.

I know I'm being the ultimate snoop, but I can't resist. I'll go through their parents' bedroom later. Right now, I need Google Translate.

I check the other drawers to make sure there's nothing I missed, except for one that's jammed so tightly it won't budge. Then I hightail it back to the Airbnb, stuff my laptop into my backpack, and set out in search of a café with free Wi-Fi. I could have done this from the rental apartment, but I didn't want to risk having Mom walk in on me and get upset all over again. Thankfully, it doesn't take me long to find a quiet seat in the corner of a café; it's a gorgeous summer day in Paris, which means everyone else at the restaurant is clamoring for a table outside on the sidewalk. As soon as I connect to the internet, I prop open the diary with an elbow and begin to type the first entry into Google Translate.

"Something to eat, *mademoiselle*?"

The waiter is here to take my order.

"Oh, um . . ." I squint at the chalkboard on the wall. *"Un pain au chocolat, s'il vous plaît."*

"And would you like anything to drink?"

Yes—but I don't want to make the same mistake as I did this morning, when I tried to place my order in French. This time, I think I'll stick to English.

"Can I just have a cup of black coffee, please?"

"*Un café?*"

"Yes, thank you."

I turn back to the diary. It's slow going; sometimes it's hard to make out certain letters, and my French isn't good enough that I can make an educated guess about what the word actually is. I end up opening a second Google Translate tab where I can enter the different possibilities until an English word pops up that seems like it fits. My glasses keep sliding down my nose because I'm hunched so low over the page.

The waiter returns with my order. One flaky pastry that looks like heaven on a plate, and one—oh no. It's another tiny coffee cup. How did I let this happen again?

"*Un pain au chocolat et un café, mademoiselle.*"

Eventually I'll get to the bottom of this, but for now I thank him and get back to work. Every time I get through a particularly dense section, I reward myself with another bite of *pain au chocolat*. I love how it practically melts on my tongue.

At last, I finish going through the first diary entry. I roll out my neck and stretch my wrists. I take a minuscule sip of coffee—Jesus Christ, that is powerful—and then I read.

I have never kept a diary before.

I am starting one now because it feels like the only way I can begin to make sense of the past few weeks. If I don't write it all down, I may not believe some of the things I have seen with my own eyes.

I found this empty notebook when I was searching for bandages to wrap my feet. Uncle Gérard said I deserved to keep it after what I'd been through. So now I am writing from the attic of Gérard's farmhouse—more specifically, from the mattress that Chloe and I are to share for the time being. Who knows for how long? My sister is complaining about the cramped sleeping arrangements (as she complains about most things), but I find this dreary little attic is the only place I can hear myself think. Between Maman, Papa, Gérard, and four of his friends who also left Paris, the house is terribly crowded and the nervous energy is too much to bear.

Where to begin this wretched story? In May, the Germans invaded France. At school they always told us not to worry, that Hitler would never get past the Maginot Line, but they were wrong.

Everything happened very quickly after that. Papa said we were leaving Paris for Gérard's farm in Jonzac. We had to pack up the car as fast as we could. Maman put on three dresses and two coats and packed a carrying case of jewelry, and told Chloe and me to do the same.

She left the apartment in her most expensive pair of high heels because she didn't want to leave them behind. I wonder what became of them.

Fleeing was meant to be for our safety, but there was nothing safe about that road out of Paris. Picture a filthy, weary current of humanity stretching as far as the eye can see. Some families pushed their belongings in teetering wagons. Others had nothing but the ragged clothes on their backs. Papa drove the car for as long as he could, inching through the congestion. Eventually we ran out of petrol near Orléans. Because there was none to be had anywhere, we had to abandon our beloved Citroën like a corpse at the side of the road—many of our things still inside it—and continue our journey on foot.

We walked for three days. Our feet ached and bled. Even with all the money Papa took out of the bank, we could not find a room anywhere. We slept—or tried to sleep—in the grass beside the road. We nibbled at the bread, cheese, and sausage we had thankfully thought to pack.

There are things I saw on the road that I will never forget for as long as I live. The crowd was a living thing. It could swallow you. There were children shrieking in terror because they'd been separated from their parents. How would they ever find them again, when they were too young to know where they were going? There were elderly people splayed out on the ground because they were too weak to go on walking. Some were alive. Some weren't. I was desperate to stop and help these people, but Maman and Papa kept marching on ahead, and I couldn't lose them. I had the food.

The worst of all was when the bombers came. We were tired, filthy, starving. And then we heard the dull drone, getting louder and louder by the second. We looked up and saw German planes flying toward a section of the road up ahead of us. Three of them. At first I assumed they were heading someplace else, but then they dove with a terrible screaming sound. They shot at the people on the ground. Innocent people who had nothing—who had been walking for days. And then they were gone.

The screaming of the planes gave Papa terrible flashbacks. His whole body trembled and he struggled to breathe, so we stopped to comfort him for quite some time. My poor, sweet Papa. Before, I had only seen him like that around fireworks.

Eventually we continued our march, but he was still shaken up. Then, as we got closer to where the airplanes had attacked, I had to run off the road to be sick. There were bodies with their insides spilling out. Grown-ups screaming like animals. I will not go into more detail because I might be sick again. I despise this war, and I despise the Germans.

I need to pause for a second to remember how to breathe. I'd never heard of this mass exodus out of Paris, but it's the most sickening thing I've ever read. So is that how the apartment became abandoned—when the family fled the city for Uncle Gérard's? No . . . that doesn't seem right, because Adalyn's diary ended up back in her bedroom somehow. The family—or Adalyn, at least—must have come back to Paris.

I turn to the following page of the diary. Adalyn's next two entries are shorter than the first, and this time, her handwriting is messier. There's a sense of urgency in the lines of text darting across the page. I need to know what happened next. I press my glasses into the bridge of my nose and start typing.

June 14th, 1940

 Today Paris fell to the Germans. The men who killed all those innocent refugees are marching unopposed down the Champs-Élysées. I don't know what is to happen. Papa is hardly speaking these days. I suspect his memories of the Great War are haunting him terribly. He lost three of his fingers at Passchendaele, but that was the least of it. He also lost his younger brother, Mathieu. Gérard says things will get worse for France. Maman is hopeful things will get better. Chloe is very afraid. She fears that our home will not be there when we return. I am afraid, too, but I am trying not to show it. I love our

apartment. I love our beautiful city. I must go—Chloe is
stirring in her sleep and says she wants me to lie down
with her.

June 17ᵗʰ, 1940

It is over. France is surrendering to Nazi Germany.
Marshal Pétain spoke on the radio tonight. (He is
running the government now.) He said it is his duty to
alleviate France's suffering. He said it is time to stop
fighting.

Maman is relieved. She trusts in the Old Marshal.
Now no more men have to die for this war, she says. I
am trying to see where she is coming from, but I cannot.
It feels like the world is disintegrating. How could
Pétain make peace with the Germans? Why are we not
defending ourselves against this force of evil?

After the broadcast, Chloe and I helped each other
climb back up to our room. We lay together and wept for
a long time before we finally fell asleep.

Now I feel guilty for all the times I complained to Gram
about having too much homework—look at what she was
going through at my age! All I want to do is reach through
the pages of Adalyn's diary and comfort my grandmother.
I want to tell her it ended up okay in the end. She found
Gramps, and they had Mom, and she had me. But then I

come back to the same questions as before: What happened to Gram's family? What happened to Adalyn? Clearly, she and Gram were as close as two sisters can be. What changed? What could have possibly happened to make Gram go the rest of her life without ever mentioning Adalyn to her own immediate family?

And most importantly, did Gram want me to find the answers?

A warning appears on my laptop screen saying I only have 10 percent battery life remaining. I glance at the time, and I'm stunned to find I've been here for nearly two and a half hours. I'll squeeze in one more entry, and then I'll go back to the rue de Marquis to keep exploring. I type the first sentence into Google Translate, expecting another gut-wrenching piece of news.

But it's the opposite.

June 18th, 1940

I take back what I wrote yesterday: It is not over. There is still hope. I can hardly keep my hand from shaking!

A French general named Charles de Gaulle made a speech on the BBC tonight. He vowed that the enemy would someday be defeated, and he called on men to come join him in London. At the end, he said the most unforgettable thing: "Whatever happens, the flame of the

French resistance must not be extinguished and will not
be extinguished."

Tonight, Chloe and I shall hardly be able to sleep
from excitement.

Do you hear that? The fight is not over!

I could jump up and cheer right now, except I'd obviously never do something like that in public. But still, I feel like I'm there with Adalyn, sharing in her excitement. I brush my fingertips against the brittle page, yellowing at the edges, and I imagine a current of electricity flowing from Adalyn through the paper to me.

I've heard of the French resistance. Mr. Yip covered it briefly in our World War II unit in European History. I remember they blew things up, like German trains and certain buildings where the Nazis had taken over. I recognize Charles de Gaulle's name, too, but only because the Paris airport is named after him. It's pretty bold that he went on the radio the day after Pétain and told the people of France to do the very opposite of what their government was mandating. How would I have reacted if I were there at Uncle Gérard's farmhouse with Gram and Adalyn, huddled around the radio during those days of uncertainty? Would I have put my faith in Pétain, like their mother, or would I have rallied around de Gaulle, like Gram and Adalyn? If I had been there on the road out of Paris—if I had seen the terrible things they saw—I know where I'd stand.

I'd want to keep fighting.

Back inside apartment five, I finish my grand tour with the master bedroom at the end of the hall. It's a very elegant room, bigger than Mom and Dad's back home. There's a wide four-poster bed and a set of dressers and an old-fashioned vanity with a round mirror. On every surface, I find more framed photos of the family, and I take them in one by one. I stare into Gram's black-and-white face, missing her more with each passing second. But now that I've read Adalyn's diary, I feel a small connection to the dark-haired girl, too. We're similar, in a way. For starters, we both loved Gram. And we both tried the best we could to hold our families together.

When I'm done taking in the photos on the vanity, I open the topmost drawer. Unexpectedly, I find myself looking at a stack of magazine clippings. They must have been cut from the society pages, because they all have photos from fancy parties, and underneath, they list the names of the guests and the designers they're wearing. I pick out Adalyn's smiling face in every single one of them, surrounded by other young people in expensive-looking clothing and jewelry.

Well, I guess my great-aunt and I had our differences, too. I'm not saying that Hannah, Camila, and I are at the bottom of the social hierarchy, but we also aren't anywhere near popular enough to get invited to the parties at Katrina Kim's mansion in Short Hills. We spend our weekends trying to replicate recipes from *The Great British Bake Off*.

I sit down at the vanity to sift through the clippings. They all seem to be dated in the late thirties and early forties, which means some of these must have been printed after the Germans occupied France. That's a little odd. Adalyn's diary made it sound like France's surrender was the absolute end of the world, but judging by this photo of her and her friends at a party in October of 1942, she wasn't *entirely* miserable during the War.

The photos are all pretty similar, and I start to flip through them more quickly. But then, toward the bottom of the stack, I come upon a photo that almost makes me fall out of my chair.

This can't be real.

I don't understand.

I don't want to.

This photo was clipped from a newspaper. In it, Adalyn is sitting at a table in what looks to be an upscale restaurant. There's a white tablecloth and fancy-looking silverware. Accompanying her are six men in military attire . . .

. . . and they're all wearing Nazi armbands.

What's more, my great-aunt looks like she's enjoying their company.

I feel like I'm going to be sick.

Leaping to my feet, I drop the clippings as if they're on fire and slam the drawer closed. My brain is in overdrive trying to process what I just saw. What . . . ? How . . . ?

This must be the explanation. This is why Gram went her whole life without telling anyone about Adalyn. She was ashamed of what she became. How long had it been since they'd seen each other, or even talked? Did they go to their graves without—

Wait a second. I'm assuming Adalyn is dead, but that isn't necessarily the case.

Gram turned ninety this year. We had a party in her condo building's multipurpose room. Judging by the family photos, Adalyn was a few years older, so that would make her, what, ninety-two? Ninety-three? It's a major long shot, but it isn't completely unrealistic. Hannah's great-grandmother is 103 years old and still with it, for the most part. For all I know, Adalyn could be living right here in Paris . . . and she could be the only person left in the world who could tell me what happened to her family. My family.

Still, something doesn't feel right about this. I pace the floor with my arms crossed, thinking. Even if Adalyn *is* alive, do I really want to spend my summer searching Paris for a Nazi supporter? A voice in my head says maybe I should leave this alone—that maybe Adalyn was out of the picture for a reason. Gram loved her family; she adored Gramps, Mom, Dad, and me. If she was willing to cut ties with her own sister, then it's probably safe to assume that Adalyn was downright terrible.

Okay. . . . But why leave me the apartment, then? If Gram *really* wanted Adalyn out of the picture, why would she give me the keys—literally—to finding out who she was? And also, what about Adalyn's diary? How could the girl in that photo be the same person who witnessed the German bombers attacking innocent refugees? How could it be the same person who wrote in her diary that her world was disintegrating? The two things just don't add up. I stop pacing in front of a photo of Gram and Adalyn when they were little, no more than ten years old, their arms wrapped tightly around each other's waists. She could still be alive . . . and maybe even close by. . . . If I found her, I could get all my answers about Gram. . . .

My head feels like it's going to explode. I massage my chest to work out the tension that's accumulated there in the last few minutes, but I can't relieve the stress.

I was just seriously thinking about trying to find the person in the *Nazi photo*.

Even though I'm desperate to learn about Gram, and about this ancient apartment that somehow belongs to *me* now, I'm not ready to go there. At least, not yet. I should get what I can out of Adalyn's diary before I consider more drastic measures.

Life is so weird. Just when you think you understand something, you realize it's way more complicated than you ever could have imagined.

CHAPTER 3

Adalyn

"Girls, are you finished getting dressed? I suspect you'll want jackets; it's cool outside."

Maman's gentle voice has a sharp edge to it. She has been waiting for us in the foyer, coat on, for five minutes now, and I know she wants to hurry up and get to Madame LaRoche's dinner, now that we have to be home before curfew. I would be ready to go, except that I'm standing in the doorway of Chloe's bedroom, watching as my fourteen-year-old sister takes as long as she possibly can to locate her stockings.

"Could they be under the bed?" I ask.

"No," she replies.

"Maybe you accidentally put them in the wrong drawer."

"I doubt it."

"Are they really lost, or is that you don't want to see Maman?"

Silence.

I had a feeling. I know Chloe better than anyone else in the world, and in any case, my sister is about as subtle as a firecracker. She's never been able to disguise her emotions, and she often blurts out exactly what she's thinking at any given moment. We're complete opposites, she and I: People complain that they *always* know what's on Chloe's mind; they complain that they *never* know what's on mine. I guess I like to calculate the risk before I end up doing or saying something I'll regret.

I motion for my sister to join me on the edge of the bed, and she does, wrapping her knees up against her chest. Her blond hair falls into her face, and she blows it away with a huff.

"This is about the soldier," I say delicately. One wrong move, and she could explode.

"She shouldn't have gotten so mad at me," Chloe grumbles.

Since we returned home from Uncle Gérard's, she and Maman have been clashing even more than usual. Maman, who went to finishing school—who always knows *just* the right thing to say in any social situation—has always been the person most offended by Chloe's unfiltered behavior. The war has only magnified their differences. Maman seems to be trying to make the best of our new reality, while Chloe seizes every opportunity to show how fiercely she rejects it.

As usual, I'm caught in the middle.

A couple of weeks ago, Chloe barged into my bedroom with a fire blazing behind her eyes. She was brandishing a crumpled piece of paper she had found on a café chair, and she wasted no time in getting to her knees and smoothing it out on the hardwood floor for me to see. The title at the top said "33 Hints to the Occupied," and what followed was a long list of ways in which ordinary people could make life more difficult for the Germans.

- IF ONE OF THEM ADDRESSES YOU IN GERMAN, ACT CONFUSED AND CONTINUE ON YOUR WAY.
- IF HE ADDRESSES YOU IN FRENCH, YOU ARE NOT OBLIGED TO SHOW HIM THE WAY. HE'S NOT YOUR TRAVELING COMPANION.
- IF, IN THE CAFÉ OR RESTAURANT, HE TRIES TO START A CONVERSATION, MAKE HIM UNDERSTAND, POLITELY, THAT WHAT HE HAS TO SAY DOES NOT INTEREST YOU.
- SHOW AN ELEGANT INDIFFERENCE, BUT DON'T LET YOUR ANGER DIMINISH. IT WILL EVENTUALLY COME IN HANDY.

"Isn't it fantastic?" Chloe exclaimed. "There are people out there who want to resist, too!"

It felt wonderful to know we weren't alone. Some of the girls at school kept remarking on how courteous the German soldiers were, not to mention handsome—how you could see their muscles bulging under their gray-green uniforms. Yes, we'd all been deprived of young men to look at for quite some time, but I was never going to trust our invaders, no matter *how* polite or attractive they were. Not after the horrors I saw on the road. I traced my fingers across the "33 Hints," hardly believing the paper was real. Without thinking, I murmured, "This is ingenious."

I should have known my reaction would embolden my sister. Yesterday, Chloe, Maman, and I were riding the metro back from the post office with another box of vegetables from Uncle Gérard when a blond-haired soldier stopped us and asked for directions in German. Before Maman and I even had time to react, Chloe stepped right up to him, planted her hands on her hips, and replied, in French, "We don't understand a word you're saying, and we don't care to, either."

The first part was a blatant lie, because Chloe and I have studied German in school since we were young. The second part, of course, was completely true. The soldier seemed to recognize that Chloe had insulted him in some way, and the polite smile disappeared from his face. He was beginning to look angry—and instead of backing down, Chloe took a step closer to the man, as though daring him to fight her. Would he do it? Would he arrest her for threatening him? I was a second away from lunging forward and grabbing her when a train finally pulled into the station. Maman, the blood drained from her face, pointed at it and shouted at the soldier in German, "There is your train, sir. We are very sorry!" Then she grabbed us each by the arm and yanked us in the opposite direction.

Maman sent Chloe to her room as soon as we got back to the apartment, and she didn't come out for dinner. They probably would have gone on not speaking to one another for much longer, had Madame LaRoche not invited us to her dinner tonight.

I place my hand on Chloe's knee.

"Maman was just trying to protect you. She didn't know how the soldier would react."

"She was trying to accommodate him!"

I sigh, because Chloe isn't entirely wrong. Maman *could* stand to be a little less friendly to every German officer we pass in the street. But at the same time, Chloe needs to stop letting her one-track mind get in the way of her better judgment. Sometimes I want to grab her by the shoulders and shake her. She would run into so much less trouble if she learned how to be subtle every now and then.

"Just try to be more careful, okay?"

Chloe groans. "You don't understand, Adalyn."

"I don't understand what?"

"How desperate I am to fight back in some way. It's like I can't sit still. I have to do *something.*"

I resist the urge to defend myself against Chloe's accusation.

Of course I want to fight back. Of course I want to do something—in fact, I *have* done something. I just had the sense to go about it discreetly, unlike Chloe's careless performance on the metro.

Uh-oh. I just heard the unmistakable sound of Maman's high heels click-clacking down the hallway. Quickly, I take Chloe by the arm and whisper, "I'm on your side, Chloe. Always. Now let's just try and get through this ridiculous dinner without any issues."

Just then, Maman's head appears around the doorframe. Her cheeks are flushed from waiting inside with her coat on for so long.

"Girls, I feel dreadful making our friends wait for us. Chloe, where in heaven's name are your stockings?"

I squeeze Chloe's arm. Begrudgingly, she goes over to the dresser and procures a pair of silk stockings from the same drawer she's kept them in her whole entire life.

"Found them," she announces.

As Chloe and I pull on our jackets, Papa shuffles out of his study to see us off. His whiskers are rough against my cheek when he kisses me goodbye. There was a time when Papa would join us on a night like tonight, but my father hasn't left the apartment very much since we returned. He's taking an indefinite leave of absence from the university, where he used to be chair of the history department. He also hasn't laughed much, or even *talked* much; he's a shell of his old self.

"I expect I'll be in bed before the three of you return," Papa says.

Maman steps forward and smooths Papa's rumpled edges, starting with his hair and moving to the creased collar of his housecoat, as though she's holding him together with her hands. When her hands pause at his cheeks, Papa turns his head to kiss her palm.

"There's soup on the stove, my love," says Maman.

"Odette," Papa replies, "you are as wonderful as ever. Thank you."

"I'll miss you very much."

"I'll miss you, too."

They share a kiss goodbye. When I get married some-day, I want us to be like my parents: two people who love each other fiercely, even in the most difficult of times. Papa gives us his two-fingered wave as he closes the front door behind us.

Maman and Madame LaRoche have been best friends since they were schoolgirls. Madame LaRoche was the one who introduced Maman to Papa, the quiet but charming professor who had fought in the same regiment as Monsieur LaRoche during the Great War. Madame LaRoche divorced her husband a couple of years ago, and she's since devoted the bulk of her time to planning lavish dinner parties for her expansive circle of friends.

Before the war began, I enjoyed going to these dinners.

It was a chance to see my two dearest friends, Charlotte and Simone, whose parents were also close to Madame LaRoche. But I haven't seen either of them for months now; Charlotte's family had the forethought to board a ship to South America last winter, and Simone's family is staying at their vacation home in Marseilles, in the Free Zone. Tonight, the only other people my age will be the LaRoche twins, with whom I have absolutely nothing in common. Thank goodness for Chloe.

"Odette! Adalyn! Chloe!"

Madame LaRoche is a vision in deep blue silk and diamonds. She kisses each of us in turn as we step through the door of her penthouse apartment on the rue du Faubourg Saint-Honoré. "You three look ravishing. These tough times are treating you well."

"We're making do as best we can," Maman replies as a maid arrives to take our coats.

With a twirl, Madame LaRoche guides us down the mirrored hallway to the drawing room, where her seventeen-year-old daughters, Marie and Monique, sip champagne on the divan. Madame LaRoche has a long face and large teeth like the horses she grew up riding, and her daughters look exactly the same, only younger. They greet us in unison. At their feet, the coffee table is set with a silver tray of bread, cheese, and butter. Maman's eyebrows disappear into her perfectly coiffed bangs.

"Ooh, Geneviève, look at all that butter! Wherever did you get it?"

But everybody knows where Madame LaRoche got all that butter. She must have purchased at least half of these items on the black market, because there's no way she got this much food on the rationing system the Germans have in place. I'm almost certain Maman has been doing it, too—just the other day I saw her returning home from the market with a very suspicious quantity of salted beef and Papa's favorite cognac.

Madame LaRoche smiles mischievously as she slathers butter on a small chunk of bread and pops it into her mouth. "You just have to know where to look," she says in a low voice.

Chloe sniffs.

Madame LaRoche doesn't seem to notice. "It's a shame Henri couldn't come tonight. We would have loved to see him."

Maman sighs. "He wishes he could have joined us, but he isn't well enough, unfortunately. He sends his regards to the three of you."

"It's his nerves, still?" asks Madame LaRoche.

"I'm afraid so. The nervous spells used to happen occasionally, but since May, they've been constant. Even the sound of their boots going by is difficult for him. . . ."

Madame LaRoche frowns and rubs Maman's arm. "That must be difficult for you, too, Odette."

Maman's smile twitches, betraying a hint of the sadness underneath. I know it breaks her heart to see Papa suffering. When his nerves are at their worst, she sits by his side and holds him until the panic subsides, whispering words of comfort into his ear.

After smoothing her skirt, Maman rearranges her face and straightens her posture. "The best thing the girls and I can do is remain positive," she says, her eyes flitting to me for reassurance. I nod supportively, not because I agree about being positive, but because I know how badly she wants to help Papa. "We have to show him there's nothing to be frightened of," Maman continues. "That we can get through this, just as we got through the last war."

"Precisely," says Madame LaRoche. "Especially with the Old Marshal on our side."

"Yes. Marshal Pétain saved France in the Great War, and he can do it again," Maman says firmly. "If he says cooperation is the best way forward . . . then we must trust him."

"I agree," says Madame LaRoche.

She dabs at her lips with a cloth napkin and I can already sense the pendulum of conversation swinging in my direction before she twists toward me. "So, Adalyn, tell us: Any exciting young men in your life these days?"

It's always the first thing Maman's friends want to know about me.

"Nobody at the moment, Madame LaRoche," I reply.

"Although I haven't been in the mood for romance, anyhow."

She shakes her head and sighs. "If only our poor men could come back home. . . ."

Thanks to the war, there are hardly any young men left in Paris these days, besides the ones who are still in school. It's a tragedy, and *not* because I haven't any romantic prospects. Those who went off to war are either dead now or being held in German prisoner-of-war camps. Our downstairs neighbor, Madame Blanchard, hasn't had word of her son since he was captured at Dunkirk in June. She looks thinner every time I see her.

Marie leans into the center of the room. She rolls the stem of her champagne glass between her fingers.

"You know, some of these Germans are rather attractive," she confesses.

"You're only saying that because you haven't seen our *own* men for so long," Monique says.

"Perhaps," Marie muses. "They certainly don't have that French charm, but they really *are* handsome. And more polite than you'd think. One of them helped me pick up my spilled groceries the other day."

"I'm sure all our men in POW camps would be happy to hear it," my sister mutters under her breath.

"What was that?" asks Madame LaRoche.

Maman shoots Chloe a warning look. "Adalyn," she says, "why don't you play us something on the piano?"

I get to my feet without hesitation, flexing my fingers. I've been playing since I was eight, taking lessons twice a week with a woman, Mathilde, who lives near the school. I like to practice on our little piano at home, the same one Papa grew up playing before his injury, but there's something extraordinary about sitting down at a gleaming grand piano like the one in the corner of the drawing room. In happier times, I would bring my song books to Madame LaRoche's and play for hours.

As I open the piano bench and sift around for something to play, I hear Madame LaRoche's voice.

"Is she still taking lessons, Odette?"

"She was, but her teacher is in the Free Zone now. Adalyn, what did Mathilde say in the last letter you received from her?"

"That she was looking at getting a permit to return to Paris," I reply.

"I hope she is successful," says Madame LaRoche. "A talent like yours shouldn't go to waste."

I find the score for one of my favorite pieces, Mozart's Piano Sonata no. 16 in C major. Papa introduced me to it; he said the sound reminded him of springtime.

As my fingers begin to dance across the keys, I let the fluttering notes transport me to a dinner party Madame LaRoche threw early last year; Papa was with us, and we talked and laughed late into the evening, as nobody had to be home before any sort of curfew. We stopped to listen to a band of street musicians on the way home, and Papa asked Maman to dance right there on the sidewalk. My eyes drift toward the window, but of course, the curtains are pulled shut so the light can't seep out. Somewhere out there stands the Eiffel Tower with a Nazi flag flying on top. Everything in Paris has changed, and I can't help but wonder if we'll ever be so carefree again.

At half past six I finish playing and we migrate to the dining room, where the staff lays out a meal of lamb and potatoes.

Amid the clinking of cutlery, we hear a car go by in the street below, and our six sets of eyes dart toward the window. The everyday purr of an engine has taken on a hair-raising quality, for it's not the French who drive cars these days. Nobody takes another bite until the sound has faded away.

Madame LaRoche looks across the table at Maman. "When you arrived, did you notice all the Germans on our street?"

"Yes, Chloe was quick to mention it," Maman replies a little pointedly. "There certainly seemed to be more of them than normal."

"No number of Germans is normal," Chloe interjects.

Maman pretends not to have heard her. "Is there a reason for it, Geneviève?"

"There is," says Madame LaRoche a bit nervously. She

glances toward the window again. "The Germans have been moving into a number of homes in the Eighth. Some of the places they stay in like houseguests; others they seize altogether."

I shudder at the thought of a German in our home—his boots on the carpet, his jacket hanging over the chair in Papa's study. A classmate of mine, Anette, has one of them staying with her family. He claimed the master bedroom, which forced Anette's parents to sleep in *her* bedroom, which forced Anette to squeeze into bed with her two little sisters. "It's lucky that you were spared," I say to Madame LaRoche.

"It's the first time we've been happy to have one of the smaller apartments on the block," she admits. "But as I've been saying to the girls, just in case it *does* happen, we must try to keep a positive attitude about these Germans. It's like you were saying, Odette: There's nothing to be frightened of."

"A positive attitude is the best way to get through this," Maman says in agreement.

"And in any case, they aren't all big bad wolves," Madame LaRoche says. She waits until she is satisfied that everybody at the table is listening, and then she launches into a story. "I was walking home with my shopping the other day, and it was so sunny out, so I thought, Why don't I take the long way home and enjoy the weather? Well, I turn the corner, and the first thing I see is my favorite bistro—a place I've been eating at since I was a little girl—with German signs

on it. Some ridiculous long name. And I didn't recognize anyone inside—they were all men in uniform. And, well, it just
hit me like a train. I can't explain what came over me—I was
weak in the knees! I thought I might faint right there in the
middle of the road!

"But then I feel a hand on my shoulder, and I look up into
the face of a *German*. I tell him, 'No, no, please leave me be'—
I'm already frazzled enough—but he invites me to sit down
at a table with him. I didn't want to be rude, so I obliged,
and I have to say, we ended up having a pleasant enough conversation. He spoke excellent French, and he told me what a
beautiful city we live in. He even asked for sightseeing rec-
ommendations."

"*And* he gave you the champagne," Marie points out.

"Yes," Madame LaRoche says with a mischievous smile,
raising her glass. "And he gave me the champagne."

Across the table, Chloe bristles.

With a smile plastered to my face, I listen as Marie and
Monique muse about the other rationed items they could try
to get from the Germans. I wonder how they would react if
they knew what I did on Friday. It's the kind of thing people would expect from Chloe, maybe, but never from me, the
one who typically follows rules to a tee. I keep the memory
to myself, turning it over and over like a shiny coin in my
pocket.

. . .

Back at the apartment, when we've both changed into our pajamas, Chloe flops face-first onto my bed.

"That was terrible," she moans into the comforter.

Gingerly, I lie down next to her, thinking about how to respond. Chloe is my best friend in the world—closer to me than Charlotte and Simone combined—but these days, it's hard to know how much of myself I should share with her. I know the way she is, and my worst fear is that I'll somehow encourage her to do something reckless and stupid again, like confronting another Wehrmacht officer head-on. Yesterday she got away with it, but the next time it could be different.

"I agree that parts of it were terrible, but it wasn't *all* bad," I say.

Chloe flops over onto her back like a fish on dry land, disbelief written across her face.

"Yes, it was *all* bad! I had to sit there and listen to stupid Madame LaRoche go on about how much she loves the Germans. She probably *wants* one of them to move in with her. More champagne to go around!"

"Chloe . . ."

"Why doesn't everybody hate the Germans like I do? Why doesn't everybody feel this . . . damn . . . angry?" She flings a pillow across the room, and it knocks over a pile of books next to the window. "Why don't you feel this angry, Adalyn? You just sit there all the time with that smile on your face."

"I don't know, Chloe." I fidget with the hem of my night-gown because I can't look her in the eye. Then, smiling wryly, I say, "The day the war is over, I'm going to tell Madame LaRoche she's insufferable."

Chloe and I made up a game when we were cooped up at Uncle Gérard's farmhouse last spring. The rules are simple: You go back and forth naming all the fun things you can't wait to do when the war is over.

Chloe rolls her eyes. "You know you could do that now, don't you?" But then, grinning back at me, she says, "I'm going break every bottle of champagne the German soldier gave her."

Soon, she and I are listing our grand plans: eating *pains au chocolat* until our stomachs hurt. Riding to the top of the Eiffel Tower on the lift, which is currently out of service. (Someone sabotaged its wiring so the Germans would have to carry their flag up on foot.) Strolling along the bank of the Seine in the evening and marveling at the blanket of light over Paris—"with a handsome boy," Chloe adds.

"Yes. With a handsome boy."

When Chloe finally leaves half an hour later, I am relieved. I feel like I've been holding my breath this whole time. I race to my desk drawer and pull out the leather-bound black note-book I found at Gérard's. It's been helpful to have a diary around. These days, it's the only place I can be completely honest about how I feel.

I begin to scribble out an entry about Madame LaRoche's dinner. Chloe was right: It *was* terrible. It was one thing for Maman to keep her spirits up for Papa's sake, and to trust in Pétain, the old French war hero; many who lived through the Great War still hold him in high regard. But it was another thing *entirely* for Madame LaRoche to speak so favorably of some polite German she met—and for Marie to be *attracted* to them. How could they look at the Germans and see anything besides evil infesting our streets? As soon as the tip of my pencil touches the paper, a floodgate opens. The anger spills out like a roiling river. It washes over everything around me.

When I'm done, I collapse onto the pillows, spent but at least somewhat calmer now. I've been writing about nearly every wretched aspect of our new reality, from fleeing Paris in the throng of refugees to returning home to find my beloved city with the life sucked out of it. I write about the curfew and the rations and the shock of seeing Germans in the places that used to be *ours*. It feels good to let it out—sometimes.

Other times, the diary isn't enough to contain my rage.

Two days ago, Friday, I was walking home from an after-school study session when I spotted three German soldiers around fifty paces ahead of me, snickering. The sound of it made my blood turn to ice. I sensed right away that it was cruel laughter, for they all had mean looks in their eyes, and one of them was jabbing his finger at something across the street.

It was a terrible sight. Monsieur de Metz, the friendly man who owns the neighborhood kosher grocery store, was kneeling helplessly on the ground in what I first thought was snow but was in fact hundreds of thousands of tiny shards of glass. Someone—or three, more like it—had smashed in the front window of his shop. Looking back on it now, I wish the LaRoches could see what some of their polite Nazis are *really* like.

Instinctively, I dropped my book bag to go help him. But just then, Monsieur de Metz looked directly into my eyes. (The soldiers were too busy laughing to take notice.) With a quiet sense of urgency, the grocer gave me a look and a twitch of the head that seemed to say "thank you" and "you should get out of here" all at once. I nodded at him, not wanting to make it worse, then scooped up my bag and hurried down a side street before the soldiers knew I'd ever been there.

I trembled with anger as I made my way down the side street, away from Monsieur de Metz's vandalized store. In that moment, I was fed up with putting on my polite smile around Maman and her friends—around *anyone*, really. I felt as though I couldn't do it anymore. Not when things like *that* were happening in Paris. The next thing I knew, tears were flowing freely down my cheeks.

When I looked up from the ground, I noticed the awful

German posters hanging along the brick wall to my right. The smiling blond-haired families with swastikas hovering around their heads. Adolf Hitler—the Germans' Führer—hoisting a Nazi flag into the air. My rage was too powerful to contain. I wanted to destroy them. And there was nobody around to see me do it.

The paper came off the wall with a satisfying rip. In one fell swoop, months of pent-up fury exploded from my fingertips. The first one felt so good, I couldn't possibly resist a second. Two became three and then four, and pretty soon, I'd torn down every damn Nazi poster in the whole alleyway. I was panting by the time I reached the end, my nails jagged from being raked across the brick.

That's when I heard the clicking of boots behind me. My stomach turned over. Somebody must have heard me.

I felt like a mouse in an open field with hawks circling overhead. My heart throbbed behind my eyes. My whole body pulsed with fear. Think, Adalyn. I wouldn't make it to the end of the alley in time to get away. Panicked, I dove into the small dark space behind an abandoned automobile and stuffed the torn posters into my book bag.

I could still hear the boots. Quiet as a shadow, I stole a glance around the hood of the car. Sure enough, a German soldier had entered the side street with two hands clasped around his rifle. Please turn back around. Please.

"Wer ist da?" Who's there?

This was it. I was sure of it. He was going to find me with the ruined posters. He was going to drag me out of my hiding place and send me to prison, if he didn't just kill me on the spot. I pictured the faces of Maman, Papa, and Chloe. Uncle Gérard and Charlotte and Simone. I would never see any of them again. I shrank back into the darkness and tucked my knees against my chest. I thought about being small enough to seep into the cracks between the bricks or the spot beneath a pebble. I didn't move. I hardly breathed.

His boots must have been within two meters of my hiding spot when more German voices called to him from the street. For a moment I feared they would join him in his search, but then, with a rush of relief unlike any I'd ever felt, I heard the first soldier turn on his heel and hurry back the way he came.

I wasted no time exiting the alleyway and tossing the papers into a sewer grate, where they disappeared forever. When I got home, I kissed my parents and chatted with Chloe about school that day. I practiced piano. I didn't say a word about what I'd done.

Nobody had any idea.

CHAPTER 4

Adalyn

That first time I tore down the Nazi posters, it nearly ended in disaster.

But the next time I do it—and the next time, and the next time, and the time after that—it goes off without a hitch. The more I do it, the better I get at slipping into the shadows when nobody's watching and quickly tearing the paper off the walls. Every time, I hear General Charles de Gaulle's message about the flame of French resistance playing in my head. Each successful operation feels like the tiniest victory for France, even if I'm the only one who knows I'm doing it.

It's a Saturday, and Maman has sent me with the family's ration cards to see what I can get from the butcher for tonight's dinner. The Germans—or *les boches*, as everyone calls them—are always closing off random sections of road, so every trip out of the apartment becomes an exercise in reorienting myself to my surroundings. Each day I wander down new streets with German signs bearing down on me; I see grand boulevards devoid of all cars and hungry people queuing for rations that may or may not be there. But what's even more harrowing, I think, is the *sound* of the Occupation. The silence sends chills down my spine. There's none of the usual automobile traffic; none of the same hustle and bustle of daily life. Only feet shuffling on the pavement and fearful whispers.

I'm nearly at the butcher's when I see them plastered on the wall of an alleyway: a fresh batch of posters. My chest tightens and my fingertips twitch. I want to take care of them so badly, but if I don't get in line now, there will almost certainly be nothing left for me when I get to the window. And so I take my spot at the end of the line, behind dozens of pale-faced mothers with hungry children swarming their knees.

An hour goes by before the butcher's window even comes into view. I have my sad ration book ready, filled with square coupons for the different food items. When I finally reach the front of the line, the butcher takes but one of my four coupons and tips a single rather skinny sausage into my basket.

"That's all for today, I'm afraid," he calls to the rest of the people in line.

The woman directly behind me lets out a short, sharp wail. I've been so focused on the posters this whole time, I never really took a look at her. She has four young children gathered about her waist, and her legs are bare and shivering in the late-November air. These days, it's impossible to find silk stockings for under 300 francs.

I place the sausage in her shopping basket.

"You should take it," I insist, and relief washes over her face. The wasted hour I spent in line gnaws at me, but so does the idea of taking this last meat ration when I know we have another package from Gérard stuffed with bacon, cheese, and vegetables. I'll tell Maman there was nothing left for me.

My empty basket swinging at my side, I hurry back to the alleyway as fast as I can without drawing attention to myself. There it is, coming up on my right, closer and closer now. At last, I dart into the gap between buildings as swiftly as a cat.

Uh-oh. This is not what I was expecting.

There's somebody else in here—a boy. And he's doing something to one of the posters. I wonder if I should slip back out to the street, unseen. But then the boy steps back from the wall, and I see that he's drawn an unusual symbol in chalk right on top of Hitler's face. It's a cross, but with two horizontal lines instead of one. My heart leaps. I need to know more. I take a step closer to him, and the boy looks up and realizes he's not alone.

He's about my height, with close-cropped brown hair and thick, circular glasses. His round cheeks are flushed pink. For some reason, he doesn't run—but he still looks apprehensive.

It's on me to make the first move, and I decide to take the risk.

"I can't stand them," I say, nodding to the posters.

"Nor can I," he replies.

We're testing each other, I think. A part of me knows it's dangerous to speak ill of the Germans to a complete stranger, but a larger part desperately needs to know what the boy was drawing.

"Sometimes I tear them down," I admit. "That's what I came here to do."

He relaxes his stance. In fact, he looks impressed.

"Really?" he asks. "Have you ever been caught?"

"Only just now, I suppose."

The boy smiles at that, so I press on.

"I must know . . . what is that symbol you drew there?"

"It's the Cross of Lorraine," he replies. "It means I support de Gaulle."

"De Gaulle!" I can hardly believe it. I nearly drop my basket. "I heard his radio broadcast in June!"

And then, as if on cue, we recite it at the exact same time:

"Whatever happens, the flame of the French resistance must not be extinguished, and will not be extinguished."

His face splits into a grin.

"I'm Arnaud Michnik."

"I'm Adalyn Bonhomme."

We shake hands.

Then he asks, "Hey, Adalyn, did you hear what happened

the other day? At nine twenty p.m. a Jew killed a German soldier, cut him open, and ate his heart."

I freeze. "Excuse me?"

"It's a joke, I promise."

"It sounds unkind to Jews," I snap.

"Adalyn," he implores, "*I'm* Jewish."

His smile is kind, not cruel, so I cross my arms and let him go on.

Arnaud makes a dramatic show of clearing his throat and continues with his joke: "What I just said is impossible, you see, for three reasons. A German has no heart. A Jew eats no pork. And at nine twenty p.m., everyone is home listening to the BBC."

I laugh—and it's the kind of laugh that comes out when you haven't laughed in a very long time. A laugh that's also relief and desperation all rolled into one. Then, looking over my shoulder to make sure no one's coming, I go to the wall, tear down a poster, and stuff it under the cloth at the bottom of my basket.

"That's clever, hiding the evidence in there."

"No one ever suspects a young girl with her shopping."

I move down the alleyway with Arnaud at my side, delighted to have a partner in crime for the first time. It takes some of the pressure off to have somebody stand on lookout while I yank down one poster after another. I would never have the guts to do this with Chloe; not only would I never want to put her in any kind of danger, but I also suspect she would tear down the posters and then run down the street waving them above her head victoriously.

No sooner do I tear the last poster from the wall than I want to know when we can do it again, but I don't know how to ask Arnaud. I don't know if this fifteen-minute operation meant as much to him as it did to me. To meet someone outside my own family who shares my views . . . it's like being lost at sea and finally spotting land on the horizon.

"I want to do more of this," I tell him point-blank.

"Walk with me to the metro station?"

What am I to make of that response? But I'll do whatever it takes to keep this ship on course, so I follow him out onto the sidewalk, where we fall into step like old friends. Two German soldiers walk past us—one of them even brushes up against my shopping basket—but they don't pay us any mind. How thrilling it is, to be hiding in plain sight!

"You should meet my friend Luc." He says it as casually as if he were commenting on the weather.

"Who is Luc?"

"Someone who thinks the same way as you and me."

"Why should I meet him?"

We've already made it to the entrance of the metro. He pulls me to the side to avoid the current of passengers.

"I shouldn't give you any more details. Just talk to him, okay?"

"Okay." My heart races as I run through my schedule. Monday, I know we're seeing the LaRoches. "I could talk to him on Tuesday, after school lets out."

"Tuesday." He nods. "There is an old shoe store on the boulevard Saint-Michel, right near the southern tip of the Luxembourg Gardens. It has a purple awning—you can't miss it. Wait on the bench outside at half past five, and he'll come and get you. He'll ask you if you made it there okay. Tell him, 'The trains ran smoothly.' Then he'll take you inside."

"'*The trains ran smoothly*'? Arnaud, what does that mean?"

"Just say it. Trust me. I have to go—it was nice meeting you, Adalyn."

"Arnaud, wait. . . ."

But he pecks me on the cheek and disappears down the steps of the metro, leaving me shivering and alone on the sidewalk. It all happens so fast that by the time I get home and tell Maman that the butcher ran out of meat, a part of me is wondering if perhaps I imagined the whole thing.

At school on Tuesday, I can barely focus. I say the same four words over and over again in my head, so I'll be primed for this afternoon: *The trains ran smoothly. The trains ran smoothly. The trains ran smoothly.* It must be some kind of password— but what for? When I meet Chloe at our usual spot after the final bell, I tell her Marie and Monique LaRoche are practically forcing me to come shopping with them for some new jewelry. As I predicted when I concocted this lie, Chloe seems relieved she was spared, and says she'll see me at home.

You can't trust the metro these days. The Germans have been closing down stations without warning, making it impossible to know if you'll ever get to where you're going. I don't even know who this mysterious Luc is, but for some reason, the thought of missing my appointment with him makes my stomach turn over, so I complete the cold hour-long journey on foot. By the time the purple awning comes into view, my eyes are watering and my nose is almost certainly the color of a ripe tomato.

I take a seat on the bench outside, wondering which direction Luc is going to come from. I don't even know what he looks like, or how old he is. Only now does it occur to me that I might have wandered into some kind of Nazi trap to catch the people defacing their posters, but I can't bring myself to get up and leave. I barely know Arnaud, and yet I'm certain I can trust him. I pull my jacket tighter around my body and hunch my shoulders up to my ears. Now that I've stopped moving, the cold air is making me tremble.

Or am I just nervous?

I steal a glance at my watch. It's twenty minutes past five. Any minute now . . .

A bell tinkles overhead, and the door of the shop swings open. *This is it. Stay calm.* A middle-aged woman in a long brown fur coat exits the shop and adjusts her scarf. She looks

at me for a moment, but then her eyes keep sliding toward the
street beyond. She sets off without a word, her shopping bag
dangling from her elbow.

A false alarm.

By now, my heart is hammering inside my chest. In two
minutes, it will officially be half past five. It's too nerve-
racking to keep jerking my head left and right, so I fix my
eyes on the second hand of my watch as it counts down the
final minute. It's so quiet outside, I can actually hear it. *Tick.
Tick. Tick.*

The bell tinkles again. Probably another oblivious shop-
per.

"Did you make it here okay?"

My breath catches in my throat, and I look up into the
dark brown eyes of a boy around my age. He's dressed in a
school uniform, but there's something about him that's more
rugged than I'm used to. His messy black hair falls down into
his eyes and curls beneath his ears. Every angle of his face
is defined, geometric. It takes me a second to remember I'm
supposed to speak now.

"The trains ran smoothly."

He smiles approvingly, and I think I may slide right off
the bench. He opens the door of the shop and motions for me
to come inside, and gently I get to my feet, praying I've done
everything correctly so far.

The store is small and dark and smells strongly of leather

and shoe polish. There is a man at the counter who doesn't look up when I enter. If Arnaud tried to choose the most random place in Paris for a covert meeting, then he succeeded. Without saying a word, the black-haired boy leads me on a winding path between the shelves, until finally we emerge in a tiny corner at the far end of the shop. He fishes a key out of the pocket of his blazer and uses it to unlock the door in front of us.

I follow him into an austere space about the size of my bedroom. There are a half dozen mismatched spindly chairs, a table, and a stack of boxes against the wall to my left. A single light bulb hangs from the ceiling. There's another door in the center of the far wall.

The boy turns the key in the lock behind us.

"You can go ahead and take a seat."

I mimic him in dragging one of the chairs into the middle of the room, and then we sit down facing each other, about a meter of space between us.

He looks me plainly in the eye.

"I'm Luc," he says.

"Adalyn," I reply.

"I heard you met my friend Arnaud."

"Yes, on Saturday. He said I should meet you."

"Did he say why?"

"No. Only that you think the same way I do."

Luc makes himself comfortable, propping an elbow on the

back of his chair and crossing his legs. He asks, "What do you suppose he meant by that?"

"I don't know what he meant, exactly." I'm still sitting rigid as a board in my seat, and I have to remind myself to exhale. Then I take another breath. "The only thing I know for certain is the feeling I get when I wake up and see the Nazi flag hanging over *our* city . . . and the women queuing for rations that aren't there . . . and the soldiers snapping up everything there is to buy in our shops."

"And what feeling is that, Adalyn?"

Luc is so good-looking, it's hard to maintain eye contact, but I mustn't seem nervous. If he decides I'm not right for this—if he casts me out of this world I've only just discovered—I don't know how I'll be able to go on. It'll feel like being shaken awake from the most wonderful dream and knowing I'll never be able to return.

"It's like there's a fire burning inside me, and if I don't do something to fight back, it might consume me. That's why I tear down their posters. I have to do something. How can I not?"

I'm breathing heavily now, and I suddenly realize I'm sitting on the edge of my seat. What is Luc thinking? Instead of responding, he's just surveying me, tilting his head this way and that as though he's examining a painting.

"You look familiar," he says at last. "Do you live around here?"

"No. My family lives up in the Ninth Arrondissement. Near the opera house."

He raises his eyebrows.

"Nice neighborhood. Expensive, though."

I don't know what I'm supposed to say to that, so I look down and fidget with my bracelet. Oh no—now I've drawn his attention to the silver Cartier bangle Maman gave me for my birthday last year. When I turn my gaze back to Luc, a look of understanding is spreading across his face.

"You're in all those fashion magazines. They're always printing your picture in the society pages," he says. "My grandmother reads them all the time and leaves them lying around the house. She loves to see what the women are wearing. That's where I've seen you before, isn't it?"

I brace myself for the note of judgment to work its way into his eyes, but it never does.

"My mother takes me along to all sorts of parties," I confess.

Luc raises an eyebrow. "Does she know that you're destroying Nazi propaganda in your spare time?"

"No," I reply quickly. "Nobody does, except for you and Arnaud."

He leans forward and rests his elbows on top of his knees, narrowing the space between us in one swift movement.

"Can I trust you, Adalyn?"

I will myself to stare into his eyes.

"Yes."

For a few agonizing seconds, he simply looks back at me. And then he stands up.

Oh no. Is it over? Am I being dismissed without ever learning why I was here to begin with? Our entire meeting flashes before my eyes, but nothing jumps out as the point where it all went wrong.

Then, right as I expect him to pull out the key and usher me back into the store, Luc goes to the stack of boxes instead. He opens the lid, pulls out a large envelope, and returns to his seat.

"Arnaud was right. I *do* think the same way you do," he says softly. The shadows cast by the light bulb make the lines of his face even more distinct, and for a moment, I have the unusual urge to lay my hand against his cheek. He continues. "I've been looking for trustworthy people like you and me— people who want to resist. We need to get our message out to as many people as we can."

"And our message is . . ."

"That not everybody in France is willing to collaborate with the enemy. That plenty of us are still fighting, with no plans to stop."

"Tell me what I can do."

Luc holds up the envelope he got from the box.

"These tracts are printed with De Gaulle's cross. You can spread these everywhere you can, in places where people will find them. On the metro. In mailboxes. In your school lavatory. And you must make it all happen without being seen. Can you do that?"

"Yes."

I shall have to find a way to do all this without my family growing suspicious.

Instead of handing me the envelope, Luc slides his chair even closer to mine, so that our knees are almost touching. When he looks into my eyes again, it's with a level of intensity I didn't even think was possible. His gaze fills every corner of my soul.

"This is dangerous, Adalyn. The Nazis arrested teenagers for marching on Armistice Day. Took them to prison, beat them, made them stand outside all night in the rain. They lined some of the them up and made them think they were going to be executed. They could do the same to us. Or worse. If you have any hesitation—any at all—you can leave now. I wouldn't think less of you."

"I'm not leaving."

"You're going to have to be careful. If they catch you, they'll do whatever it takes to get information out of you. And you can't tell a soul what you're doing—do you understand that? Not a soul. Not your family. Not even people you think are loyal to our cause. Paris is crawling with Nazi informants."

I swallow hard. "I can keep a secret," I say firmly.

He searches my face one last time. I let him. I need him to

know how badly I want this. Then, finally, he hands me the envelope, and I tuck it inside my book bag. I straighten up.

Luc smiles for the first time since I arrived, and I feel my own shoulders relax. I didn't even realize they were up by my ears. I passed the test. I'm in. I'm a part of something bigger than myself, bigger than angry diary entries and torn-down posters. It's like the tension has evaporated from Luc's body, too. He springs to his feet, strides to the door on the far wall—the one we didn't come in from—and gives it three short raps. It bursts open from the other side, and there is Arnaud, grinning and rosy-cheeked in the cold evening air.

"You're one of us!" he cries, and my heart swells.

"Were you standing out there the whole time?"

"I was waiting for Luc's signal," he says. "It was three knocks if he approved of you, two if he sent you packing."

I turn to Luc, beaming. I suppose I should be afraid right now, but I feel almost drunk on excitement.

"Thanks for not sending me packing."

"It's my pleasure, Adalyn," Luc replies. When he says my name like that—with such confidence—I feel a jolt of excitement in my chest that has nothing to do with the assignment he's just given me. Being around Luc makes me nervous, but at the same time, I'd like to stay in this strange room and talk to him for hours. Which reminds me:

"Luc, where are we right now?"

"My parents' store," he says. "They've always let me use this place to do whatever I want while they're working."

"Do they know what you're doing here now?"

He shakes his head.

"They think I'm just back here with friends."

"Little do they know you're stuck back here with two people you absolutely can't stand," Arnaud chimes in, throwing his arm around Luc's shoulder. Luc laughs and musses his friend's hair affectionately. Then he clears his throat and jams his hands into his pockets. He's back to business.

"You two get going," Luc says. "Remember, Adalyn: Don't say a word to anybody."

Arnaud holds open the door for me. It's like I'm stepping out into the world as a new person. I lock eyes with Luc one last time before I leave for the night.

"And what shall I do when I'm done?"

"You'll come back here and let me know."

His voice is like a sip of tea that warms me from the inside out.

"Thank you," I whisper.

"Good luck."

As the sky goes purple and pink in the fading daylight, Arnaud walks me back toward the Right Bank. It used to be the time of night when Paris would truly become the City of Lights. Now it's the time when Parisians hurry home to drag the curtains over their windows. It's all so very quiet. People roll past us on bicycles, now that we haven't any cars left in the city. Exhausted housewives trudge home with vacant expressions after another fruitless day at the markets. Now that I've left the whirlwind of the shoe store and settled back down onto land, the very real, very terrifying questions start to creep into my mind. Things I wanted to ask Luc but didn't, for fear of seeming afraid. He said that if the Nazis catch me, they'll do "whatever it takes" to get information from me. Would they torture me? Or worse—and this thought really makes me feel sick—would they harm my family? As the panic mounts behind the brass fasteners on my coat, I interrupt the story Arnaud is telling about his two younger brothers.

"Arnaud, do you think I'll end up arrested?"

He snorts. "I think we'll *all* end up arrested."

I stop in my tracks as the reality of what I've just committed to sinks in. What on earth am I doing, toting around these anti-German tracts?

"Don't look so gloomy!" he says, clapping me on the shoulder. "It'll all be worth it in the end."

When still I refuse to move, Arnaud says, "Come on, I'll buy you an ice cream."

Sure enough, I start walking again, but then I realize his mistake.

"There's hardly anywhere to buy ice cream in Paris anymore," I point out.

"Ah, right you are," Arnaud concedes. "Well then. Ice cream's on me when this goddamn war is over."

I scatter the tracts.

I carry them with me everywhere, hiding them in my shopping basket and the pages of my schoolbooks, waiting for a chance to drop them without anybody seeing. Just the other day, on a crowded metro platform, I left a stack of them sitting on a bench! The papers are nothing, just a sheet with De Gaulle's cross inked in the middle, and yet they are everything to me.

Unfortunately, the work is slow going, as it's hard to get time alone. I'm with Chloe on my way to and from school, and in the evenings I'm in the apartment. If only Charlotte or Simone were still here, I could at least feign plans with one of them; instead, I must cram all my work into the hours I'm out fetching rations alone.

Yesterday I returned from the market triumphantly, the last of the papers slipped into housewives' shopping baskets when they weren't looking. I'm ready to see Luc for more, but that will mean sneaking back to the Latin Quarter without Maman and Papa wondering where I've gone. Even if I ride my bicycle or take the train, I shall still be gone for at least an hour in the evening.

Sitting in a history class I'm only half paying attention to, I make up my mind that I want to do it tonight. I cannot put

it off any longer. If I sit around waiting for the perfect opening in my schedule, Luc may think I've lost interest in our
cause, so when classes let out, I meet Chloe on the front steps
of the school and tell her I can't walk home with her today.

"There's a really big history test coming up, and a few of
us are getting together to review," I say calmly. Inside, I feel
terrible for lying.

Chloe puts her hand on her hip. "Can't Papa help you
study?"

Improvising, I tell her, "He doesn't know this material
very well. It isn't the Revolution or Napoleon. It's medieval
stuff."

"You could also not study at all," Chloe points out. "Your
perfect grades are making the rest of us look bad."

We both laugh, and I know I've pulled it off.

"I'll see you soon, okay? I won't be gone long."

"Okay. I'll miss you on the walk home." She frowns at the
Germans patrolling with a big brown bulldog nearby. "You
help take my mind off *les boches*."

"If Papa isn't asleep already, let's play songs when I get
back. You can sing, and I'll accompany you."

"I'd love that. Although be warned," she says with a note of
sarcasm, "my choir teacher said I sounded 'screechy' today."

"'Screechy'? You're never screechy. I promise."

"Thank you. I *told* her she was wrong." Chloe smiles and
shoulders her book bag. "She should have agreed with me

instead of sending me out into the hall. Anyway, I'll see you at home, Adalyn."

"See you, Chloe."

I watch Chloe until her blond head disappears around the corner at the end of the street, and then I turn on my heel and hurry to the nearest metro station. It's going to be tough coming up with a different excuse every time I go to Luc's— not only because I'll have to get creative, but because I hate keeping secrets from my sister. She's safer this way, I remind myself.

When no one is looking, I scurry down the alley to the right of the purple awning. Arnaud said I could go around the back this time. He also taught me the special knock they do on the door: one hard rap, followed by five that are light and quick. *Rat-tat-tat-tat-tat*. A minute goes by while I worry that Luc isn't here, that I wasted a perfectly good studying excuse for nothing, but then he opens the door. His dark brown eyes glitter as though he was hoping to find me here.

I hear boys' voices in the room behind him.

"Adalyn," he says. My name sounds like music when it's in his voice. A rich baritone.

I have to get straight to the point—I'm too excited to keep it in. "I finished, Luc. I came back for more."

"Excellent," he says. "Come in, we just made a fresh batch last week."

Luc steps aside so I can enter. It's more crowded than the last time I was here, owing to the presence of two boys I haven't met yet. One is tall, gangly, and curly-haired, a human dandelion. The other is small and baby-faced. They're seated around a table with Arnaud—or at least they were, for as soon as I walk into the room, Arnaud leaps out of his chair.

"Adalyn! I was worried I scared you off last time."

"I managed not to get arrested yet," I joke.

Luc motions to the gangly boy with the curls and says, "This is Pierre-Henri." Pierre-Henri performs a mock military salute, and we both giggle—the drunken excitement has definitely returned. Then Luc motions to the small boy, who's already grinning and waving. "This is Marcel," he says. "The four of us go to school together. We started meeting in September to talk about the war, share any broadcasts or pamphlets we've come across, make plans to resist however we can . . . that sort of thing."

"We're essentially trying not to go mad," Arnaud chimes in.

Luc smiles. "Exactly," he says. "And Marcel's dad has a mimeograph machine he smuggled out of his print shop before the Germans closed it down, so we've been able to make our tracts, as you know."

I nod, trying to take it all in. My brain is buzzing with new information.

"Boys, this is Adalyn," Luc continues. He sounds like a

captain addressing his lieutenants. "Arnaud found her tearing down posters of the Führer—"

"Actually, *she* found *me*," Arnaud says, holding up his index finger. He and I exchange a knowing grin.

"Adalyn has been helping spread our papers around the city, and she's excellent at avoiding detection," Luc says. "She's an asset."

An asset, he called me. I look down at my hands. I suppose I *am* an asset, the way the Germans never suspect me. . . .

"Welcome to the team!" Marcel chirps.

"Thank you," I tell him. "It's such a pleasure to meet you."

"We're happy you're here," says Pierre-Henri. "I know our tracts don't seem like much, but trust me, it feels good to do *something*."

"I know exactly what you mean."

My heart swells. Marcel and Pierre-Henri barely know who I am, but they welcomed me in immediately. It's clear that Luc, the most serious of the bunch, is the unofficial leader here. They must trust his vetting process.

"We meet here every Monday," Luc says. "You should join us whenever you can."

"I'll be here," I answer immediately, even though I still haven't worked out how I'm going to pull it off. Getting down here every Monday, on top of sneaking around spreading tracts? That's a lot of time outside the apartment, and it's especially suspicious nowadays, with the city making everyone so claustrophobic. People don't go outside unless they have to.

Luc pulls out a chair for me, and I sit down with them. Only now do I notice the random assortment of novels strewn across the table.

"They're a decoy," Luc says without my having to ask. He must have been watching my face. "If anyone finds us and asks questions, we can say we're a book club."

"It was my idea," Marcel says proudly.

The group falls naturally into conversation, and I drink it all in. I've been parched for so long, holding my tongue around Chloe so she won't be emboldened; around Papa so he won't become nervous; around Maman because she trusts in Pétain and wants to think positively.

The boys talk about the possibility of getting their tracts across the demarcation line, from Occupied to Unoccupied Zones.

"They need 'em more down there than they do up here," says Pierre-Henri.

"Why is that?" asks Marcel.

"Because their streets aren't crawling with *les boches*. Up here, the Germans do half the propaganda work for us."

Arnaud's wristwatch catches my eye; I've been gone for

nearly two hours now. "I need to start heading home," I whisper to Luc, so as not to disrupt the others' conversation. "I don't want my parents to ask questions."

Luc nods. He gets up, goes to the boxes, and returns with another envelope. My next batch of deliveries.

"Thank you."

"Thank *you*."

The intensity in his gaze makes it hard to look away, but I tuck the tracts into my book bag, say farewell to the others, and exit through the back door into the dark and bitterly cold evening.

Our elderly concierge is like a cat, in that he naps for the majority of the day. When I let myself into the building, the thud of the front door jolts him awake; he blinks, looks left and right, and finally locates the source of the noise.

"Miss Bonhomme," he says sleepily, "a letter for you."

"Thank you, Gilles."

When he hands me the envelope, I immediately recognize the slanted cursive of my piano teacher, Mathilde, who's been living with an aunt in the Free Zone since May. In truth, I haven't missed our twice-weekly lessons all that much; she's very strict, rapping my wrists with a ruler when I don't have them lifted enough, which takes the joy right out of playing. That's why I prefer practicing on my own. As I walk up the stairs, I open the envelope and read Mathilde's message.

Dear Adalyn,

I hope that this message finds you and your family well. I am writing to inform you of my decision to remain with my aunt here in Avignon for the foreseeable future. She is unwell and in need of care, and in any case, it isn't easy obtaining an Ausweis *in order to travel. I regret that our lessons must come to an end, but trust that you shall find time to keep up with it on your own.*

Sincerely,

Mathilde

The apartment smells like roasting meat, and Maman is setting the table for dinner when I walk through the door with the letter in my hand. I stop under the dining room archway to say hello, like normal. Like I haven't just come from a secret meeting in the Latin Quarter.

"How was studying, my darling?"

"Quite helpful. Thanks, Maman."

She looks at me adoringly, and I feel rather guilty for lying to her.

"Did someone send you a letter?" Maman asks, noticing the piece of paper.

"Mathilde," I reply.

"Oh! Did she say when she'll be returning?"

"It sounds as though she won't be coming back to Paris,"

I tell her. "She says she's staying in the south to care for her aunt."

Maman stops positioning silverware and puts her hands on her hips. "I feared this might happen," she says with a sigh. "What are we to do about your lessons? We really ought to find you somebody else. . . ."

And then the plan comes to me, fully formed and perfect. A simple idea that could make my whole new life possible. Before I say anything more, I slide the letter into my pocket so Maman won't think to reach for it.

"Mathilde actually referred me to a new teacher," I lie. "She's a wealthy widow who gives lessons for free—she's just happy to play the piano with somebody. She can take me on Mondays and Wednesdays, just like before. Mathilde already made the arrangements."

Maman looks surprised. "That is very kind of her."

"It is, isn't it? She says it's important I continue my lessons."

Maman walks around the table, and I panic that the jig is up. She's going to ask to see the letter, and she'll see that Mathilde made no such arrangements. But instead, she lays her cool hand on my cheek.

"I agree with Mathilde," she says with a smile. "You have a real talent, darling."

"Thank you, Maman. I'm looking forward to going."

"Good," she says, smoothing my hair. "Now go wash up

for dinner. I paid an arm and a leg for this chicken tonight."

Later that night, when everyone else has gone to sleep, I creep into the kitchen with Mathilde's note tucked inside my nightclothes. As quietly as I can, I open the door of the stove, prod the dying embers until they glow red, and place some fresh coal on top of them.

Kneeling on the floor, hoping that no one comes in, I manage to conjure up a small, bright flame. Next to it I put the letter, the only proof that my piano teacher didn't, in fact, arrange any new lessons for me.

Soon enough, the fire licks the top of the stove. Impatiently, I wait for the flames to go down again, my heart pounding relentlessly. When at last they do, I crawl forward and peer through the grate.

Mathilde's letter is nothing but ash.

CHAPTER 5

Alice

It's full steam ahead on Operation Learn about Gram's Secret Childhood, and I need to find a place where I can hunker down with my laptop and get through more of Adalyn's diary. Maybe I'll check out the Latin Quarter, on the opposite side of the river. Camila and her family stayed there over spring break, and I remember her saying it was full of cute cafés. She also said it was full of cute boys, at which point her boyfriend, Peter, squirted his water bottle over her head.

It's a gloomy, overcast afternoon, but I'm not focused on the bad weather. I was up until two in the morning toiling over another chunk of the diary, and now my great-aunt's perfect cursive sentences swirl around my head as I traipse across a very gray Seine. It's amazing to read all these stories about Gram that I never could have imagined. Like the one where she and Adalyn performed songs for their parents in the drawing room—I didn't even know Gram could sing! I know it sounds weird, but it almost makes me feel like a part of Gram is still alive, waiting to be discovered. Like Gram isn't gone all the way.

Zoom! A guy on a Vespa nearly runs me over as I set foot on the Left Bank. I should probably pay more attention to my surroundings, because the streets over here are jammed with people. I pick my way around clumps of tourists, wondering why Camila sent me here. All I see are souvenir shops and restaurants promising "authentic French cuisine" in big, bright letters. The waiters try to lure me in, yelling, *"Mademoiselle! Mademoiselle!"* as I walk by.

Dodging more traffic on the boulevard Saint-Germain, I contemplate turning back and going to the same café as yesterday, but then the neighborhood changes. The crowds thin out, and there are considerably fewer sightseers with cameras slung around their necks. I've found my way to a more intimate section of the Latin Quarter, where the streets feel like a maze you *want* to get lost in—narrow and twisting and full of surprises, like pint-sized coffee shops with space for just one or two tables out front, where people my age read novels and stir sugar into tiny cups of espresso. Everyone here looks so, well, *French*. Like they threw on the first thing they pulled out of their closet, and yet somehow, they're better dressed than anyone I've ever seen at my school.

Okay, Camila. You were onto something. This area is really cool.

Also, sorry, Peter, but Camila was definitely right about the cute boys—they're everywhere. There's one cutting into a *croque monsieur* at an outdoor table, another walking his bike over the bumpy cobblestone. The guys at school are always doing the dumbest things to get girls to pay attention to them, like throwing erasers at their heads or jabbing them with the ends of their rulers, but these Parisian boys are so effortlessly cool. They would know not to try and swallow a girl's face during a slow dance to Adele. That being said, they would probably never be interested in me, Alice Prewitt, when they could date another cool, attractive French person instead.

It starts to drizzle, and I know I should probably pick out a place to sit down, but there are just too many enticing cafés to choose from. I wander the streets some more, hoping the perfect place will present itself to me. But now the rain is getting heavier, so I pull out my phone to google a good place with free Wi-Fi.

There's a sudden crack of lightning and the rain starts to fall in thick drops, ten times harder than it was before. I should get inside soon, otherwise my clothes will be soaked for the rest of the day. Wait, forget the clothes. I just remembered I'm carrying a very expensive laptop in a very non-waterproof backpack right now. I dart through the door of the closest shop on my right.

A bell tinkles merrily over my head. The warm, sweet smell of freshly baked bread washes over me like a wave. I seem to have stumbled upon the most beautiful little bakery—and just in time, because right as the door swings shut, a raging thunderstorm starts to pelt the front window hard enough that I can hear the glass rattling in its frame.

"Bienvenue!"

A singsong voice greets me from somewhere up ahead. I can't find its source until a petite, fairy-like girl pops up from behind the counter like a jack-in-the-box. There's white flour smudged across her apron and her cheek.

"Bonjour—avez-vous le Wi-Fi?"

"Oui!" She points to a piece of paper taped to the wall. It has the network name and password written out.

"Merci beaucoup," I say with a smile. I got lucky. This place is perfect.

I go to put my things down. The bakery only has room for a single communal table, and currently, there's only one person sitting there. It's a young guy with a mop of reddish-brown hair, and he's bent over a sketchbook with a ballpoint pen in hand. He briefly looks up when I unzip my bag, just long enough for me to catch a glimpse of olive-green eyes behind round tortoiseshell glasses like mine. He's very handsome. In fact, he's probably the best-looking guy I've seen all day, which is saying something.

I go back to the counter with the intention of explaining once and for all that I want a regular-sized cup of black coffee, but when I get there, I pause. If Sketchbook Guy happens to be looking at me right now, do I really want to come off as the loud tourist who doesn't know what she's doing? No. I want to be the sophisticated lady who orders her coffee in a microscopic cup like everyone else in Paris.

Not that I think Sketchbook Guy is interested in me in any way. But strangely, when I return to the table armed with my caffeinated slap in the face and a croissant, Sketchbook Guy looks up again. This time I notice his lips, specifically how the upper one dips down in the middle as though somebody pressed a thumb there.

He smiles.

I sip my coffee and try not to wince.

He goes back to drawing, and I open my computer, where last night's translations are still pulled up on the screen. I left off in the fall of 1940, when Gram and her family were still settling into their strange new existence under Nazi Occupation.

The city is claustrophobic. As Chloe and I walked
to the butcher's on Saturday morning with our ration

coupons, we remarked for the hundredth time on how foreign our familiar streets felt. The German soldiers reading German signposts, the random checkpoints and road closures, the boarded-up windows of apartments whose owners have fled. . . . It makes you feel as though you're trapped in a nightmare.

In any case, there isn't nearly as much to do these days in the way of entertainment. Charlotte remains in South America, Simone in Marseilles. And the Germans have closed the Grand Rex cinema to Parisians! Needless to say, I cannot imagine what I would do without Chloe. In this upside-down world, we anchor each other to the ground. Last night, after I had already gone to bed, she crept into my room and climbed under the covers with me. She said she couldn't sleep.

I asked why not.

Chloe said a classmate had told her the Germans could be in France longer than any of us will be alive, and she couldn't stop thinking about it.

I pulled her in close and assured her it wasn't true, and that Charles de Gaulle was taking care of it. To help get her mind off the frightening thought—and my mind off it, too!—we played our usual game. We went back and forth until Chloe's voice trailed off, and I hoped she was dreaming of a decadent slice of chocolate cake.

And here's another one:

Today Maman and I passed Madame Blanchard
in the lobby of our building, looking despondent and
awfully pale. She'd become a ghost since we'd last seen
her. We asked if anything was the matter, and she said
her son had been killed. Shot by the Germans for some
kind of infraction. I didn't know him, but I am just
so devastated for his family. The man had a wife and
children. It isn't fair. I hate, hate, HATE the Germans.

Maman said I couldn't bring up Madame
Blanchard's son in front of Papa. It was too upsetting.
My uncle Mathieu was shot and killed, too. I love my
parents so very much, and I understand why we must be
strong for Papa, but I will say it here, in private, that it
is getting harder and harder to hold my tongue around
them—to hear Maman go on about Pétain and nod my
head as though I agree with her. I don't care what the
Old Marshal did in the Great War. . . . In THIS war, he
forced France to give up without a fight! I hate him, too.
However, not as much as I hate the Germans.

At dinner we made polite conversation about how
lucky it was to find butter at the market today. We also
saw a mother begging for medicine for her sick baby, but
we didn't bring that up. All through the meal, I felt as
though I might explode from sadness.

Chloe must have sensed it. Afterward, she led me
to her bedroom, and as soon as we were alone, I broke
down and cried. For poor Madame Blanchard and the
desperate mother at the market. I couldn't get their faces
out of my head.

Chloe held me for I don't know how long—a long
time. We said how grateful we were to feel the same
way about the state of things. I don't know what I'd do
without her.

The part at the end warms my heart, even though it's sad.
It makes me proud to be Chloe's granddaughter, and also
makes me want to have a sister, in a way. I love how much
they loved each other.

As I brave another sip of coffee, the thought gnaws at me
again, like it did last night.

The thought that I should try to track down Adalyn.

I set the cup down and swirl the brown sludge in a circle.
On the one hand, I have a very good reason not to: the photo.
It *must* be the reason Gram never talked about her.

On the other hand, Gram and Adalyn used to be so, so
close. And Gram wouldn't have left me the apartment if she
didn't want me to know about Adalyn . . . right? I mean,
maybe she actually *wanted* me to find her.

I almost wish I'd never opened that stupid drawer, because
if I hadn't found the photo—if I only knew Adalyn as the

person who wrote this diary—this wouldn't even be a decision. I'd be in full great-aunt-stalking mode.

But that's a pointless hypothetical, because I *did* open the drawer.

But—but!—according to the diary, Adalyn didn't *always* support the Nazis. And she could talk to me about Gram. She could help me make sense of everything.

It can't hurt to just poke around, can it?

I start with the obvious. I google "Adalyn Bonhomme." The results are a Pinterest board for a baby's birthday party and a list of Twitter accounts that definitely aren't right. I try "Adalyn Bonhomme France" and "Adalyn Bonhomme Paris" to narrow the scope, but the results are similarly unhelpful. I try "Adalyn Bonhomme Nazis" just to see what happens, but all I get is an essay on Nazi zombie movies by a film professor with the last name Bonhomme.

Wow, there's a weirdly high number of Nazi zombie movies out there.

Next, I pull up Facebook. My heart leaps when I search her name and get one result, but it sinks again when I realize this particular Adalyn Bonhomme is a thirteen-year-old girl in Cardiff, Wales. I try Instagram, too, but it's no use. How many ninety-three-year-olds are actively using social media, anyway? Gram's crowning technological achievement was learning to put spaces between the words in her text messages.

I try the white pages. I search obituaries. I do everything I can think of, to no avail. Older people just don't have the same digital footprints we do. My friends and I can spot a random person in the background of an Instagram photo and figure out their name, age, school, and whether or not they're dating anybody in a matter of minutes.

There's no chance I'm going to find Adalyn on the internet. If I wanted to find her, I would need some kind of lead, but where would I even begin? I wish I knew more about the time period. That way, I could put myself in Adalyn's shoes and figure out where she might have ended up by the end of the war. I google "Paris during World War II" and find a Wikipedia page that's ten thousand words long. It isn't much of a plan, but on the bright side, it'll help me understand more of the references Adalyn makes in her diary. I need a crash course in Nazi-occupied France, anyway. I start by reading about Germany's invasion of France in the spring of 1940—the same time that Adalyn started writing.

An hour into my research, my attention starts to waver. I realize I've read the same sentence about the French government retreating to the spa town of Vichy three times in a row. I need a distraction, so I peek over at Sketchbook Guy, who's been drawing this whole time. I don't know if it's because he saw me look over, but for the first time since I got here, he sets down his pen and sits back in his chair to admire his work.

Wow.

It's the most captivating drawing I've ever seen. I don't know where to look first—a million tiny abstract shapes fit together in intricate patterns, like the world's most complicated puzzle. And he did it all with a single ballpoint pen, even the shading. I can't stop staring at it, and sure enough, he catches me in the act. He smiles, and I smile back. Something flutters in my chest. Then he looks down at the table, redness creeping up over the collar of his white T-shirt.

And then I can't believe what happens next. The fairy-like girl flits over from the counter and deposits a coffee in front of him—not a tiny cup of sludge, but a regular mug of coffee with steam rising off the top.

I have to ask him. I hope he doesn't think I'm weird.

"Excusez-moi—parlez-vous anglais?"

"I do, yes," Sketchbook Guy replies in a French accent.

"What's the name for that kind of coffee?"

"Un café américain."

American coffee. Great. Now I *definitely* look like a stupid tourist, but at least he finally solved the mystery for me.

"Thank you very much," I say to him. "I've been trying to order that all week, but I keep getting it wrong."

"You are very welcome," he says with a laugh. Then he points to the tiny coffee cup next to my computer. "You did not seem to be enjoying this *café noir*. Do not worry—it is too strong for me, too, and I am French."

We smile at each other and go back to our work. Eventually

the rain dies down, and he packs up his things to leave. He gives me a small wave before he gets up from the table.

It isn't until I'm walking home for dinner, my brain drowning in details about the armistice signed between France and Germany, that I stop and think about my conversation with Sketchbook Guy. His accent really was incredible. Camila is going to freak out when I tell her. And there's a moment I keep coming back to at the end—the part when I thanked him, and then he said . . . what was it, exactly?

That I didn't seem to be enjoying my coffee.

Doesn't that mean that Sketchbook Guy was looking at me, too? The more times I replay it, the more I get the fluttering feeling inside my chest.

The next day brings beautiful blue skies, and even though I know I'm being ridiculous, I'm a little disappointed. I wanted to go back to the bakery in the hope of running into Sketchbook Guy again, but now I assume there's zero chance I'll see him there—not when everyone in Paris is outside enjoying the sunshine.

The only reason I ultimately decide to go back is that I heard him address the girl behind the counter by name, and she wasn't wearing a name tag on her apron. I checked on my way out. If he's that close with the staff, it means he has to be something of a regular, right?

But when I arrive at the bakery in the early afternoon, he's not there.

Obviously.

The only people at the big square table are a harried-looking couple with two squirming toddlers, both of whom have chocolate smeared across their cheeks. One of them lets out an ungodly shriek. My stomach sinks. I'm embarrassed for thinking I could find him again so easily. I kind of want to leave, except the woman at the counter has already asked for my order, and I don't want to offend this already-stressed-out family, so I ask for a *café américain* and gloomily dump my backpack onto the table.

After half an hour, I'm ready to pack it in and find someplace else. I'm trying to focus on the rationing system the Germans forced upon the French people, but I keep getting distracted by the sounds of kids' toys clattering to the floor. Yes, it's definitely time to go. I'm finishing the last sips of my delicious American coffee—the only good part of this whole experience—when the bell tinkles over the door.

I almost drop the mug.

It's Sketchbook Guy.

Right as he enters, Toddler Number One shrieks again. Toddler Number Two bangs her Tupperware container on the table, and Cheerios explode out of it like a geyser. Sketchbook Guy fidgets with the strap of his messenger bag and backs toward the exit.

"Wait!" I cry out. Oh god, that was louder than I meant it to be—and it wasn't even in French. But I must have gotten his attention, because he stops moving and takes his hand off the door.

"*Un moment,*" I say, sweeping my bag to the side so fast, it nearly falls onto the floor. I wouldn't normally make such a public show like this, but I guess I'm just going to go with it. I clear off a section of table that isn't covered in Cheerios, enough room for him to open his sketchbook and create another one of his dreamlike drawings.

We lock eyes from behind our identical glasses, and a familiar smile appears on his face. Sketchbook Guy remembers me from yesterday. He walks over to my corner of the table—our corner now—and slings his bag over the back of a chair.

"Thank you," he says.

"*De rien,*" I reply.

"You found the right coffee this time."

"All thanks to you."

He goes to the counter and comes back with a *café américain* of his own. I pretend to get back down to reading, but instead I peer over the top of my laptop to watch as he opens his pad to a fresh page and uncaps his pen. He picks a spot near the middle and starts drawing small spirals, then a cluster of perfect spheres, then a checkerboard pattern. It's hypnotizing. Sometimes his hand pauses for a moment, and I can't be sure, but I think he's stealing glances at the notes I'd been taking by hand as I read.

What I *do* know is that the toddlers' screams have become a lot more bearable since Sketchbook Guy arrived, because now, every time one of them shrieks like a banshee, he looks at me and winces dramatically, and I have to stifle a laugh. We go on and on like this in secret—our very own inside joke—until the family eventually packs up their things and exits the bakery like a traveling circus.

"Now we will at last be able to focus," he says to me.

"Yes, finally," I reply.

But a few seconds go by, and neither of us returns to our work. We just keep looking at each other. I'm pretty sure it's supposed to feel awkward to stare at a stranger like this, but it doesn't—not at all. His gaze makes me feel comfortable. It says, *Make yourself at home.*

"I'm Alice."

"Paul," he says.

When we shake hands, a tingling sensation dances up my arm.

"Your artwork is incredible."

He seems to be genuinely surprised.

"This?" He surveys his latest creation like he's seeing it for the first time. "This is just a random drawing. I wasn't really thinking about it."

"Well, it's a *very good* random drawing."

"Thank you," he says, the redness creeping up his neck again.

From the corner of my eye, I see the girl behind the counter dust the flour from her hands. Then, out of nowhere, she skips over to the table and greets Paul with a kiss on the cheek.

She might as well have dumped a bucket of ice water over my head.

The two of them start chatting in French at much too fast a pace for me to keep up. The girl keeps saying things that make Paul laugh, and it isn't lost on me that she's incredibly pretty. Well, now I know why Paul came back to the same bakery two days in a row. I go back to my reading for real this time, feeling deflated.

"Would you like something to eat?"

Silence.

I look up to see what's going on, only to discover that the girl is addressing me. Paul is staring at me, too.

"You should get something," he says. "My sister, Vivienne, is the best baker in all of Paris."

She's his sister! Even though Paul and I barely know each other, I won't pretend I'm not relieved. Now that I see them side by side, they clearly have the same auburn hair and green eyes. They even have the same patch of freckles dotting their noses.

I squint in the direction of the counter. The croissant I had yesterday was amazing, but there are at least a dozen other glistening pastries that look just as good.

"I think it may be impossible to decide," I tell them.

"Which are you deciding between?" Paul asks.

"I think the *pain au chocolat* and the *tarte tatin*."

He fishes for change in his pocket and hands it to his sister.

"Les deux, s'il vous plaît. Merci, Vivi."

Vivienne winks and skips off to the counter, and before I even realize what just happened, she's back with both pastries: the *pain au chocolat and* the *tarte tatin*. I can feel myself blushing.

"Merci beaucoup. You didn't have to do that."

"Well, I didn't want you to miss out."

"I think you might have to help me finish these."

I've never struck up conversation with a random person in public before—and *definitely* not with an extremely good-looking boy—but it ends up being easy to talk to each other, even with the language barrier. Paul's English is good enough that I only have to dredge up the occasional vocabulary word I learned in French class. He's from Lyon, but moved to Paris last year for school. He just finished his first year of university—not college, as I mistakenly call it, which turns out to be the French word for middle school.

"Are you an art major?" I ask, nodding at his sketchbook.

"No," he says. "Graphic design." He smiles wistfully and looks at the window. "I was accepted to an art school, but my parents said they wanted me to have a job after graduation."

"What do your parents do?"

"Both are heart surgeons."

"Whoa."

Paul laughs. "I know. I think maybe Vivi and I were switched with other babies at the hospital."

He changes the topic, asking me all about my life in New Jersey. Of course, he also wants to know why I'm in Paris for the summer, so I tell him all about Gram's perfectly preserved apartment and the mystery of why it ended up that way. I tell him I'm trying to learn what I can through Adalyn's diary, but I leave out the part about the photo I found in her mother's vanity. It's too shameful.

"If I were you, I would want to know very badly what happened to my family," Paul says, sliding the edge of his fork into the last piece of *tarte tatin* and dividing it in half. We each take a piece.

"That's why I'm doing all this research," I reply through a mouthful of baked apple.

"Have you found anything useful so far?"

"I'm off to a decent start," I tell him. "I know my grandmother and her family fled the city with millions of other people shortly after the Germans invaded France. I know they camped out in a town called Jonzac while they waited to see what the government would do. And I know that this old military hero named Pétain became prime minister all of a sudden, and he signed an armistice with Germany—and after that, France was split into Occupied and Unoccupied

Zones. Pétain still ran a French government out of Vichy, but he essentially did whatever the Germans wanted him to do. My grandmother and her family ended up going back to Paris after the armistice. That's about as far as I've gotten."

"I wonder . . . is it possible your grandmother's family got into trouble with the Nazis? Many people were arrested and deported in this time, and they would simply disappear."

I pick at a spot on the table, picturing the photo of Adalyn.

"I don't know. Maybe."

Paul clears his throat, and when he speaks again, his voice wavers.

"Just so you know . . . I am working this summer in a little bookstore near here," he says. "We have a very good history section, and many books on this particular time period in France . . . if you ever wanted to come by and look at them."

Oh my god. I think Paul just asked me to hang out again.

My fear of him finding out about Adalyn is completely trumped by nervous excitement. My palms start to sweat. I think I might be having a heart attack. Play it cool, Alice. But I have no idea how to play it cool! So I blurt out the first thing that comes to mind: "Wouldn't they all be in French?"

Where did that come from? Oh god, why did I say that? Paul's beautiful face falls. He looks embarrassed. He busies himself with stacking our empty plates and cutlery.

"I'm sorry," he mumbles. "You barely know me. . . ."

"No!" I need to turn this around, and fast. I want to see

him again more than anything. "I only ask because I'll probably need you to help me translate."

Paul looks up at me. A beat passes, and then he grins.

"I definitely can do that. We have some in English, too."

I smile back.

"I can't wait."

CHAPTER 6

Adalyn

Luc told me once that the trick isn't trying to hide from them—it's *not* trying.

It was hard to follow this advice in the first year or so, and even now, it isn't easy. Walk down the street with a stash of illegal flyers printed on a mimeograph machine hidden in your friend's attic, and all you want to do is leap into the shadows whenever *les boches* appear. It's human instinct to want to hide; the Germans have executed scores of resisters since the start of the Occupation. They print their faces on posters and hang them around the city as a threat. One of them, a Communist named Guy Môquet, is said to have been just seventeen years old when he died.

I can hear Luc's words as my bicycle crests the hill and a checkpoint comes into view up ahead. My chest tightens. There are two soldiers standing in the middle of the road, examining people's papers and inspecting their belongings before letting them pass through. I can't turn back now. They've surely spotted me, and if I look like I'm trying to avoid them, I'll give them all the more reason to be suspicious.

My palms almost slip off the handlebars as my wheels grind to a halt on the gravel. Stay calm. My eyes flit to the basket on the front of my bike, where underneath a checkered cloth and a few books sit two things: a spool of thread, and an envelope stuffed with the flyers we printed at Marcel's on Monday. They won't know what to make of the spool, but if they find the tracts, there will be no way to explain them away. All of them either have de Gaulle's cross or a big letter V for victory, two symbols you always see scrawled across German posters in Paris.

I need to think fast.

I mustn't look scared.

But I am scared.

There's another piece of advice Luc gave me: Always play the role of the person I am in the fashion magazines. Be the pretty young socialite who goes to parties—who has money—who isn't troubled by this silly Occupation.

"Nobody will ever suspect that girl," he said.

The first soldier waves me forward. He's a young man with smooth skin and a patchy blond beard that doesn't connect to his mustache. The second one—the handsomer of the two—can't be much older. As I present my identification card to the first soldier, I can't help but notice his partner eyeing me hungrily, from my divided cycling skirt to my red lips and my hair twisted into a chignon at the nape of my neck. At last, I have an idea.

"Where are you going today?" the first soldier asks.

I flash what I hope comes off as a flirtatious smile.

"To find a nice place in the grass to read my books." I run my fingers along my exposed collarbone. "Why? Do you care to join me?"

The second one laughs. He sidles over to my bicycle, his chest puffed out like a rooster's, and peers into the basket. He takes a closer look at my reading material and clucks approvingly. Not a banned book in sight.

"Goethe and Miegel," he says, raising his eyebrows. "Two fine German authors."

"I must have good taste," I reply.

The soldier smirks. He seems to be enjoying this coy little game we've started playing. He slings his rifle over his shoulder, hooks his thumbs into the waistband of his pants, and juts out his hips.

The first man, blushing now, clears his throat.

"That is a large basket, *mademoiselle*," he says. "What else are you carrying with you today?"

My heart thuds. But it's clear that the second soldier still can't take his eyes off me. So I say, in as facetious a voice as

I can muster, "Oh, terrible things. Lots of *highly* illegal propaganda."

Silence. This must be it. I'm going to be the next condemned resister pictured on a German poster. But then, miraculously, both soldiers erupt into fits of laughter. The first one hands me back my identification card, and the second one pats me on the small of my back.

"I'll tell every man in the Wehrmacht to watch out for you," he says.

"You should notify the Führer himself!" cries the other.

I'm so relieved, I laugh along with them.

"Have a wonderful day, gentlemen," I say to them, and they step aside to let me pass. I pedal away in a daze, amazed at my own quick thinking—and dumb luck. I cannot wait for my next Monday-night "piano lesson," when I can tell the group what just happened. Arnaud will probably stage a reenactment of the whole thing, with Marcel and Pierre-Henri's help. Luc, in his serious manner, will probably tell them to knock it off, as I could have been killed.

Luc. I've been successfully sneaking off to my "piano lessons" for a year and a half now, and each of our encounters still shines in my mind like a dream I can remember in the morning. His perpetual intensity—his determination to do as much as we possibly can—keeps the fire stoked in my chest, even as the Germans crack down on resisters. And he's broadened the scope of our work, so we're not just disseminating tracts anymore.

We're couriering secret messages.

Around six months ago, at his cousin's birthday party, a trusted aunt of Luc's pulled him aside for a private conversation in the study. Already well aware of his feelings toward the Germans, she said she could introduce him to a man running an intelligence network out of Paris, if he was interested. Speaking in a hushed voice so the other guests wouldn't hear, she explained that the network's goal was to ferry information between resistance groups throughout France, and also back to London, where Charles de Gaulle was leading his Free French Forces. Luc's aunt wasn't personally involved, it being too great a risk for a mother of four with a husband detained in Germany, but the man running the network was a personal friend of hers. He went by the code name "Geronte."

Since then, we've had so much more to do. Through Geronte, Luc brings us messages to deliver, each one concealed in a cleverer way than the last.

"I need you to deliver this pencil," Luc said to me at one of our recent meetings. "He'll be wearing a brown beret on a bench by the river, just east of Pont Neuf, under the poplar trees."

I stared at the writing implement he handed me, perplexed as to what its purpose could be. The others looked on, equally confused.

"Watch this," Luc said.

Our hands touching, he unscrewed the metal piece that held the eraser until it popped right off. The pencil turned out to be a hollowed-out cylinder with a message rolled up tightly inside. Arnaud's jaw was about an inch from the floor.

I can tell the new resistance work is taking its toll on Luc, though, even if he won't admit it. Last Wednesday, when I stopped by the shoe store to pick up another delivery, I noticed creases in his forehead that hadn't been there before—worry lines that were cast into sharp relief by the single bulb dangling from the ceiling. We've all been busier than ever, and in that moment, it showed.

"You look exhausted," I remarked.

"I'm okay," he replied with a weak smile. "I just haven't been sleeping much."

"Why not?"

"I can't stop thinking. I run through the deliveries we all have to make the next day, and I obsess over every detail."

He sighed. Then he added, "It's that, *and* the fact that I'm constantly starving."

"My sister and I play this game where we fantasize about the food we're going to eat when the war is over."

He looked at me curiously. "How does it work? You just list the foods you miss the most?"

"You make a plan of it," I tell him. "Like, 'I'm going to eat a warm baguette with butter and a big wheel of Brie.' Or, 'I'm going to drink *real* coffee, not hot liquid that tastes like dirt.'"

Luc smiled again, bigger this time. "I love that," he said. Then he rubbed his chin. "Let's see . . . I'm going to make my grandmother's duck à l'orange recipe. You can have some, if you like."

"How kind of you."

Something stirred in my chest, perhaps because he had dropped his guard for once, or perhaps because the two of us were in there alone, which was rare. But I pushed the feelings aside as I got down to business.

"So what do you have for me today?" I asked him.

This time, Luc pulled a wooden spool out of his pocket. We'd used these before; the message was curled around the center, then concealed beneath layer upon layer of thread wrapped around it. You would only know the paper was there if you unwound the whole thing. The messages were always written in codes I didn't understand. The fewer people who could give up vital information if captured and tortured by the Gestapo, the better, apparently.

Luc said, "I know Mondays and Wednesdays are best for you, but we need to get this to one of Geronte's contacts in Créteil on Saturday. It should take you about an hour each way by bicycle, and the handoff itself will be quick. Do you think you can manage?"

"I'll find a way," I replied. I would have to invent a lie about shopping for rations, and pray Chloe didn't try to come along with me. (That wasn't likely to happen, given how much Chloe hated standing in the food lines.)

He placed the spool in the center of my palm, then curled my fingers around it. For a moment he cradled my hand, as though he was hesitant to part with it—or perhaps he just wanted me to keep it safe. Neither of us acknowledged the physical contact, and a few seconds later he let go of me, reached back into his pocket, and produced something unexpected: half of a train ticket.

"Take this, too," he said quickly. "Geronte says your contact will have the other half. Hold your ticket against hers, and if the numbers match up, you can proceed with the delivery."

"That sounds easy enough."

I opened my book bag and tucked away the spool, the train ticket, and another envelope of tracts. The meeting was over as soon as it began; in what felt like no time at all, Luc was showing me to the door. I didn't want to leave him—not with the stress lines deepening across his forehead again. He looked like a teenage boy with the weight of the world on his shoulders.

"I'm okay, Adalyn," he said, as if he could tell what I was thinking. "I want you to worry about yourself. You're the one cycling an hour out of the city on Saturday."

"I'll be fine," I insisted.

"I know."

...

I still can't believe I got past the checkpoint. How those Germans underestimated me! I speed along the country road, grateful for the sunshine and the fresh spring air on my face. It was another brutally cold winter, with hardly enough coal to go around. The stores ran out of warm winter clothing, but thankfully, Chloe and I still fit into our coats from last year. We were the lucky ones; I saw plenty of women padding their old overcoats with newsprint to keep warm. Arnaud said he and his younger brothers all slept together in one bed. These are the kinds of adjustments that have to be made nowadays; at their store, Luc's parents are selling clunky wooden clogs, because rubber is impossible to find.

I follow the road until I reach the sign announcing my arrival in Créteil. Just off the main street, I see the café with the green awning—the one Luc told me about. My contact is supposed to be waiting for me at a table by the door. I lean my bike against a lamppost, take off the basket, and go inside.

There is a handful of tables one could consider being "by the door," each with a patron sipping some watery concoction meant to replicate coffee. But only one of them is a middle-aged woman in a pale blue coat and matching cap. She is examining her lipstick in a compact mirror, just as Luc said she would be.

I approach the table.

"What a surprise to see you."

The woman smiles politely.

"Why don't you sit for a moment?"

So far, so good. I lower myself into the chair and place the basket under the table, next to her valise.

Then the woman asks, "Did you get my card?"

I reach into my pocket for the small fragment of paper Luc gave me on Wednesday, while the woman slips hers out from under the powder puff in her compact. We slide the two halves of the train ticket together on the surface of the table, our hands obscured by her cup. They fit.

She leans in and places her hand over mine, the way close friends might share a secret. "Go to the counter and order a coffee with milk," she says in a measured tone. "The owner is one of us. He will go into the back room, and when he comes back, he will tell you he's all out of both. Then you may return to the table, take your basket, and leave."

I do exactly as the woman commands. I drum my fingers on the counter, waiting for the coffee I know isn't coming— and out of the corner of my eye, I see her reach under the table. I can't make out exactly how the woman pulls it off, but when I pick up my basket and bid her farewell, I don't feel the spool rolling around inside it.

When I walk in the door an hour later, Papa looks up from his armchair in the drawing room. He's holding a copy of *Les Nouveaux Temps*, the French newspaper favored by supporters of Pétain. Sometimes when we're all together in the drawing room, I catch him staring at a page without moving his eyes, his mind clearly elsewhere.

"Did you have any luck?" he asks.

I'm perplexed by his question, until I realize he isn't asking about the delivery. "I'm afraid not," I tell him, remembering my cover story. "The baker ran out just before I got to the window. I'm sorry we won't have any bread on your birthday."

Papa sighs, and I feel a sharp pang of guilt. On top of his terrible nerves, he has a daughter who lies to him. I know it has to be this way, but it doesn't make it any more bearable. Lying to two German soldiers is easier, in a way, than lying to your own family.

"It's no matter. I'm grateful that you tried at all," he says vacantly. When Papa isn't having a nervous spell, he seems to detach from his surroundings as a means of self-protection; I suppose the less he's aware of what's going on, the less his mind (and body) can react to it. "And besides, it sounds like your mother is preparing something interesting," he adds, nodding toward the kitchen before turning back to stare at his newspaper.

I find Maman at the counter, preparing an apple cake for tonight's dessert. She is grinding up a gnarled pile of apples to use as a sweetener, even though she never has any trouble finding sugar from her various contacts involved in the black market.

"I saw the recipe in one of Suzette's columns," she says,

referring to her favorite writer in *Les Nouveaux Temps.* "I expect it will end up tasting dreadful, but I thought it would be fun to try it out."

I consider pointing out that for most Parisians, these makeshift recipes are a matter of necessity, not *fun*, but I don't want to hurt Maman's feelings when she's trying to do something nice for Papa's birthday. Maman can be somewhat blind to reality, even if her intentions are pure. As she mixes the batter, her new silver charm bracelet dangles from her wrist. I was with her when she told the jeweler she wanted something to commemorate the struggle we were all going through—something to show her solidarity with the other housewives in the bread line. The charms are shaped like tiny baskets, one for each item of food the Germans have rationed.

"I'll tell you it's delicious either way," I promise her.

Maman kisses my cheek.

"Of course you will. Your sister, on the other hand, will no doubt tell me *exactly* what she thinks of it."

In school, I learned that every action has an equal and opposite reaction, and that is exactly how I would describe Maman and Chloe's relationship. The more Maman tries to make the best of the Occupation, the more Chloe reveals her desperation to resist it. Recently, my sister has taken to hanging out at the Café Pam Pam with a new group of friends—*zazous*, they call themselves. I've started seeing them around, the girls with their short skirts and bright lipstick; the boys with their big, billowing jackets and long hair slicked back with vegetable oil. Chloe says they're protesting the Vichy government's idea of how young people should dress and behave. The whole idea, she proudly explained to me when she got home the other night, "is to show that old skeleton Pétain that we're not going to follow his rules."

I laughed when she said "old skeleton," for it was the perfect descriptor for the ancient marshal. A rattling bag of bones without a brain or a heart.

"Just make sure you stay out of trouble," I told Chloe. "When you're all dressed up like that, keep away from *les haricots verts*." (This was another name we'd taken to calling the Germans, because they looked just like string beans in their gray-green uniforms.)

"I will," my sister said breezily. Then she flashed me a bright red smile. "Admit that you like the lipstick, though."

"I *do* like the lipstick."

Chloe giggled. "I know. I borrowed it from your room."

When we are finished with dinner, Maman sets the cake down on the table. Papa is the first one to take a slice, it being his birthday. When he swallows his first bite, he doesn't say anything—just furrows his brow and reaches for his glass of water. I try some for myself, and it immediately becomes clear why Papa had no comment. The cake is dry and tastes oddly like soap.

"It's good," I tell Maman.

Then it's Chloe's turn. Tonight, she's wearing her blond hair in a big bouffant that must be six inches high, and her lips are a garish pink. I watch them as she chews the foul-tasting cake, bracing myself for whatever bomb is about to go off.

"I tried one of Suzette's Ration Recipes for fun," Maman announces to the table. "It has no sugar at all!"

Oh no. It didn't take long. Chloe stops chewing, sets down her cutlery, and swallows the cake in what appears to be a long, tortured process. After washing it down with a sip of water, she rounds on Maman.

"This is a disgrace," she snaps.

Papa looks stupefied. Maman is livid.

"How could you—"

Chloe cuts her off.

"How could *you* just skip out on sugar when you have a perfectly good bag of it sitting in the cupboard? Do you know what some of my friends and their families would give for—"

"Your friends aren't poor either," Maman fires back. "They're just spending their money on ridiculous costumes. It's no different than—"

"It *is* different. We're protesting. You're just finding ways to make the Occupation *fun*."

Maman's lip trembles for a fraction of a second. She only wanted Papa to enjoy his evening. Chloe can be somewhat

blind to reality, too; she forgets that our parents are also trying to survive this war, in their own way. She and Maman
have some iteration of this fight at least once a week, and it
always ends the same way.

"Clear your dishes and go to your room," Maman orders.

My sister is about to object when the noise from outside
makes everybody stop what they're doing. It's the sound of a
car rolling to a stop.

What could the Germans be doing on our street, at this
time of night?

Oh my god. I lied my way past a checkpoint and smuggled
a concealed message to Créteil today.

What if they're here for *me*?

The argument over the apple cake is forgotten.
"Odette . . . ," Papa murmurs, and Maman leaps out of her
seat to attend to him. As his hands start to shake, she helps
him to his feet and steers him into the hall, probably toward
the quiet of their courtyard-facing bedroom. I rush to turn
off all the lights, and Chloe and I hurry to the window to
peer out from behind the curtains. Down on the street is a
sinister-looking black automobile. The front doors open, and
out step two men in unmistakable gray-green uniforms. But
they don't turn in our direction. Instead, they barge through
the front door of the building across the street. I'm safe. I
feel a rush of relief, which is almost immediately followed by
terror for our neighbors.

Minutes go by in silence. I wonder how many others are watching from their windows like we are. All is eerily quiet down on the darkened street. And then—

"YOU CANNOT TAKE HIM!"

The doors of the building fly open and four people come spilling out onto the sidewalk. Two are the hulking Germans in their big black boots. One is the old man in pajamas the Germans are forcing—violently—toward the car. The fourth is the old man's wife, reaching for him and shrieking at the top of her lungs. The bigger of the two Germans pushes her against the wall, while the other shoves her husband into the back seat. The woman continues to scream.

"WHAT IS HIS CRIME?! TELL ME WHAT HIS CRIME IS!"

"He is a Jew," snaps the man who pushed her. "Now get inside before we arrest you, too."

I want to go down there and kill the Germans with my bare hands. I want them to die. Right now. Chloe must feel the same way. She's bitten her fingernails down to the quick. Her breathing is all shallow. I can feel our two bodies trembling against one another. And then, in one impulsive movement, she wrenches open the window, sticks her head out, and screams into the night:

"LEAVE HIM ALONE, YOU MONSTERS!"

Chloe. No. I don't know why I wasn't thinking. I should have thought to pull her away before she did anything careless. My world goes dark at the edges, and all I can see is my sister, exposed. Someone is going to see her and recognize her big bouffant. My heart hammering in my chest, I seize her by the waist and drag her onto the floor before anyone can tell where the cry came from. We land with a crash, and Chloe's forehead collides with one of the wooden table legs.

"What the hell is the matter with you, Adalyn?" She untangles herself from my grip and clambers to her feet. There's a thin trickle of blood above her eyebrow, which she wipes away with the back of her hand. "You're acting like Maman," she spits. "It's like you're perfectly fine with all this!"

If only she knew. *If only.*

"I'm not fine with all this. I'm just trying to keep us both from being killed," I hiss back.

Chloe spins on her heel and stalks off to her room. The car outside drives away. I'm too shocked to cry, too scared to move. I sit on the floor with my knees tucked against my chest until Maman tiptoes in to see if I'm all right.

Chloe and I have never been able to stay mad at each other for long. The following day, after ignoring me on our way to and from school, she finally changes her mind and comes knocking at my door before dinner.

"Come in!" I say immediately, recognizing the sound of her footsteps. I put down my novel and sit up in bed, eager to talk to her again.

As soon as Chloe enters the room, an apology bursts from her lips. "I'm so sorry, Adalyn. Can we please be on speaking terms again? I hate this."

"Of course we can. I hate it, too."

The tension between us melts away. Thank heavens. I pat a spot on the quilt, and my sister comes and joins me on the bed. She crosses her legs carefully and looks down at her hands.

"I was just so angry, I couldn't keep it in," she confesses. "It makes sense why you pulled me away from the window."

"I was just worried about you, that's all."

"I know. It was the right thing to do."

"I'm sorry I made you hit your head."

"It's all right. It was better than getting caught."

It feels good to be back to normal—so good, I slide over and rest my head on her shoulder. Her hair mixes with mine, blond and brown woven together as one.

"Chloe?" I ask.

"Yes?"

"I was angry, too."

For weeks, I can't get the arrest out of my head. I think about it all day at school, while the other girls talk excitedly of our upcoming graduation. I even have nightmares about it, my brain coming up with terrifying visions of where the man from across the street could be now. Is he in prison? Is he still *alive*? It especially haunts me when I'm with Arnaud, for if it could happen to our innocent neighbor, who's to say it couldn't also happen to my friend?

I think Arnaud is worried, too, even if he tries not to show it. Besides arresting Jewish people for no reason, the Nazis are enacting one repugnant law after another. Next fall, when Luc, Pierre-Henri, and Marcel begin studying for their bachelor's degrees, Arnaud won't be able to join them, as Jews are now forbidden from enrolling in university.

"This is absurd," Marcel protests on a warm Monday night in June, when he first learns the news.

"I know, but it's the law now," Arnaud says. "Like how my dad can't work at the hospital. And how they make me ride in the last carriage on the metro."

"It's evil, is what it is," says Pierre-Henri darkly. Luc and I both nod in agreement.

"Listen, it's fine," Arnaud insists. "I'll just have more time to work on everything we're doing here. I'd rather resist the Nazis than try to get through the first year of medical school anyway. Believe me, I've heard stories."

We all do our best to laugh for Arnaud's sake, and the mood really does lighten when Pierre-Henri shows us the new camera his grandfather gave him as a graduation gift. Arnaud asks if he can see it, and proceeds to take a photo of himself with his tongue sticking out. This time, everyone laughs for real.

Still, when I say goodbye to Arnaud later, he does something he's never done before: He hugs me.

"I'll see you next week?" he asks.

And even though he shouldn't have to wonder, as I've seen him nearly every Monday since the fall of 1940, I sense he might need a little reassurance.

"Of course you will," I tell him.

Rat-tat-tat-tat-tat. A week later, I show up in back of the shop and tap out our secret code on the door. It creaks open to reveal Arnaud's bespectacled face, bearing an oddly disoriented expression—no, worse than that. It's as if somebody has snuffed out the bright light usually shining behind his eyes. My first thought is that something happened to Luc or Marcel or Pierre-Henri, but no . . . I can see all three of them in the room beyond.

"Arnaud, what . . . ?"

But then I spot it. It's sewn onto his shirt, directly over his heart. A six-pointed yellow star with the word "Juif" in the middle. I touch the fabric gingerly with my fingertips, like it's a wound.

"Why . . . ?"

"Another new law," he says flatly, stepping aside to let me in. The four of us watch silently as he trudges over to a chair and sits down, his face in his hands. I know how hard Arnaud tries to keep his spirits up, how he doesn't want to make it any harder for his parents or his two little brothers. I try to imagine how he must feel right now. I can slip from one disguise to another to suit my needs; Arnaud is stuck with a dangerous label he can't take off.

Luc draws up some more chairs, and we all sit in a semi-circle around our friend. I rub his back, and Luc pats his knee. Arnaud reaches up and unpins the yellow star from his breast pocket. Holding it in his lap, he stares down at the awful thing with a mix of sadness and contempt.

"You know, I thought about refusing to wear it," Arnaud says quietly. "But then I saw my parents going out into the street with their heads held high, and I thought, I must not be a coward. I will wear this star, and I will be brave. What do I have to hide? I am proud to be a Jew."

"And we are proud to know you," I whisper.

"Thanks, Adalyn." He sighs, twisting the yellow fabric this way and that. "Things are getting really bad. It feels like we're being . . . hunted."

This time, Marcel chimes in. Though his heart is in the right place, and he's easily the best at operating the mimeo-graph machine, he isn't the brightest of the group.

"I'm sure you'll be okay," he says. "You were born in France, right?"

"*I* was," Arnaud says, "but my parents came here from Poland. And besides, it doesn't matter who's French and who's not. At the end of the day, we are all Jews, and they would prefer it if we didn't exist. Don't you remember the exhibition?"

Everybody winces. Last winter, we all witnessed the grotesque advertisements for *Le Juif et la France*, some revolting exhibition at the Palais Berlitz about the Jews' supposed thirst for world domination—organized by the Germans, of course. The five-story sign plastered to the front of the building showed an old man with a hooked nose and a claw-like hand clinging to a globe. It was grossly unrealistic and meant to be frightening. Between that, the new laws, and the senseless arrests that keep happening, there can't be any doubt that Arnaud is right. I put on a brave face for him, even as despair creeps in.

"Well, I'll kill any damn Nazi who comes near your family," says Pierre-Henri, who's become very fixated on the prospect of killing Nazis. Arnaud laughs weakly, but it sounds to me like he's dangerously close to crying. I feel so helpless, and scared, and *angry* that no matter how many flyers I spread, nor how many secret messages I pass along, there's nothing I can do to take away Arnaud's pain. He was the one who brought me into this whole world. I would trade places with him if I could.

Then Luc, of all people, claps his hands enthusiastically.

"Okay, enough of this for now," he declares. "It's beautiful outside. We shouldn't be cooped up in here. Who feels like a trip to the park? I know I do."

I've never heard him sound so upbeat, but it's just what we need right now. Everybody is on board, including Arnaud, who sheds a single tear as he pins the star to his shirt. He very quickly wipes it away with the back of his hand.

We step outside into the late-afternoon sunshine. "Good light," observes Pierre-Henri, who's wearing his camera around his neck.

I don't think I'll be seen, as nobody in my normal life lives on this side of the river, but I keep my head down all the same, just to be safe. The five of us walk across the boulevard Saint-Michel to the Luxembourg Gardens, where we flop onto the grass under a chestnut tree. The water in the fountain sparkles in the sun. Luc disappears for a few minutes, and when he comes back, he's carrying lemonades for the group. Being here feels surreal, like a dream.

"I just realized something," I say to Luc as I take my drink.

"What's that?"

"With the exception of the first ten seconds we met . . . I've known you for a year and a half now, and I don't think I've ever seen you outside."

Luc nearly chokes on his lemonade as he starts to laugh, which only makes the two of us giggle even more. The break in our usual routine makes the war seem borderline absurd.

"Did you think I was a vampire?"

"I was beginning to worry."

He sits down next to me in the grass and tries to cross his legs. It looks uncomfortable. "I don't fold up very nicely," Luc confesses, before abandoning the mission and reclining on his elbow instead. I find myself noticing how the muscles in his shoulder flex under his shirt.

"Do you come here often?" I ask.

Instantly, I wish I thought of a more original question.

"I did when I was younger, with my parents," Luc says. "Sometimes on the weekends, they would close the shop for lunch and we would walk over for a picnic."

He gazes at his chest and smiles to himself.

"What is it?"

"I just remembered: My father used to tell me I should bring a girl here someday." He looks up and studies my face, which suddenly feels hot, and not from the sunshine. "I never got around to it . . . until now," Luc says. "He was right. It's nice."

We smile at each other.

I don't regret my boring question anymore.

"Luc!" cries Marcel. "Tell Arnaud about Jacques throwing the paper airplane at Stéphane when he was reading in Latin. Arnaud doesn't believe me that I intercepted the plane and threw it right back at Jacques's head."

Before he answers, Luc holds my gaze for one last second. Then he shifts toward his friends. "I can confirm it's true!" he says. "It was the finest operation I've ever witnessed. A work of art, if you will. Jacques looked like he didn't know what hit him."

Marcel beams.

"I remember another fine operation: when you wrote the wrong answers on that test because you knew Jacques was copying you."

"A classic!" cries Pierre-Henri.

I gape at Luc in disbelief. "You purposely failed, just to get back at this person for cheating?"

"Of course not," replies Luc. "I corrected my test as soon as Jacques handed his in. He was furious!"

It doesn't happen right away, but after about half an hour, we manage to get Arnaud laughing again like his old self. Luc and Marcel take turns telling stories about the pranks they've pulled at school, each tale more ridiculous than the last.

Pierre-Henri, who's now determined to become a professional photographer, wanders around snapping pictures of us. Occasionally, he directs us to strike poses.

"Luc, smile. More," he says. "Arnaud, poke Luc in the face until he smiles. Yes—perfect." *Click.*

Luc dodges out of the way as Arnaud goes to poke him again, and somehow the two of them end up play-wrestling like lion cubs. Arnaud takes it to the theatrical extreme, bellowing out battle cries as he launches each offensive maneuver, so that by the time the two boys eventually call a truce, I'm doubled over with laughter and gasping for air.

Pierre-Henri continues to take photos of us. Here and there, butterflies drift through the air, and Arnaud's face lights up when one of them lands on his finger. *Click*. Luc leans over to examine it, and when he does, he rests his hand on my lower leg. For three magical seconds, it feels like the whole entire universe exists in that spot below my knee. *Click*. His hand is in the grass again, just an inch or two from mine. *Click*. There's that stirring again inside me. Luc really is handsome, especially with the golden sun hitting the ridges and planes of his face.

In this moment, I wish the world didn't exist beyond the walls of the park. Because if not for the war—if not for the horrors we've endured, and the ones that still may come— this would be the most perfect afternoon.

CHAPTER 7

Alice

Mom's mood isn't getting any better. I've been trying my best to cheer her up, but Gram's death is still clearly weighing on her. We've been in Paris for two weeks now, and she's spent most of that time in the Airbnb, doing nothing. There's this sad, vacant look on her face that just won't go away, not even when I tell her I've made a new friend.

"He's working in a bookstore this summer. He's been letting me read all about French history, and he's helping me figure out what happened to Gram and her family."

Mom takes a sip of her tea. She's curled up in the corner of the couch with her knees to her chest, staring at a spot on the living room wall where the paint is chipping away. I wait for her to react to what I'm saying about Paul, but she never does. It's like she's trapped inside a thick glass box that muffles the outside world, and I can't break in, no matter how hard I try.

I'm starting to get worried, because this is exactly how Mom gets when she's entering one of her dark phases. They happen pretty rarely, only once every few years or so, but they're unbearable when they do. It's like somebody turns off a switch in her head, and she totally powers down.

Her *darkest* dark phase happened when I was in the first grade. We haven't talked about it since, but I remember my lively, loving mother suddenly going despondent for months. The others have been shorter and less intense, but still awful. For a couple of weeks, she won't want to go outside, or even get out of bed. Worst of all, there's nothing Dad or I can do to turn the switch back on. We can only act positive and wait for Mom to gradually get her energy back.

Maybe I'm overreacting. I doubt Mom's actually in a dark phase right now. I mean, we *know* what's bothering her. It's Gram's death, and discovering all the secrets she kept. Plus—and Mom's too nice and conflict averse to say this out loud—I suspect she's also hurt that Gram left the apartment to me, and not her. I still feel guilty when I picture the look on her face when we read the will.

I want to take her mind off things, and the first step is getting her to talk to me.

"Paul's really sweet and smart," I press on. "And he's an

amazing artist. You should see his drawings."

Still more silence.

"Diane, are you listening to Alice?" Dad peeks over from the kitchen, where he's been up to his ears all morning in paperwork for Gram's estate; it's spread across the surface of the table like a patchwork quilt. "It sounds like she has some real news to share."

Mom blinks. She looks at me, confused.

"Sorry—what did you just say?"

"I met a boy named Paul. We've been hanging out for like a week now."

"That's nice."

Her gaze drifts back to the wall, and she's sealed inside the glass box again.

I hate that a part of me feels this way, but I'm kind of relieved when noon rolls around and it's time to see Paul again.

One thing I like about Paul is that it's easy to be around him. I don't have to think about what to say; I don't have to pick up on what kind of mood he's in and plan my behavior accordingly. In fact, the only thing that's complicated about my relationship with Paul is figuring out what, exactly, our relationship *is*.

I've visited Paul in the bookstore twice now. Even though we have a good time when we're together—and even though I'm pretty sure he *might* have flirted with me—so far, nothing has . . . happened. Both times there have been long stretches when it's just the two of us in there, sitting shoulder to shoulder behind his desk, and he hasn't made a move. To be fair, I haven't either, but I'm the one with next-to-zero experience. Paul has probably been with tons of girls, so I've been waiting for him to take the lead. I can't tell if he's shy, or if he's concerned about acting unprofessional at work . . . or if he's just not into me that way. Maybe he wants to be friends, and that's it. All I know for sure is that my stomach is Butterfly Central whenever I'm with him. I even feel them fluttering when his name pops up on my phone.

I messaged Hannah and Camila last night about how confused I was, only I didn't give them details in case it ended up going nowhere. That was the most likely scenario, judging by my love life thus far—namely, the Pomorski Incident. I texted them: "When two people like each other, how long does it usually take for someone to make a move? Is it supposed to happen immediately?"

Camila was the first to reply. "Why??? Did u meet someone???"

That was classic Camila. She *loved* love.

"Not important at the moment," I wrote back. "Just need your wisdom." Anxiously, I watched her type. Of the three of us, Camila knew the most about relationships. She and Peter had just celebrated their seven-month anniversary.

"Some people don't make moves right away," she said, and

my spirits lifted instantly. "Remember how Peter didn't kiss me until after our mini-golf date?"

"Yes!" I typed back. I was tremendously relieved.

Then I realized she was still typing.

Her next message hit me like a ton of bricks.

"Still, if nothing steamy has happened by like the third hangout, I feel like maybe the right chemistry just isn't there?!"

As the weight of her words sank in, Hannah finally chimed into the conversation.

"Hey you guys!!!!!!!!!!!!!! I agree with Cam!!!"

My heart plummeted. I quickly thanked them and put away my phone. Paul and I were at two hangouts, and that wasn't counting either of the times we sat in the bakery together. According to Camila's rule, a lot was riding on our third arranged meeting.

At exactly 11:59 a.m., I lace up my Converse sneakers, say goodbye to Mom and Dad, and head downstairs to meet Paul. Since it's such a nice day outside, he offered to meet me at the Airbnb and take me through the Tuileries Gardens on our way to the bookstore, where I'm going to hang out with him during his shift.

As soon as I open the door, I hear his voice.

"Alice!"

He's waiting at the curb in his usual white T-shirt and jeans, two American-sized cups of coffee in his hands. He's smiling, and the sun makes his hair shimmer like copper. There go the butterflies again.

"For you," he says, handing me a cup. Did *he* feel that jolt of electricity as our fingers touched, or was it just me? Would Camila say that was chemistry?

"Thank you! That's so sweet."

"Of course."

We grin at each other stupidly for a second.

"Well . . . should we walk?" he asks.

"Okay," I reply.

We set off down the sidewalk, sipping our drinks. I notice he's holding his coffee in his right hand, leaving his left hand free to potentially hold mine.

"Paul, I've never asked you, is your apartment around here?"

"No, it's down near my school. In the Latin Quarter."

"You mean . . . you walked all the way up here just to walk back down again?"

"Yeah," he says happily.

My cheeks flush. Then again, it *is* a beautiful day. Who wouldn't want to go for a long walk outside? Paul leads me down to a spot on the rue de Rivoli where the sidewalk becomes a sandy path, the Louvre on the left and the Tuileries Gardens on the right. When I came here with Mom and Dad, we went straight to the glass pyramids and the museum ticketing line; I never turned around and marveled at the sprawling green lawns that seem to stretch on forever. It's beautiful geometry, the way the bright yellow tulips and white marble statues form rings around the circular fountain in the middle. There are flowering trees with bright pink blossoms, and small clusters of daisies peeking out from the grass.

"It's incredible," I say, feeling like no word could truly do it justice.

"I know," Paul replies. "When I first moved to Paris, I could not believe all the beautiful things just sitting in the middle of the city, you know?"

"It's so funny you just said that. I've been thinking the same thing since I got here."

"Maybe we are reading each other's minds?"

"I think so."

Maybe I should try it out. *Paul, If you really are reading my mind right now, I wouldn't object to holding hands.* Hmm, no response. We walk around the fountain, then along a shady, tree-lined path that emerges at yet another big water feature. We compare our favorite things at the Louvre, and laugh about how tiny and underwhelming the *Mona Lisa* is when you finally see it through the crowds. Sometimes there are lulls in our conversation, but not in an awkward way— they're more like pleasant pauses, giving us time to take in the scenery.

"Have you always loved art?" I ask as we exit the gardens and head for the nearest bridge across the Seine.

"Yes," Paul says. "I was always drawing, from when I was little. My teachers would be angry at me for making pictures during class, but actually, it helped me focus."

"You seemed really sucked into your sketchbook when I saw you in the bakery the first time."

He nods. "Drawing is very calming to me."

"Oh, Paul, this is beautiful!" I stop in my tracks, floored by the view from the center of the bridge. The water is a stunning turquoise, and over on the Left Bank, the Musée d'Orsay rises like a royal palace. "I think I have to stop and take a picture. Do you mind?"

"Of course not."

I set my coffee cup down on the balustrade and pull out my phone. Paul steps to the side so I can capture the whole scene. I'm working on taking the perfect shot when a warm breeze sails in, and my near-empty coffee cup skids toward the edge of the wall. Paul lunges for it at the same moment my finger taps the camera button—and the result is a blurry action shot of Paul leaping through the air with an expression of utmost intensity on his face.

It's the funniest thing I've ever seen. Wiping tears from my eyes, I show it to Paul, who bursts into laughter, too. He doubles over, gripping my shoulder for support, but no sooner does his hand touch my skin than it falls down to his side again, a little stiffly. Is he trying to minimize contact with me? I don't get it.

We make our way to the bookstore. La Petite Librairie, as it's called, might be tied with Vivi's bakery for my favorite spot in Paris. The orange awning is tucked on a quiet cobblestone street, a hidden gem among the rows of residential buildings. When I first went inside, it seemed there were too many books for the small space; the stacks were so close together you had to turn sideways to pass between some of them, and the smell of yellowing pages was overwhelming. I loved it immediately.

After the clerk from the morning shift hands over the keys and heads out, Paul retrieves an extra stool, and we both sit down behind the front desk. Sometimes I peruse the English-language history books when we're here, but mostly I like to be next to him. Right now, our shoulders are almost touching. I can smell his laundry detergent.

Paul dives in to cataloguing a new shipment of books, and I decide to pick up on my translations. Adalyn's diary is long, and her writing is small, but I'm making good progress; I'm in early 1942, and my great-aunt just finished writing about another frigid winter without enough heat. Apparently, she and Gram used to huddle under the covers to keep warm, sometimes sleeping together on the coldest nights.

I still haven't told Paul the whole truth about Adalyn. It's why I keep waving away his offers to translate the entries for me; I'm scared my great-aunt could go bad at a moment's notice, so I have to be the one to read them first. By now I've read enough about the Occupation to get the picture: France is still pretty ashamed that a bunch of its own people collaborated with the Nazis. If your family member was one of them, it's not the kind of thing you want to go telling the world.

I roll out my wrists and start translating an entry from July 20, 1942.

Oh no. This one is really upsetting.

I can hardly write. My hand is shaking as bad as Papa's. But I must keep a record of everything that has happened. I apologize if I am scattered. I cannot think straight—not when my friend's whereabouts are still unknown.

There was a massive roundup on Thursday and Friday. It began very early in the morning. Thousands of Jews were forced onto buses and taken to the Vélodrome d'Hiver, where they are now being held in the most frightening conditions. One hears sickening snippets of information in the bread line and on the metro—people crammed inside the bicycle arena without any food or water or a place to use the lavatory. Many are said to have died already. And what will become of the living? What if they are all deported, and he is among them?

I am trying my best not to cry right now. I don't want Maman and Papa to hear me.

I had to pause to cry into my pillow.

The stories of the arrests are terrible. Parents ripped from their children. Once they are separated, how shall they ever find each other again?

A family of five poisoned themselves so as not to be taken—a mother, a father, and three little children. All dead now. Another woman threw herself from a window. There are tales of policemen being shot for refusing to comply with the roundup orders.

Every account is appalling, but nothing frightens me more than not knowing what has become of my friend. I have neither seen him nor heard from him since the day before the roundup. It does not help to know that many Jews in the Vel' d'Hiv are Poles.

Sometimes when I learn of the cruelty that is happening, I think it must be happening in another world. But it is right here, in Paris. And they say it will only get worse. Today I sat by two Jewish women on the train who seemed to be very shaken up. I overheard one of them whisper to the other, "They will come for the French citizens next."

I would give anything for this madness to end.

I stare at the screen feeling nauseous. Paul and I read about the Vel' d'Hiv roundup the last time we were here together.

The Jews were held in the stadium for five days without food or running water. They were living in filth. There were women who gave birth on the floor. Eventually they were shoved into cattle cars and sent to concentration camps.

"Alice? Are you okay?"

Behind his glasses, Paul's olive-green eyes study my face. He looks concerned.

"I'm so confused," I tell him.

"What is the matter?"

The *matter* is that Adalyn eventually became a Nazi sympathizer, which presumably led Gram to cut her out of her life. But in July 1942, when she wrote this diary entry, Adalyn had a Jewish friend who was a victim of the Vel' d'Hiv roundup—someone she cared about a lot, apparently. What in the world happened to her?

"Paul, there's something I need to tell you."

I can't keep it a secret anymore. I need somebody to talk to. In a hushed voice, so no customers can overhear us, I tell him about the photo I found in my great-grandmother's vanity. As I go through the details, Paul's expression moves like a time-lapse video from concerned to horrified to downright confused, just like me.

He reads the latest diary entry two times through.

"So you are telling me this person . . ."

". . . became a Nazi sympathizer. Yes."

"I cannot believe it. I don't understand."

Still staring at the screen, he furrows his brow and sticks out the very tip of his tongue, a habit I've noticed. He does it when he's very focused on something, like his drawings. Seeing him in that pose—so goofy and so serious at the same time—helps me to relax.

"I was nervous to tell you about Adalyn because I only just met you, and I didn't want the fact that I'm related to this person to scare you off."

"Scare me off? You could never."

Blushing, I watch as Paul fishes inside his backpack for his sketchbook. When he finds it, he opens it across his lap and starts scribbling something on a fresh page.

"What are you doing?"

"I'm making a list of everything we know about Adalyn so far."

"You're amazing, Paul. Okay, let's see. She was beautiful . . . rich . . . went to a lot of parties . . . and she hated the Germans when they first invaded. She also hated Pétain for striking a deal with Hitler. And she loved Charles de Gaulle's speech about the flame of French resistance."

Paul jots everything down as I talk.

". . . She had at least one friend who was Jewish, and it sounds like he was deported to a concentration camp. . . ."

". . . And then somehow, she changed sides," Paul says, completing my train of thought. "Is there anything else?"

"No, that about sums it up."

We both stare at the list, as perplexed as ever.

"This is really bizarre," Paul concludes.

"Tell me about it."

At five o'clock Paul locks up the bookstore. We wander around the corner for an afternoon snack at Vivienne's bakery, where she plates two slices of apricot tart fresh from the oven—"on the house," she insists. I try to get Vivi to accept my money, but she pushes my hand away, and Paul just shrugs helplessly.

As we scrape the last crumbs from our plates, Paul says, "Now I keep wondering about Adalyn, too."

"Right? It's like a whole other mystery in and of itself," I reply. "I want to know all about Gram *and* Adalyn."

"What are you going to do?" he asks.

"I feel like I should go back to the apartment and look for more clues. If I already found the diary and the photos, maybe there's something else I haven't seen yet. Something my grandmother wanted me to find. Who knows?" I fidget with my glasses for a second. "You could come with me, if you wanted. It would be cool for you to see it."

"I would like that very much," Paul says.

There go the butterflies. Paul has invited me into his world, and now I get to bring him into mine. He smiles, and the distinctive curve in his upper lip is enough to make me melt on the spot.

And then a red warning light flashes in my head. Oh no, I

just remembered Camila's text messages. Our third hangout is about to be over, and absolutely no steamy advances have been made. Well, that's just great. While I'm over here fawning over Paul, he's probably looking at me as nothing more than a friend.

"Are you sure you want to come?" I ask him. "I know it's a far trip from your apartment."

"I don't mind," he says with a smile. "I am just happy to go someplace with you."

Maybe there's still hope for me.

Paul and I make plans to meet tomorrow, and then I head back to the Airbnb to see what Mom and Dad are up to. I've been gone for over six hours, and they're still in the exact same places as when I left them. The only difference is that Dad's hair is standing on end, presumably from all the times he's raked his fingers through it in frustration at all the paperwork. Mom is a little more lively than before; at least, she seems to register my presence when I plop down next to her on the couch. It's a far cry from the person who sings along to her *Best of Broadway* CD in the car, but I'll take it.

"Did you and Dad have a nice afternoon?" I ask her.

"Your father is in over his head," she says. "He hasn't been able to get up from the table."

"It seems really complicated."

"Your grandmother certainly didn't make it easy for us."

Your grandmother. Mom must be feeling angry today. I get

up from the couch and pop my head into the kitchen.

"Dad, is there any way I can help?"

"That's nice of you to offer, honey, but I think I should be okay," he replies. "Why don't you go keep Mom company? I think she could use it right now."

I go back to the living room. Mom is picking at a thread dangling from the frayed sleeve of her cardigan.

"Do you want me to grab scissors for that?"

"When I die," she says quietly, catching me off guard, "you can be sure I won't do something like this to you."

"Mom, what are you talking about?"

"I mean I'll make it easy for you and Dad to take care of things—I won't leave you with a mess of a will to sort out!"

Where the heck did that come from? She's talking like she only has days left to live. I'm kind of alarmed that Mom would bring up her own will—but then again, I have to remember, everyone handles grief differently. When someone close to you dies, it's totally possible that you'd start to think more about your own mortality, right? Maybe all she needs is a distraction; I mean, she's been cooped up here all day with nothing to do but think about Gram.

"Let's go do something," I suggest. "We can walk to the market and pick something out for dinner." Mom would love that. I know it. She's always showing me what to look for in the produce section of the grocery store: bananas with a hint of green, avocados with just the right amount of squish.

"If you want," she says simply.

I go to my parents' bedroom to find her a pair of shoes. Then, with some effort, I manage to pull her up from the couch. By the time we get outside, the first wisps of pink have appeared in the evening sky. It's a clear night; I should finally do what that taxi driver said and take Mom up the hill to Sacré-Coeur. You never know—a beautiful summer sunset over Paris may be just the thing to brighten her mood.

The next morning, I turn the corner onto the rue de Marquis to find Paul standing with his hands in his pockets outside number thirty-six. His freckled face brightens when he sees me coming down the block.

And then I realize I have a minor emergency. How are we supposed to greet each other? The other times we met up, there was an automatic barrier between us: Paul's desk at the bookstore, the cup of coffee he handed me yesterday. This is the first time we've met without any obstructions, and it occurs to me that I have no idea what to do. We're obviously not going to shake hands—too formal. But do we hug? We've never hugged before. I know I'd *like* to hug him, but does he want to hug me? Do friends hug each other in France? Oh, this is bad! And I'm getting close now. I wish he would give me some kind of cue.

"Hey, Paul!"

I'm not exactly sure how much distance to keep between

us, so I pick a random spot to stop walking. Oh no, I think I messed up—now there's a weirdly large gap between us. Paul inches forward. Are we hugging? Is this happening? His arms seem to be moving, but I can't tell for *sure* what they're doing, so in a panic, I do the only sensible thing I can think of in the moment: I wave at him from two feet away, like an idiot.

He drops one of his arms and waves back.

"Hey," he says.

Real smooth, Alice.

I try to move past the awkward moment, and lead him into the building and up the five winding flights of stairs. I open the door of apartment five, and a look of amazement appears on Paul's face. His lips open and close a few times without any words coming out. Finally, he manages to say, "Alice, *c'est incroyable!*"

I take him through the living room to the dining room, then through to the kitchen. Paul keeps mumbling words of disbelief as he turns his head in every possible direction.

"I could look at everything for hours," he says.

"I'm glad you like it. When I came to see it with my parents, my mom wanted to get out of here pretty quickly."

He sets down the brittle old stack of recipes he was examining.

"How is she doing, by the way?"

It's sweet that he thought to ask. The other day we were

talking about my parents, and I mentioned that Mom's been having a tough time since Gram died. He said he was really sorry to hear it—and not in that rehearsed voice some people use when they're responding to bad news that doesn't affect them. It sounded like he really meant it.

"Still not great," I tell him. "Yesterday she basically sat inside all day and stared at the wall. I took her to the market and to watch the sunset when I got home, because she'd normally like that kind of thing, but she was just, like, detached."

Paul frowns.

"That doesn't sound good."

"I know. I wish there was something else I could do."

"Have you and your dad tried talking to her about it?"

"A little here and there," I mumble, crossing my arms. "Talking about feelings isn't exactly my family's strong suit."

"It might help," he suggests.

He sounds so hopeful. Paul clearly hasn't met the Prewitt family.

"Maybe," I say politely. "Anyway, do you want to see the rest of the apartment?"

I take him to the master bedroom and lead him over to my great-grandmother's vanity. After warning him to brace himself, I open the top drawer and show him the photo of Adalyn surrounded by Nazis. He reacts the same way as I did, even though he knows exactly what's coming. The picture is so disturbing, it's like you don't even want to touch it; he holds it between the very tips of his thumb and pointer finger, like he's trying to minimize skin contact.

"Do you think she was dating one of these men?" Paul asks.

"It's possible," I say with a grimace.

"They could have even gotten married."

"I hope not."

As Paul inspects the photo, I notice something in the drawer I didn't see before: a hardcover day planner from the year 1943. Curious, I flip through the pages. Just as she saved the magazine clippings, my great-grandmother documented every social engagement in her calendar. At least once a week, there's some kind of *dîner* or *fête* in the books. Every few weeks, the words "Hotel Belmont" appear in the square for Saturday.

"Paul, have you ever heard of this place?"

"Yes. I think it is near here, actually."

I show him how often it appears in the day planner. "I'm going to look it up."

I whip out my phone and search "Hotel Belmont WWII Paris." The first result is a booking site for the Hotel Belmont in the Eighth Arrondissement, nearby. The second result is a review in the *Guardian* of a book about resistance and collaboration in Nazi-occupied France. Bingo. I click the link and scan the article for any mention of the Belmont, and when I find it, I read it out loud to Paul: *"LeGrand*—that's the author—*goes inside every walk of life, from the hungry families*

queuing for rations to the socialites who flocked to the Hotel Bel-
mont to dance the night away with German officers."

"Oh my god," says Paul.

"My great-grandmother was in on it, too," I say bitterly. "I
guess I shouldn't be surprised."

I put the datebook in my backpack for closer inspection
later, and then I take him across the hall to Adalyn's bedroom to show him the place where I first found the diary. I
remember how excited I was, back when I didn't know the
awful truth about her. I also remember having trouble with
the drawer closest to the floor.

"Hey, Paul, I couldn't open this one before." I tap it with
the toe of my sneaker. "Any chance you could try?"

"Sure," he says, crouching down. He seizes the knob and
pulls it hard, his biceps flexing under his T-shirt. "Wow,
it's really stuck." He shakes out his arm and pulls it again.
There's an encouraging squeak, and then with one final tug,
the drawer shoots open. We both peer inside.

"Look," Paul says, "there's a note."

He carefully retrieves the piece of paper and holds it up to
the sunlight.

"Is that stationery from the Hotel Belmont?"

"It is," Paul says, moving closer so we can both see it.

Underneath the hotel's crest, there's a short message written in French. It's signed by a person named "Hauptmann
Ulrich Becker III."

"That is a very German-sounding name," Paul whispers. "I think 'Hauptmann' is a military rank."

"What does the message say?"

Paul adjusts his glasses and looks at the card closely.

"His French was not very good," he says. "Okay, let's see: My most dear Adalyn, I give thanks for the many evenings I have spent by your side. . . ."

I groan.

". . . Your beautiful eyes and your wonderful stories make better the pain of being so far from home. If I cannot be in Berlin, I am glad to be here in Paris with you. I give you this gift in the hope it will keep you warm during the winter. Yours truly, Hauptmann Ulrich Becker III."

Paul sets down the card and looks at me with a grimace. I feel the same way. We just read a Nazi love letter addressed to someone in my own family.

"She must have met him at the Hotel Belmont with her mother," Paul says.

"Well, if it's like you said, and she ended up marrying one of them, I bet it was this guy," I say gloomily.

"We can try to find him, too," Paul says.

"That's a good idea," I reply—and then I shake my head in disbelief. "I can't believe I'm about to go tracking down a Nazi. I feel like I need to cleanse my soul somehow."

"What is the exact opposite of Nazis, do you think? Oh! We should go to the Museum of National Resistance," Paul says. "It's in Champigny-sur-Marne. I have always wanted to go."

I look at him standing there in his jeans and plain white T-shirt—a cute Parisian boy who could be anywhere right now, but he's here with me, helping me solve the most bizarre mystery on the planet. The strange thing about being around my parents, especially in these past two weeks, is that I still end up feeling alone, even when we're together. Being with Paul is the opposite; it's like having a teammate who's always on my side.

"I'm really happy I met you," I blurt out—and I'm embarrassed right away. Today has *not* been my smoothest performance; first the awkward wave on the sidewalk, now this.

But Paul smiles.

"I'm really happy I met you, too."

I slide Ulrich's card into the front of Adalyn's diary for safekeeping, and we go back down to the street. Paul has to get to La Petite Librairie, and I have to get home to make sure Mom has remembered to eat food today, which isn't a guarantee.

I walk with him back to the metro station. But instead of saying goodbye, Paul says, "Hey, Alice . . . do you know about *le quatorze juillet*? I think they call it Bastille Day in America?"

Where is he going with this?

"I think I've heard of Bastille Day—it's like the French Fourth of July, right?"

"Yes—well, sort of," he says. "It's our national holiday, on the fourteenth of July. It is maybe not as big as the American holiday, but there are still parades . . . fireworks . . . no competitions to see who can eat the most hot dogs, though."

"You're missing out on a great tradition," I point out.

Paul laughs. Then he looks at his shoes and clears his throat.

"So my sister, Vivi, loves to celebrate *le quatorze juillet*," he says. "Every year, she and her friends rent an apartment in Versailles—very near to the palace—and Vivi spends the day cooking for everybody. . . ."

My heart is beating faster all of a sudden.

". . . Anyway," Paul continues, his voice a little bit shaky, "Vivi says she would love to have you join us this year. And I would, too, of course. It's only a forty-minute train ride from here, and her friends are all really nice, and of course I will bring you home whenever you want, and—"

"Paul, I would love to go!" I clasp my hands together.

He looks surprised—then relieved. "You would?"

"Of course I would! I mean, I'll have to ask my parents first, but if they're okay with it, then I'm in."

For a few seconds, we both just stand there smiling at each other on the sidewalk. People are sidestepping around us to get to the stairs leading down to the metro, but I'm barely paying attention.

"Well," he says, "let me know what they say."

"I'll text you as soon as I get an answer."

"Sounds good. See you, Alice."

"See you."

Paul looks like he might say something else, but then the moment is gone. He gives me a quick wave goodbye before he walks down the stairs, his hands stuffed into the pockets of his jeans. It almost aches to be away from him, and I just wish I knew for certain if he feels the same way about me.

CHAPTER 8

Adalyn

I wanted to believe this summer was the hardest thing I would ever have to go through. But as Papa says, things never get any easier during wartime. Either the war ends or life gets worse.

Two months have passed since they took Arnaud, and still I miss my friend every minute of the day. Sometimes I hear a voice that sounds like his and I spin around, longing to laugh with him again, only to find myself staring at a jumble of strangers. I don't think I've laughed since July—not really. Not in the red-cheeked, doubled-over way we laughed in the Luxembourg Gardens that day.

Luc got the details from Arnaud's neighbors about a week after the roundup. It was the concierge of his building who sold the family out. She told the officers exactly when his parents would be home, and when they arrived, they took

Arnaud, too. The neighbors didn't know where his two younger brothers ended up, but they assured Luc they never saw them get shepherded onto the buses headed for the Vel' d'Hiv.

August brought more bad news. Luc got word through Geronte that the resistance group in Créteil had been compromised. The Gestapo dragged one of its members in for questioning, and under the threat of his whole family being deported, he turned over the names of three of his accomplices. We were safe, as no one in Créteil knew our names, but the three unlucky people were promptly arrested and sent to the prison of Fresnes. The woman in the pale blue coat, the one I met in the café, is among them. It is said that at Fresnes, resisters are beaten and starved for the smallest infractions—that they're hung from the ceiling by an arm and a leg and tortured for information. The name "Fresnes" alone makes my stomach drop.

Rat-tat-tat-tat-tat. It used to feel like a game, scurrying down to the Latin Quarter when school was out and rapping on the back door of the shoe store. We felt ecstatic—invincible—like the five of us could take down Nazi Germany if we just put our heads together. I know better than that now. We all do—those of us who are left. What I'm doing is risky. It could cost me my life.

But if Arnaud could be brave in the face of danger, then I must be, too.

Luc opens the door. He's the only one in the room. I try not to look at the table, where Arnaud's feigned "book club" scene is still on display.

"You don't look well," Luc says.

"I'm fine," I mumble.

"Adalyn, I know you well enough—"

"I just miss him, Luc."

And then he does something unexpected. In nearly two years of knowing him, Luc and I have never more than grazed each other's skin by chance. Now, in the dim light, he pulls me into his arms and holds me against his chest. My cheek makes a nest in his shoulder, and his fingers find roots in my hair. Every heartbeat could be his or mine—it's impossible to tell the difference.

"I know you miss him," he says softly. "I do, too."

"Sometimes I wonder if we should just stop all this," I whisper, my voice catching. "I look at what happened to Arnaud, and I ask myself . . . I ask myself what difference we're really making."

I feel his hands on my shoulders, and the next thing I know he's holding me at arm's length.

"We have to do the opposite," Luc says with determination. "We have to look at what happened to Arnaud and let it be the reason we *don't* stop all this."

He's right.

We stare into each other's eyes for what feels like an

infinite stretch of time. At some point—I can't quite say how long it's been—a single tear rolls down Luc's cheek. He doesn't wipe it away. I follow its glimmering trail until it dries at the corner of his perfect lips.

"Adalyn," he says, "I have to tell you something."

"What?"

"It isn't good."

An unwelcome chill settles about the room. It isn't good? What more bad news could we possibly endure? He leads me over to the two chairs, and I take a seat, shaking.

"I can't stay here anymore," he says quietly. "I have to leave."

"What do you mean?"

"It's the Compulsory Work Service," he replies. I can tell he's trying to keep his voice steady. "Any able-bodied men over eighteen years old are being sent off to work in Germany."

I shoot to the edge of my seat.

"Oh, Luc, you mustn't—"

"I'm not going to do it. Of course not."

"Good."

"But that is why I have to leave."

My body droops against the back of the chair as I gradually comprehend what Luc is saying. I can tell from the pained look in his eyes that he doesn't have a choice: If he wants to keep fighting, then he has to hide. Our prolonged embrace from a moment ago suddenly takes on new meaning. I think Luc is really going to miss me.

"Where will you go?" I ask.

"Underground. Into hiding. I hear there are bands of guer-rilla fighters forming in the south. Perhaps I'll join them—we can find out how good I am with real weapons." He laughs weakly, but his eyes still look sad. "Geronte is helping me figure out what to do. Which reminds me—he will be your contact now, Adalyn. I think you will like him . . . eventually. He has a tough shell."

"What about Marcel? And Pierre-Henri?"

"They must leave, too."

While Luc goes to the table to scribble on a small scrap of paper, I try to make sense of everything that's happening right now. It is too much information to process all at once. I have so many questions I want to ask him, I don't even know where to begin. . . .

But then I realize there is only one that really matters to me right now.

"Luc, when will I see you again?"

He returns from the table and places the scrap of paper in my palm, along with another half train ticket.

"I don't know," he answers.

"Wh-what?"

"This isn't goodbye forever," he says hurriedly. "I'll be in and out of the city, I think. I just can't say for certain when it will be."

Just like the first time I met him, here in this very same room, I have the urge to run my hand along his cheek, thinner now than it was at the time, but no less beautiful. I might even like to touch my mouth to those perfect lips. . . . And with the way he embraced me earlier, I think he might feel the same way. . . . But no—he has already cried tonight—I mustn't make this goodbye any harder for him.

I step out into the chilly September air feeling sapped of all my energy. I am a girl made of stone.

Life keeps on getting worse, just as Papa said it would.

A couple of days later, I'm sitting in the drawing room reading a novel—just glancing at the pages, really—when I notice that something feels off in the apartment. At first, I can't put my finger on it: Maman is reading Suzette's latest column with great focus, her red lips slightly parted, mouthing the words; Chloe sits at the table across the room, her sewing equipment spread out at her fingertips. It isn't until I gaze from one to the other that I realize . . . what's so strange about this scene is that neither of them is shouting at the other.

Now that I think about it, Chloe has been oddly calm all day; even her hair isn't as tall as it usually is. Which is strange, because Maman informed us over breakfast that we'd been invited to a very important salon at the Hotel Belmont tonight. Madame LaRoche and the twins are going to be there, along with a few of Maman's other friends. Apparently, there will be writers and actresses and fashion designers and musicians in attendance. Even Suzette is expected to make an appearance.

It's the exact kind of thing Chloe would despise.

I hope she isn't up to something.

"Chloe, what are you sewing?" asks Maman when she finishes the column.

"My outfit for tonight," Chloe replies in a singsong voice.

Oh no.

"Can I help you with anything?"

"No thank you, Maman! I should be fine."

When Maman looks at the clock and says that it's time to get ready, Chloe gathers up her things and skips off to her bedroom with a smile.

As I comb my hair in front of the mirror, there's a knock at the door. Maman enters, wearing a lovely green dress with a cinched waist and full skirt. "Oh!" she says, noticing the dress I've laid out on the bed is a similar shade of green. "We're going to match—shall I go change?"

"No, Maman. Don't be ridiculous; you're dressed already. I'll pick something else."

"But you look so beautiful in that dress."

"Well then, why don't we both wear green? I don't mind if we match."

Maman beams in the reflection of the mirror. "I'm so lucky," she says. Then she walks over, eases the comb from my hand, and begins to pull it through my curls herself, as she's done so many times before. I relax into my chair, enjoying the familiar repetition: a drag of the comb, followed by Maman's hand smoothing my hair. She's done this for me ever since I was a little girl.

"How are your lessons going, darling?"

"They're good, Maman. Challenging, but good."

Maman and Papa encouraged me to enroll in university so that perhaps I can teach music someday, and I took them up on their gracious offer, although it seems like such a small, selfish goal compared to what really matters now. I drift between classes, barely registering the lessons, feeling miserable that Arnaud didn't get the same opportunity. Now that they're leaving the city, I suppose Luc, Marcel, and Pierre-Henri won't get it either. The only upside is that Maman and Papa are much less aware of my class schedule now, meaning it will be easier for me to sneak off and do work for Geronte—whom I am meeting tomorrow morning for the first time.

"Did anything fun happen this week?" asks Maman.

"No . . . actually, there was something rather upsetting," I confess.

"Oh no," she says, frowning. "What was it?"

"A professor in the music department didn't come in on Thursday . . . and then yesterday, we found out he'd been arrested. His wife, too."

Maman inhales sharply through her nose. "For what?" she asks.

"They were apparently sheltering Jews in their apartment."

Maman stops what's she's doing and grips my shoulders as though to steady herself. She looks like she's trying not to faint. With Papa around the house, she rarely shows this kind of emotion, but ever since the Vel' d'Hiv roundup, I think it's been harder for her to trust that everything will be all right in the end. She brings up Pétain less than she used to, and even though she hasn't openly said such a thing, I wonder if her confidence in the Old Marshal has finally been shaken.

Maman takes a deep breath to restore her composure and resumes her work on my hair. "That's terrible, Adalyn. Did you know the man?"

"No. I only saw him in the halls a few times. People said he was lovely, though."

Maman just shakes her head sadly.

After a minute or two, she says, "Let's talk about something more uplifting. It's wonderful to see your sister looking forward to a party for once."

Oh, yes. Chloe. What is she up to on the other side of the wall? I still don't know, so I nod at Maman in a noncommittal sort of way as she sets down the comb and begins pinning my curls in just the right place.

Maman and I, as usual, are the first to arrive in the foyer with our coats. Chloe's door is still shut.

"Chloe, dear?" Maman calls. "Are you almost ready?"

"Just about!" Chloe answers.

It hurts me to see the joy twinkling in Maman's eyes. I can tell how excited she is to spend a night with both of her daughters. Chloe rarely accompanies us to dinner parties at Madame LaRoche's anymore—there's usually a fight, and then my sister stomps off to join her friends someplace, or to shut herself in her bedroom. Each time, I see how it shatters Maman, who just wants everybody to get along and make the best of things. I can tell Maman thinks this time will be different, that maybe at last, her youngest daughter has come around. And maybe I'm wrong—I hope I'm wrong—but I know Chloe very well, and I know she would sooner walk back to Jonzac on foot than go to the Hotel Belmont tonight.

The bedroom door swings open. Chloe is wearing the long violet dress she was sewing in the drawing room earlier. Her hair is styled in an elegant chignon, and she's even wearing a non-blinding shade of lipstick. I am desperately relieved—until I see the yellow star stitched to her chest. It looks exactly like the yellow star Arnaud was made to wear, except instead of the word "Juif" in the center, Chloe's says "zazou." I have seen other young people wear stars like this to protest the Nazis' anti-Jewish policies.

Maman is elated at the sight of her daughter all dressed

up, until she sees what Chloe has done. It would be easier to watch if she spiraled into a fit of rage, but instead, her face crumples in disappointment.

"I'm ready," Chloe says defiantly, a smirk playing on her lips.

"Darling," Maman says in a low, controlled voice, "you cannot wear that to the Hotel Belmont tonight."

"Why not?"

"You just *can't*," she insists.

I wonder if she's thinking about the music professor.

"Because everyone who's going to be there *agrees* that the Jews should be singled out and deported?" asks Chloe.

Maman looks affronted.

"Chloe," I chime in, desperate to avoid a big fight, "of course we don't think that. But you could get in trouble if a German sees you on the way there."

Chloe plants her hands on her hips. The color rises in her fair cheeks.

"Well, if I can't wear it, then I don't want to go," she says.

"Fine," Maman says. "Adalyn and I will go by ourselves."

I'm in the middle, once again. Chloe looks at me expectantly, as though daring me to side with Maman.

"You really won't change outfits?" I ask, taking her by the hand. "Please, Chloe—I want you to come." It's true. These events would be much more bearable if Chloe was with me, and besides, we haven't spent as much time together lately, now that I'm in university and Chloe has a whole new cohort of *zazou* friends.

But she yanks her hand away.

"No thank you."

I sigh. I never want Chloe to be upset with me. At least she still lets me hug her goodbye, and then Maman and I set off for the Eighth Arrondissement.

"So who is hosting the party?" I ask Maman, trying to lighten the mood as we walk down the boulevard Haussmann. The wide, tree-lined street is mostly deserted. At certain intersections you used to be able to see Sacré-Coeur off in the distance, but not anymore, with Paris in the dark.

"Madeleine Marbot," Maman says, "of the Marbot diamond family. Madame LaRoche and I happened to be seated next to her at Madame Agnès's runway show. And then we ran into her again at Cartier, where she and Madame LaRoche had their eyes on the same clock, and that's when she invited us all to the salon tonight."

"That was generous of her."

"She really is an admirable woman," Maman says. "Madame LaRoche told me the whole story. She's one of these people who came back to Paris to discover the Germans had requisitioned her apartment. I still can't imagine what that must have been like. . . . But in any case, Madame Marbot kept her head held high. She took up residence at the Hotel Belmont and has been hosting these salons ever since."

"How interesting."

"Yes. I suppose that's the spirit, isn't it? We all have to adapt, because who knows how long this will last. . . ."

We go in through the grand front doors, Maman leading the way. As we descend the short flight of stairs into the lobby, I spy them everywhere, infesting the place like rats: Germans. They sip wine and smoke cigarettes in the plush red chairs, and some even have their big black boots up on the tables. I despise them even more now, ever since Arnaud, but we both pretend not to notice them as we cross the marble floor to the lift.

We can hear the din as soon as we get off on the fifth floor. The doors of the suite open to reveal a glittering chandelier, and underneath, a party in full swing: hordes of people—mostly women—in their evening finery; a live band playing in the corner; hors d'oeuvres and drinks being passed around as though rationing were not in effect.

Not five steps into the room, we are greeted by a somewhat stout woman in a voluminous turquoise dress and matching feathered hat. She kisses Maman twice on each cheek.

"Odette Bonhomme! I am delighted to see you again."

"The pleasure is mine, Madeleine," Maman says. "I *adore* the hat."

"It's Madame Agnès, of course," Madame Marbot says with a wink. "And your marvelous clutch?"

"Boucheron."

Madame Marbot nods approvingly. Then she turns to me, laying her gloved hands upon my shoulders.

"And who is this charming creature?"

"My daughter Adalyn," Maman answers.

"It's lovely to meet you," I say.

"Lovely to meet you, too, darling," Madame Marbot replies airily. I can tell that her eyes have already latched onto another new arrival. "You two go and enjoy the party, now."

And just like that, she's gone.

"Odette! Adalyn!"

A flush-faced Madame LaRoche waves to us as she navigates her way through the crowd with the twins in tow. Along the way, she snatches two flutes of champagne off a passing tray and gives us each one.

"This party is incredible, isn't it?" Madame LaRoche says breathlessly. "Odette, come with me. Suzette is over there by the window, and she's just *lovely* in person." She seizes Maman by the hand, and the two of them go off toward the group of middle-aged women clustered around the obliging—though perhaps slightly overwhelmed—columnist.

Now, once again, it's just me and the twins. I really do wish Chloe were here. I still feel hopelessly sad from my meeting with Luc, and it would help to have a friend at my side, even if I couldn't tell her exactly what was wrong.

"What shall we do?" I ask them.

"Maybe we should go to the room in back," Marie suggests, eyeing Monique. "The one we were in earlier."

Monique shrugs. "If you want."

Marie takes me by the hand and guides me and her sister toward a set of doors. But when I see where she's taking me, I recoil. The sitting room is smaller, quieter, and more comfortable than the main entrance, with a roaring blaze in the fireplace. But reclining on the divans, and leaning against the mantel, are a half dozen German officers in black jackets adorned with medals and leather gun belts. They stand out like roaches on a white-tiled floor.

"I know, I was surprised, too," Marie whispers. "But they're really very friendly."

They deported one of my friends.

"It's quite nice when you can forget about the war for a while and just be *people*."

Frozen at the threshold of the room, I watch as Marie strikes up a conversation with a blond-haired, blue-eyed German on the sofa. His red Nazi armband is glaring, but she doesn't seem to mind as she tries a sip of his cognac, then wrinkles her nose in what's meant to be cute expression of disgust.

Monique is still standing next to me, like a beachgoer deciding if she wants to get into the water. Of the two LaRoche girls, she is the one I get along with *slightly* better. Surely, she sees how wrong this is.

"Are you going to go join them?"

"I . . . I suppose so," she says. "I know it isn't right, because they're the enemy, but at the same time, the Occupation is the Occupation, is it not? We can't change that. We might as well interact and see if we can get something out of them."

"Like what?"

"Food. Wine. Maman says the black-market prices are getting steeper and steeper."

Monique seems ready to join her sister. I am not. "You go ahead," I tell her, spying a corridor that looks as though it might lead to a lavatory. "I want to powder my nose first."

"Okay, see you soon," she says. "I swear it isn't as bad as it looks."

I dart for the corridor, intent on spending as much time as I possibly can in the toilet tonight. But I'm about to turn the corner when I career headfirst into another body—one that emits a clinking of metal upon collision. The crash sends a wave of champagne splashing down my front, and my glass flute plummets to the floor and shatters into a million pieces.

The room goes silent as everyone turns to look at us.

I am mortified.

"Gut gemacht, Uli," teases the blond-haired Nazi on the couch. *Well done, Uli.* The other Germans in the room point and laugh at us. Great—now they have all seen us together. If I sneak away now, people will notice.

Uli, as he must be called, is crouched on the floor and

using his leather gloves to sweep the glass into a pile and deposit it in a nearby trash can. Instinctively, I bend down to help him, but he holds out his hand to stop me.

"Vorsicht—es ist sehr scharf," he warns. Careful—it's very sharp.

He can't be much older than I am. He has smooth, pale skin with rounded features and a full head of sandy-brown hair. I notice, with the tiniest bit of relief, that he isn't wearing the swastika on his arm.

When the glass is all gone, he gets to his feet, his cheeks flushed with embarrassment. Then he takes one look at my dress, now wet with champagne, and launches into a string of apologies in mangled French, his cheeks growing more and more crimson by the second.

"It really is fine," I assure him for the tenth time.

At last, he is calm.

"I do not have very much experience at big parties," he says with a chuckle. "You see? I still have not introduced myself to you. I am Ulrich Becker. What is your name, miss?"

I cast around for Marie and Monique, but they are deep in conversation on the couch. Well, if I must stay at this party until Maman is ready to go home, better I pass the time with Ulrich, who isn't an armband-wearing party member, than with the blond-haired Nazi.

"Adalyn Bonhomme."

"You have very beautiful eyes, Miss Bonhomme."

"Oh. Thank you."

"We must get you something else to drink."

"Okay."

I let Ulrich lead me to a pair of empty chairs near the fire and pour me a glass of cognac. It feels good to let the flames dry my damp clothes—but what am I to talk about with this damned *boche* all evening?

"Tell me about yourself," he says.

"All right. What would you like to know?"

He takes a long, slow slip of his drink and stares into the blaze. I can see tendrils of fire reflected in his eyes. "Anything."

I sense that Ulrich does not want to learn; he wants to be distracted. Well, so do I. I pick a safe, neutral topic—school—and in a meandering sort of way talk about my first few months of university.

"It is nice that you enjoy it," Ulrich says. "I must admit, I never liked school."

"Why was that?"

"I was not good at sports—the worst in the whole school. My classmates called me weak. I . . . I never had very many friends."

"Oh. That certainly makes things more difficult." Like school after Charlotte and Simone left. "It isn't fun to feel lonely every day."

"No. It isn't."

"What do you do now?"

"I work at the rail yard."

"Are you happier?"

Silence. Ulrich chews his bottom lip. "Can I tell something to you, Miss Bonhomme?"

"Yes. You may say whatever you like."

He tips his glass against his lips once more, his eyes never leaving the hearth. "I must speak softly," he says, nodding toward his compatriots. "You see, I am grateful for my position . . . and I believe it is the right thing, the natural thing, for Germany to rule over France . . . but if I am to be honest, Miss Bonhomme, I miss very much my home in Berlin."

I try not to let my reaction to his comments about Germany and France show in my face.

"Is your family there?"

"*Ja*. My mother, my father, and my baby sister. My sister, Klara, she is my very best friend. We are normally talking to each other all the time. It is not easy to be away from her . . . and it has been two years now."

His words stir up an unexpected flurry of emotions in my chest. They remind me of Chloe, and the look in her eyes as she yanked her hand out of mine in the foyer, and all the secrets I've been forced to keep from her in the last two years. The war has driven a wedge between us, which frustrates me terribly, because we are still the same people at our cores.

"My younger sister is my best friend, too," I tell Ulrich, and when he finally looks at me, I can see that his eyes shine with tears.

"Thank you for understanding. . . ."

"Of course. That must be very painful."

"*Ja*," he says again, nodding. "Very painful."

There is nothing left for me to say about school, so Ulrich talks about his work instead. I learn that he is in charge of train schedules at the Gare de l'Est, the railway station not far from my home. He makes sure that important supplies from Germany—weapons, ammunition, building materials, and the like—make it into Paris safely to be used by the Occupation forces. Despite missing home, he says he enjoys his job, and it isn't long before he's getting into the finer details of organizing train schedules. When he mentions the specific timing of a firearm shipment coming in later this week, my ears perk up. Perhaps under the influence of an evening's worth of cognac, Ulrich is revealing very specific details about the German war effort—details that could be useful to us.

My head starts to pound with adrenaline.

I need to memorize everything he's said.

"Adalyn?"

Ulrich stops talking, and we both look over to find Maman standing in the doorway. She looks back and forth between us, assessing the situation. She must be doing some mental calculation over how it's okay to feel about a German officer being kind to her daughter. In the end, she smiles, albeit somewhat cautiously.

"Are you ready to go, darling? Madeleine has arranged for a German staff car to take us home." She pauses. "It's easier than walking all the way back."

Earlier in the evening, I might have leapt at her arrival, but now I wish I could stay and get more information out of Ulrich. He helps me out of my chair and guides me to Maman, past Marie and Monique, who are now more than a little drunk and taking turns trying on the blond Nazi's uniform hat.

"You have a lovely daughter," Ulrich says to Maman. "We have very much enjoyed talking this evening."

"Thank you," Maman says. "It's nice to see us all getting along."

"I hope to see you again, Miss Bonhomme," Ulrich says to me.

"I hope so, too," I reply.

Maman and I retrieve our coats and make our way to the door, stopping along the way for a few final goodbyes. I don't know what makes me do it, but right before we leave, I glance over my shoulder for one last look at the party. There's Ulrich, standing at the entrance to the sitting room and gazing in my direction. When our eyes meet, he smiles.

He waves to me.

I wave back.

On the car ride home, the cool September breeze blows our hair this way and that. Maman recounts the highlights of the evening with the air of someone trying hard to assure themselves of something.

"I think we deserved a night out, didn't we? It was nice to just *relax*. With the way things are now, we have to let ourselves eat and drink like that when we can." She nods, as though agreeing with herself. "The band was excellent—and there was so much champagne—and Suzette was brilliant; I would love to meet her again."

I nod along, too, my mind on Ulrich's train schedules. I'm also thinking about my meeting with Geronte, which is happening tomorrow morning.

"Madeleine said we *must* come to her next event," Maman says, reaching across the seat and squeezing my hand.

I can tell she's conflicted. She knows it isn't right to go to parties with Nazis, but tonight, she had fun. Maman wants to adapt to our new normal—not to the same lengths as Madame Marbot, of course, but enough to make our lives under the Germans a little more tolerable. I think she wants me to help justify our return to the Hotel Belmont—and luckily for her, I have a vested interest in meeting Ulrich again.

"Of course we'll be at the next one," I tell her, squeezing her hand in return.

The automobile turns onto our darkened street, its covered headlights casting an eerie blue light onto the pavement. I don't know what makes me do it—maybe it's purely by chance, or maybe I really am attuned to my sister's every impulse—but as the car rolls to a stop outside number thirty-six, I gaze up toward our apartment on the fifth floor.

There, staring down at the street with her head hanging out the window, is Chloe.

It's too dark to read the expression on her face, but perhaps it's better that way. For I can only imagine what's going through my sister's head as we climb out onto the sidewalk in our evening wear—Maman giggling about some joke she heard at the party—and the shiny German car drives off into the night.

CHAPTER 9

Alice

Another evening at home. Another rigid dinner around the kitchen table with Mom sitting in sullen silence, and me and Dad taking turns trying to start some kind of conversation.

"So, Alice, it sounds like you and Paul have a fun day in Versailles planned tomorrow. He seems like a good guy, doesn't he, Diane?"

"Mhmm."

"It was really nice of him to invite me," I chime in. "He did it out of the blue, as we were leaving Gram's apartment."

Shoot. I wasn't thinking—it just slipped out. The second I mention the apartment, Mom's body visibly tenses. She stops chewing, her jaw clenches, and she squeezes her fork so tight her knuckles turn white. Oh no, no, *no*. I feel terrible. Mom's still so sensitive to anything involving Gram, and I just dropped that bomb without any warning.

"I'm sorry, Mom. I've been trying not to talk about it."

"It's fine," she says, swallowing her food with what looks like difficulty. "It's fine."

But it clearly *isn't* fine. Nobody speaks for the rest of the meal; the only sound is the forks and knives scraping against china. When we're finished, we clear our plates, and Mom returns to her corner of the couch; Dad, to his laptop. Mom probably needs a little space right now, so I go to my room to keep translating Adalyn's diary.

Tonight, I have the diary open on one side of my lap and my great-grandmother's day planner open on the other. I've been cross-referencing dates to see if I can find any links. Suddenly, I find something that makes my heart leap.

There's a diary entry dated September 26, 1942. The day before, Adalyn's mom visited the Hotel Belmont for the first time. What if Adalyn went with her? And what if she wrote about Ulrich Becker III? I start typing into Google Translate as fast as I can.

September 26*th*, 1942

I thought Chloe would yell at us when we came in from the party, but it was worse. She was standing in the foyer, looking like she was about to cry. Then she stormed to her room and slammed the door.

So I guessed right. Adalyn *was* there.

I hated knowing that I disappointed her, so the next morning I begged her, please, come for a walk with me down by the river. The river is the only place that doesn't feel claustrophobic in this city, where the buildings give way to wide-open water and air. You can think there. You can breathe. It was a long walk to get there, but the weather was agreeable, and since Maman and Papa were handling rations that day, I said, what else did we have to do?

She was reluctant, but she agreed. I bought us two cups of so-called coffee along the way, which tasted terrible, but our mutual revulsion broke the ice. We played our old game again, starting with a cup of rich, dark espresso for me and a steaming mug of hot chocolate for Chloe.

At the river, we returned to the more serious matter. She of course said, How could you? They are the enemy! And I said, I know they are the enemy, and so does Maman. People have different ways of dealing with the Occupation. Different things they must do to survive.

And then I made a mistake: I told Chloe the truth, which is that I never would have gone in the first place had I known les boches *would be there.*

Now I dread what will happen when she learns I intend to go back.

I double-check the translation, certain I made a mistake. It's the ending that I don't get: Adalyn says she wouldn't have gone to the Belmont if she'd known about the Germans—but then why in the world does she want to go *back*? Strangely, it all seems correct, so I keep going.

October 6th, 1942

I could not focus in class today at all. It was sociology, which I tend to enjoy more than other lessons, but my mind was simply untethered. The professor called on me and I had to ask him to repeat the question—it was embarrassing.

I know why, though: because I miss him. I long for another evening together. I didn't expect to miss him this much, but I do.

I stare at what I just typed for about fifteen seconds.

Oh my god.

Gross, gross, *gross*.

I slam my laptop closed and shove the diary into my backpack, out of sight. I finally found it. The point when Adalyn went bad. I'm not translating another word of that thing.

My heart races as I put it all together into a plausible story line.

I know that Adalyn used to hate the Germans. She *despised*

them. Then, in 1942, she went to the Hotel Belmont . . . and even though there were Germans there, she decided she wanted to go back.

Was it because she met Ulrich Becker III? That *must* be who she was daydreaming about in the second diary entry. My stomach churns as I imagine them falling in love, and Ulrich writing Adalyn the note we found in her desk drawer.

There's a gentle knock at the door. I jump about a foot in the air.

"Alice?" It's Dad.

"Hey—come in."

He slips into the room and closes the door behind him with a soft click.

"What's up?" I ask, trying not to show how shaken up I am from the diary.

Dad sits down as close to the edge of the bed as possible. He crosses and uncrosses his legs, but he can't seem to figure out how to arrange himself comfortably. Finally, staring at my knee, he says, "I want to talk to you about something."

"Okay."

"It's about Mom."

I sigh as the guilt from dinner ricochets around my chest again. "I'm really sorry I brought up the apartment earlier. I feel so bad. . . . It just slipped out. . . ."

"It's okay, Alice." He pats my shin with the world's stiffest hand, before clearing his throat. "That's, ah, that's actually what I wanted to talk about." He pauses to take a deep breath, and suddenly I get nervous. "Given how Mom has been doing, I wanted to gauge your interest on . . ."

". . . On what?"

He rubs the back of his neck. "On potentially selling Gram's apartment."

Whoa.

He wants to . . .

He wants to *what*?

"S-sorry," I stammer, searching for words, "I'm just kind of—kind of stunned."

"Ultimately, it's up to you," Dad jumps in. He's talking faster now, and I can tell he's in selling mode. "I know you were close with Gram, and I know it means a lot to you that she left you the apartment, but I think you should at least consider it. I mean, aside from everything with Mom, it'll also be worth a lot—not just the apartment itself, but everything inside it. You could make a lot of money."

I sit there blinking as the words sink in, and the next thing I know, there's a lump in my throat. This is what Gram left to me; she wanted me to have it. If we sold the apartment, we might never find out what actually happened to her family. We might lose important clues. We'd be sweeping away history.

But I also get it. Completely. If everything about the apartment makes Mom sad, then why not just get it out of our lives for good? Start fresh. Mom would feel relieved—and I would feel so much less guilty about the inheritance. And really, do I still *want* to track down Adalyn, after what I just read in the diary? Do I *want* to hang on to an apartment that used to house a Nazi sympathizer? I feel like I'm back at square one, not knowing which way to go.

"You don't have to make a decision right away," Dad continues, "but maybe in the next two weeks? I've started doing some poking around on potential agents, and I'd like to get in touch with someone before we leave."

I reach for the comforter and drag it onto my lap. I have no idea what to say right now, because I honestly see the value in both options.

"Does Mom know?" I ask.

"I mentioned it to her," Dad says. "She said it's your decision . . . but . . ."

". . . She probably doesn't want to pressure me."

"Right."

I think Dad might be downplaying Mom's reaction. Let's be real—she was probably *thrilled* at the prospect of selling Gram's apartment. I sink into the headboard, feeling crushed by the weight of this decision. At least I have two weeks to make it.

"I'll let you know, Dad."

He flashes me a double thumbs-up and springs to his feet, no doubt delighted for the difficult conversation to be over.

"What time do you leave for Versailles tomorrow?"

"Oh . . . um, I'm getting up early so I can pick up food before I meet Paul, so if I don't see you . . ."

"Have fun tomorrow, honey."

"Thanks, Dad. And hey . . . will you make sure Mom has fun, too? I made her promise me she'd make an effort, but . . ."

". . . I'll make sure," he says. He smiles, but sadly. "Night, Alice."

"Night, Dad."

It's only eleven o'clock in the morning, but the streets are already crowded with people, some of them sporting a French flag tied around their shoulders. I'm supposed to be meeting Paul outside the Musée d'Orsay train station, but the crowds are so dense, I'm having a hard time spotting him. Someone jostles me from behind, and the forty-five pounds of French cheese I'm carrying come dangerously close to flying out of my hands.

"Alice! Over here!"

I follow the sound of his voice, and I finally see Paul jumping up and down and waving something in the air to get my attention. Oh my god—it's a baguette.

I'm still giggling when I make it over to where he's standing.

"I appreciate your resourcefulness," I tell him.

"I just didn't want you to get lost," Paul says, blushing.

Then he takes in the sight of my arms wrapped around the massive shopping bag like I'm hanging on for dear life, and his eyes go wide. "Alice, is that entire bag full of cheese?"

"Cheese . . . and olives, and nuts, and dried fruit, and these cute mini pickles the guy told me to buy, and some other things I can't even remember right now. I might have gone a little overboard at the market. We don't have this kind of selection in New Jersey."

"Is it heavy?"

"Extremely."

He takes the bag from my arms and gives me the baguettes to carry instead, and I follow him down the stairs to buy our tickets at the machine. The train is crowded, but Paul and I squeeze through to the upper level and manage to find two seats together. It feels very grown up, to be sitting next to a boy with our groceries at our feet. My heart lurches as the train pulls out of the station.

After making a few more stops within Paris proper, our train cruises through the suburbs toward the town of Versailles. As we fly past clusters of houses built into the hillsides, I fill in Paul on the disturbing entries I read in Adalyn's diary. I leave out the part about selling the apartment, because I don't want to get into everything with Mom—and besides, I don't even know what I'm going to do yet. Finally, I pull out my phone to show him what I did as soon as I woke up this morning: dig around Facebook for Ulrich Becker III.

"I could be completely wrong," I say, "but there's a chance I found him."

Paul leans over to watch, our bare arms pressed together.

"At first I was like, 'Shoot, there are a lot of Ulrich Beckers.'" I say, typing the name "Ulrich Becker" into the search bar and scrolling down the page to show him the endless list of matches. "But then I remembered we're looking for Ulrich Becker the Third. So I tried getting a little more specific. . . ."

I add the Roman numeral three to the name in the search bar.

". . . There didn't seem to be any Ulrich Becker IIIs who fit the age we're looking for, but then, out of curiosity, I clicked into this guy's page—Ulrich Becker IV. . . ."

I go to the profile of the seventy-something-year-old man.

". . . I obviously knew he wasn't our guy, but then I happened to see the most recent photo he posted, and . . ."

I show Paul the picture. It takes him a second, but eventually, he gasps. He actually pulls the phone closer to his face, which happens to involve him grabbing me by the hand. It's a lot to process at once.

"So you think it could be him?" Paul asks in disbelief.

The photo is of a group of men and boys holding fishing rods at the edge of a lake. They must be family, because the man tagged "Ulrich Becker IV" has his hand on the shoulder of a younger man tagged "Uli Becker V." Plus they look alike with their sandy hair and dull, rounded features. But the most intriguing part of the photo is the wizened old man sitting in a chair in the center of the front row. He isn't tagged—I mean, there's no way the guy has Facebook—but thankfully, the caption hints at who he might be. I hit the translate button for Paul, and together we read the German text in choppy English:

"Annual wilderness journey to Three's ninety-fifth birthday! He is still strong. He caught more fish than anyone else."

"They call him Three," I point out.

"And he would be the right age," Paul adds, sounding mystified.

My heart is racing—one, because Paul is as excited about the discovery as I am, and two, because he still hasn't let go of my hand. We both seem to realize this second point at the exact same time, because Paul immediately lets go and busies himself with straightening out his glasses. I should probably keep talking so he doesn't know I'm paying such close attention to our every bit of physical contact.

"I want to send him a message," I say quickly, "but I don't even know where to begin. I mean, he obviously speaks German."

"We can use Google Translate," Paul points out.

"True. But also, what do I even say? How do you ask someone out of the blue if their dad happened to be a Nazi who fell in love with your long-lost French great-aunt? He's going to think I'm a freak—or get really angry! You can't just go asking people if their parents were Nazis."

Paul rubs his chin.

"Yes," he concedes, "we will have to think about how to phrase that correctly."

"I'm not good at that," I admit. "I'm already stressed out from thinking about it."

"Then we will save it for later," Paul declares. "Tomorrow, we will sit down at the bookstore and figure out exactly what to write to this man, okay?"

"Okay."

"*Today*," he continues, "we worry about nothing except celebrating your first *quatorze juillet*. Now, let's have something to eat, yes?"

He tears off a still-warm hunk of bread and offers me half.

Pretending to be distraught over the state of the baguette, I ask him, "But now how will I find you if I get lost?"

Paul puts on a serious thinking face that makes me giggle again.

"I suppose we will just have to stick together," he says.

We learned about Versailles in history class this past year. Mr. Yip made a slideshow of all the most opulent parts of the palace: the front courtyards; the Hall of Mirrors; the ridiculously symmetrical gardens in back . . . but nothing could have prepared me to exit the train station, turn just *one* corner, and see the enormous place for myself, looming in the distance.

"Oh my god, it's huge!" I exclaim.

"Just wait," Paul says. "We're still a ten-minute walk away."

It's the kind of thing that throws off your entire understanding of size and space, like the Grand Canyon. Up close, the palace is so big, I have to turn my head to see it all. The sprawling front courtyards are teeming with people, so we set down our bags near the statue of Louis XIV on horseback and soak in the sight from there.

"In the French Revolution," Paul says, "women marched here all the way from Paris to protest the price of bread."

I remember Mr. Yip telling us about that, but the significance of it didn't really sink in until right now. "I would have given up instantly the second I saw this place!"

"You? Given up instantly? There is no chance," Paul says, nudging me with his elbow.

"Oh yeah? What makes you think that?"

"I see you trying to solve your grandmother's mystery. You are determined. I like this about you."

I smile to myself the whole way to the apartment.

Paul mentioned on the train this morning that Vivi is very serious about holidays, and he wasn't kidding. When we arrive at the top-floor apartment, she opens the door looking like a tiny human firecracker. She's in a red-white-and-blue sequined dress, and her hair is in pigtails with metallic party favors wedged into either side; she's wearing dangly earrings in the shape of disco balls, and shiny silver bracelets that jangle every time she moves her arms. When she hugs us each in turn, she leaves behind glitter on our clothes.

"Vivi, tu es ridicule," Paul says as he dusts off the front of his shirt. Then, to me, he explains, "The French don't usually dress up like this. Just Vivi."

Practically bouncing with every step, Vivi leads us down the hall into a wide-open space with a kitchen, dining room, and seating area all combined. The smell in here is intoxicating; it might be even better than the bakery, which is saying something. Sure enough, the table is set with a feast that could probably feed twenty people, but as far as I can tell, there are only three other people in the apartment: a guy and two girls who are chatting outside on the balcony.

"I think I might have gone overboard this year," Vivi confesses.

"I think you go overboard every year," Paul jokes. He plunks the shopping bag down on the counter. "Well, at least Alice and I will have plenty of cheese to eat on the train ride home."

Vivi calls the other three inside to introduce us before we sit down to lunch. The guy is her boyfriend, Theo, an art student with multiple piercings in his ears and colorful tattoos from his wrists to his shoulders. The girl with the long brown braid is Vivi's best friend, Claudette, and the other girl with the blond curls is Claudette's girlfriend, Lucie.

I like them instantly. Considering that I'm used to quiet meals with Mom and Dad, Vivi and her friends are so outgoing that it's almost overwhelming. They do their best to speak in English so I don't feel left out, and they go out of their way to learn all about me, the random girl who crashed their annual celebration. What's New Jersey like? How did I meet Vivi's little brother? And the obvious question: What am I doing in Paris for the summer?

Paul and I work together to answer that last one. Now and then, he jumps in to relay certain details in French, so that everyone can understand. I surprise myself by opening up about the photos we found of Adalyn, and the recent diary entries, and to my relief, nobody recoils in horror and forces me out of the apartment.

"The French do not like to admit how deeply many of our people collaborated with the enemy," says Theo. "There were French policemen who enforced Nazi law . . . French citizens who revealed their Jewish neighbors to the Gestapo . . . French bus drivers who drove Jewish families to the Vel' d'Hiv to die. . . . And yes, French women who hooked up with Germans."

"You know, you can't judge *all* the women who did that," Claudette interjects.

"What do you mean?" asks Theo.

Claudette sighs. "After the war, they made a big show of

punishing French women for *'collaboration horizontale.'"* She makes air quotes on the last words.

"What does that mean?" I ask.

"You know . . . like . . . sleeping with the enemy," she explains. "They would drag the women into the street and shave off their hair . . . draw swastikas on their foreheads in lipstick . . . and then parade them through the streets naked."

"And it's disgusting," her girlfriend chimes in, "because they weren't all just sleeping with the Germans for fun. Maybe their husbands were gone, and they were very poor, and they needed money or food to survive. . . . Or maybe they were forced to have a German come live with them, and the German didn't give them a choice. . . ."

"I'm sorry," says Theo. "That's horrible."

"It's really messed up," I agree. "But do you guys think it applies to Adalyn? She had money, and she lived with her family."

Everybody sighs.

The mood lightens again when I tell them about my discovery on Facebook, and how Paul and I are going to sit down tomorrow and figure out what to write to Ulrich Becker IV.

"What would *you* guys say?" I ask the group.

"Howdy there," says Theo in his best attempt at an American accent, which is already hilarious. "You don't know me, but we might be secretly related. Any chance your dad wrote this love letter that made me throw up?"

We take turns tossing out funny ideas and gorging ourselves on Vivi's amazing cooking until no one can possibly
stomach another bite of food, at which point she skips to the
kitchen and returns with a tray full of chocolate-chip cookies.
When Claudette tries to wave her away, Vivi looks positively
affronted.

"You still have seven hours until dinner," she says sternly.
"Eat!"

The rest of the day goes by in a haze of sunshine and
laughter and the freedom of having nothing to do but enjoy
being with Paul. After lunch, the six of us decide to go for
a much-needed walk through the palace gardens. Claudette
points out that the sections in back have free admission, but
Vivi will hear none of it. She wants all or nothing. She convinces us to buy tickets for the fancy gardens right behind
the palace, where you can roam through the hedges to the
soundtrack of classical music.

"I promise it's worth it," she tells me, her disco-ball earrings swaying side to side.

As soon as we're through the ticketing line, I realize Vivi
was right. The manicured greens seem to stretch to infinity,
like they take up the whole world. At the base of the stairs
cascading from the main building, we naturally start to pair
off: Vivi and Theo; Claudette and Lucie; me and Paul. Since
he's been here before, I let Paul lead me down the main lawn
to a beautiful pond with a fountain in the middle. We take a

lap around the perimeter, laughing at the ducks as they skid on the surface of the water with their feet out.

There's a young boy sitting on his haunches at the edge of the water, his small, pudgy hand reaching for one of the birds. He starts to teeter dangerously far forward, at which point his father runs over and scoops him into his arms. It brings back a funny memory from when I was little.

"When I was a kid, I fell into the pond in Central Park," I tell Paul.

"Oh no!" he says. "Were you okay?"

"Yeah, totally fine. My mom yanked me out as soon as I went under—I barely realized what happened."

"How did you fall in the first place?"

I smile to myself. "It's a little embarrassing," I say.

"Now you *have* to tell me," Paul insists.

"Fine. I . . . I was trying to talk to the turtles."

Paul snorts with laughter.

I nudge him playfully. "I was like four, okay?"

"Sorry," he says, smiling at me and shaking his head. "It's just the most adorable thing I've ever heard."

After the pond, we explore the shady groves off to the side. I can barely hear what Paul is saying about the design of the gardens, because all my focus is on the fact that my fingers keep grazing his. I know it's been more than three hangouts, but I'm certain the right chemistry is here—I can *feel* it. Finally, as we start to meander back to the palace, he takes my hand in his, and even though I'm too shy to look at him, I can sense that we're both smiling.

Later in the evening, after another outrageous meal, Vivi leads the party up to the roof deck with a bottle of wine in one hand and yet another tray of homemade desserts balanced in the other. I curl up in the chair next to Paul's, perfectly full and deliriously happy.

As if on cue, right as Vivi pops the cork, there's a dull crackling noise in the air. Paul taps me on the shoulder and points into the distance, and I gasp as red, white, and blue stars explode in the night sky over Versailles. Vivi cheers and throws her arm around Theo's shoulders; Claudette and Lucie leap up and clap their hands. I keep glancing at Paul as I watch the show, and every time, I catch him looking at me instead of the fireworks.

The display goes on for a while, and after a few minutes, everybody settles back into their seats. The conversation lapses into French, which I don't mind—they've stuck to English all day, and I'm happy just to listen to the language and nibble at a cookie and watch Paul sip his wine.

Nobody here drinks alcohol in the show-offy way the kids back home do. Katrina Kim and Bethany Mackler split a beer before the fall semiformal and proceeded to do cartwheels around the gym, just so everyone would know what they'd done. Paul, Vivi, and the others aren't in it for the spectacle; they sip it during conversation like an afterthought. I've tried red wine at Hannah's place a few times, because her parents are big collectors. I liked it, although I stopped before it gave me any kind of buzz. I didn't want to have to explain anything to my parents. I don't see the harm in having some now— Mom and Dad will probably be in bed when I get home. So the next time Vivi offers refills, I hold out my glass. The familiar fruity, leathery taste warms me from the inside out.

My phone buzzes with a text message. Earlier in the evening, I texted Mom and asked if she and Dad were watching the fireworks. Her response is only five words long:

"Not really in the mood."

It's like a cinder block dragging me back down to Earth. A minute ago, I was reliving the memory of my hand in Paul's, the sun shining and the scent of citrus in the air, but now all I can picture is Mom sitting in that corner of the couch with her knees tucked up to her chest, like always. It makes me want to cry.

I type a response:

"You promised you'd try to have fun tonight!"

I'm just so helpless right now. And scared. I don't completely get what's going on with Mom. It's like I'm back in the first grade, when Gram would drop me home and I'd run to see Mom, back from another doctor's appointment, and she just wouldn't seem excited to see me. She seemed . . . nothing. Empty. Numb. Dad told me not to ask questions. All I could do was try to cheer her up, but nothing worked. Even though I'm older now, even though I know nothing has *ever* worked during Mom's phases, I feel like there has to be some way to make her feel better, if I just think hard enough. A few years ago, during the last one, I tried writing poems to let my feelings out, but they didn't actually make anything better. They just ended up stashed at the back of my desk drawer, the ashes of my pent-up emotions.

The wine makes me feel light-headed. It's nice. It puts a sort of wall between me and the bad feelings. When I see Mom typing her reply to my last message, I take a big swig. And then another. Oh—I just drained the whole glass. This is more than I've ever had at Hannah's.

Mom's message appears on the screen:

"Sry I let you down. Guess I'm a disappointment to everyone."

My fingers fly across the keys.

"You're not a disappointment," I type. "We all love you, Mom!"

"K," she writes back.

I'm not scared anymore—I'm frustrated. Angry. I wanted Mom to at least *try* tonight. I mean, maybe if she actually left the Airbnb, she wouldn't be so miserable. I lunge for the bottle of wine, but it's empty. I want more. There must be more downstairs. I should go downstairs and get it. When I stand up, my legs feel wobbly, but my head feels clear, and that's good. I don't have to think about Mom's texts. Where are the stairs? Oh, there they are. I grab the railings.

"Alice? Are you okay?"

That's Paul's voice.

"I'm fine. I'll be back in a second."

The stairs take focus. They turn and turn. I hold the railings with both hands. Finally, I'm back on flat ground. There's a bottle of red wine on the counter, but I don't know how corkscrews work. Aha—it's a twist-off. Success. I fill up my glass. I bend down and suck a sip off the top so it doesn't spill. That is really delicious. I should finish this one and fill up another before I go back upstairs. Yes, that's what I'll do.

"Alice, what are you doing?"

It's Paul again. He's at the foot of the stairs. He looks concerned, but he shouldn't be. I'm totally in control. I'm just irritated.

"I promise, I'm fine," I say.

"Who were you texting upstairs?"

"My mom."

"Is something wrong?"

"It's not a big deal."

"It seems like a big deal."

"It *wouldn't* be a big deal if she just tried to help herself."

Paul opens his mouth to say something, but I cut him off.

"I know what you're going to say, Paul." The words are flowing faster than I can keep track of them. "You're going to say the same thing as last time, which is that my dad and

I should sit down and talk to her."

Now Paul is at my side. His hand is on my shoulder. I really don't want to hear the same advice again, so I grab my wine and march out onto the balcony. Paul follows. I lean against the railing, watching fireworks erupt across the city.

"Alice, can I tell you something? It's something I haven't told very many people."

I wish he would just come and watch the fireworks with me. I don't want to talk about this anymore.

"You know that my parents are both doctors, yes? And that they didn't want me to go to art school?"

He waits for me to say something, but I don't feel like actively participating in this conversation.

He keeps going.

"What I didn't tell you is that they *really* wanted me to go to medical school. But you see, French medical school is ridiculous. To get from the first year to the second year, you have to take an impossible exam, and almost everybody fails. Maybe fifteen percent make it through. To put yourself through that, you have to really want it . . . and I didn't. Not at all. I wanted to be an artist. We ended up settling on graphic design school, but I still felt my parents were not very proud of me—especially my father.

"And so last fall, when I started at the university, I was very, very stressed out. I had all of these projects, and I was working very, very hard, but at the same time, I felt like I was disappointing my father. Every minute, I felt like I was doing the wrong thing.

"So eventually, I start to really feel the stress. I am walking down the street or sitting in class and I have these horrible episodes where I cannot breathe all of a sudden. My whole chest gets tight and it's hard to see, and I really believe that I am dying. This happens at least once a day. And of course, I become scared that I will have more of these attacks, so I stop going outside unless I have to. I just stay in my apartment alone . . . not making friends . . . not finishing my school-work . . . not really doing anything. And I did not talk about what was going on because, you know, I am already scared that people are disappointed in me.

"But then one day, Vivi shows up at my room. I think I missed her Christmas party the night before. And she says, 'Paul, I am not leaving until we talk about what is happening to you, and we figure out how to make it better.' Alice, I *never* would have brought it up if she did not say this to me. She made me talk about it for the first time, and she made me go see a therapist, who was very, very helpful."

He's standing next to me, gazing out at the sky.

"If Vivi did not have this conversation with me, then I never would have fixed the problem. I never would have gone to the bakery and used my sketchbook just for fun . . . and I never would have met you. So . . . I think you should try."

Paul tries to hold my hand again, but I pull it away and retreat to the corner.

"Alice?"

His speech stings like salt in a wound.

I'm about to explode from the pain.

"Paul, do you think I haven't been *trying* until now?" I am seething. "My mom's been having these weird episodes on and off since I was in the first grade. What do you think I do every time she—"

"Alice . . . I didn't know . . . I didn't mean to offend you . . . I was just trying to—"

"Tell me I clearly don't care about my mom as much as your sister cares about you?"

Paul looks as though I've just slapped him. Good. He thinks he can waltz in and fix my family just like that, but he doesn't know us. He doesn't know our problems. And he doesn't get that my family has never talked about a single feeling ever, in history—not once.

"That's not what I meant," Paul says quietly.

He's trying to make peace, but I'm still fuming.

"I do the absolute best I can to help her—"

"I believe you, I'm sorry—"

"And I don't need your criticism," I snap. "I can handle it on my own. I'll probably just sell the stupid apartment and move on."

"What?" Paul asks.

I don't feel like explaining.

The fireworks have mostly died down. It's quieter now. The sky is black. I stand there with my arms crossed, breathing heavily. I can't believe that earlier today, we were holding hands without a care in the world.

"I'm really sorry," Paul says after a minute or two. "Can we talk about what just happened?" He pauses and chews his lip. His beautiful lip. I can't look at it right now. "Do you want to tell me about your mom? And what do you mean, 'sell the apartment'?"

Talk, talk, talk. Paul must think he can solve everything just by talking. He probably wants to demonstrate how *productive* it can be.

"I think I just want to go home," I reply.

His face goes from desperate to defeated.

"Are you sure?"

"Yes."

We go upstairs and say our goodbyes to Vivi, Theo, Claudette, and Lucie, who are spending the night. Then Paul calls a taxi to take us to the train station. On board, I slump against the window and close my eyes to the dark landscape passing by.

We ride the whole way back to Paris in silence.

CHAPTER 10

Adalyn

At half past ten, I follow the directions on the scrap of paper to the southern edge of Parc Monceau. I count out the park benches and find the one third from the end, next to the lamppost. I take a seat, trying to appear nonchalant, but my heart is hammering. Is he watching me right now? There are people all around, and he could be any of them: the businessman with the black umbrella, the elderly gentleman with the wooden cane, the father reading a picture book to his young daughter.

A shadow falls across my lap, and just like that, there's a man sitting next to me. He's in his sixties, maybe, with an unkempt gray beard and a face like a gnarled tree trunk. There's a deep scar that runs down his cheek, as though the bark had been struck by a bolt of lightning.

So—this is the man they call Geronte.

"If you're planning on taking the train, I hear they're running behind schedule today," he says gruffly.

This is my cue. In one swift movement, I pull the half ticket from my pocket and pass it to him. He holds our two pieces together, nods curtly, and stuffs them into his breast pocket.

"I need you to memorize what I am about to tell you," he grunts. "Can you do that?"

"Yes," I reply.

"You will go to 27, rue Cambacérès tomorrow morning," he says. "Tell the concierge you are collecting a package for your uncle, and she will hand you an envelope. There will be letters inside, and addresses. You will deliver them by the end of the week."

This must be the kind of work that Luc was doing. I remember the bags under his eyes and the worry lines that formed on his handsome face.

"Yes, sir."

Geronte grunts.

"So you're the girl they put in all the magazines—the one who goes to all the parties," he says, still staring straight ahead. "Luc speaks very highly of you."

My heart beats even faster. "That is very kind of—"

"I will have to judge you for myself, of course."

Luc always saw it as an advantage that I kept an active social life. Geronte, I can tell, is more skeptical. I understand; for all he knows, I could run and tell the Germans at Madame Marbot's next party about the package at 27, rue Cambacérès. But I need him to know he can trust me. I need him to see what an asset I am.

I must tell him the idea that came to me as I listened to Ulrich the Hotel Belmont.

"Geronte, last night I met the German who manages the train schedules at the Gare de l'Est."

I pause to make sure he's interested.

"Go on," he says.

"I have as little interest in fraternizing with Germans as I'm sure you do, but this man revealed many details about supplies coming in and out of Germany."

"And why do you suppose he did such a stupid thing?"

"Because he thought he was talking to a harmless girl."

Geronte grunts again. He must not be interested. This must be his way of dismissing me. Embarrassed for going beyond the simple task he asked of me, I tighten my scarf and stand up.

"Where the hell do you think you're going?" Geronte growls, stopping me in my tracks. He pats the spot on the bench where I was just sitting. "Sit down and tell me every damn word that man said."

. . .

Two weeks later, Madame Marbot plans another salon. I agonize for hours over how to explain myself to Chloe, until at last, I come up with a plan: I tell her I'm going to the salon so I can keep an eye on Maman, to make sure she doesn't come into direct contact with any Germans. Incredibly, Chloe not only believes me—she *likes* the idea.

"I wish she didn't go to those parties at all, but this makes me feel a tiny bit better," she whispers through the darkness. It isn't a terribly cold night, but we decided to share her bed anyway. "Maman needs someone to keep her in check," Chloe continues. "She'll talk to *anybody*. Especially when she's been drinking champagne."

"The LaRoches will be there," I tell her. "I can make sure we talk to them all night."

Chloe groans into her pillow. "Another whole evening with the LaRoches? Oh, Adalyn," she says, "you're a saint."

So Maman and I return to the Hotel Belmont. I find Ulrich in the same spot by the fire, and he is still homesick, and therefore still very happy to see me. I let him talk to me all evening long, absorbing his words like a sponge.

The very next day, I meet Geronte on the park bench to wring out every last detail.

September becomes October, and the country careens closer and closer to what is sure to be another brutal winter. In November, we learn that Germany has invaded Vichy France, dissolving the border between the Occupied and

Unoccupied Zones. We are all together in the same prison now. Down in Toulon, the French Navy deliberately sinks dozens of its own ships to avoid them being captured by the Germans. This small victory buoys my spirits, if only for a little while.

At least everyone sees that Pétain is nothing more than a German puppet now. For anyone who was still telling themselves the Old Marshal would rescue France like he did back in the Great War, it's now impossible to suspend their disbelief any further. Geronte says that more and more people are joining the resistance movement.

At home, Maman doesn't praise Pétain at all anymore, but she's still trying her best to stay positive. After reading the news of the invasion in *Les Nouveaux Temps*, she calmly folded up the newspaper and placed it on her lap. In the armchair next to her, Papa—who had also seen the story—was staring at the ground numbly. Maman reached over and squeezed his hand. "We'll be all right, my love," she said. "We'll just keep living our lives and wait and see what happens."

Meanwhile, I carry on passing information from Ulrich to Geronte, while also making time to complete my new assignments. I courier messages from one location to another, from one strange hand to the next. I am perpetually exhausted from running and hiding all over the city, but the memory of Arnaud pushes me to keep fighting, just as Luc said.

One snowy morning in December, Chloe and I pile all

our blankets onto my bed and huddle underneath them to keep warm. We sleep this way, too, on the colder nights. The frigid cold is already settling over Paris, and there isn't enough fuel to keep the apartment as warm as we'd like. When I went to collect our rations the other week, the man handed me only three sacks of coal.

"This is to last the month?" I asked him in disbelief.

"No," he replied, "this is to last the winter."

Today, to pass the time, Chloe and I read Baudelaire's poems out loud to each other, taking turns flipping the pages so our fingers don't get too cold. We're wearing our warmest coats indoors, and we're still shivering.

"I never want to leave this burrow of ours," Chloe says.

"Neither do I, but I have to go out later," I remind her. There's another party at the Hotel Belmont tonight.

"I expect the Germans will be there?" Chloe asks darkly.

"Yes, I think so," I tell her. "I'm going to distract Maman all night."

This keeping of secrets never gets any easier. How I would love to tell Chloe why I'm really so eager to go to these parties—how I would love to see the relief, the *excitement* spread across her face . . . but I know that I mustn't. Just the other day, Geronte told me a terrible story about the husband of a resister he knew. The Gestapo knew the man had information, so they dragged him in for questioning. They tortured him with a knife, and they cut him too deep.

The man bled to death in their custody.

"Adalyn," Chloe says, "do you *promise*?" Her eyes search my face.

"Do I promise what?"

"That you really are just keeping an eye on Maman. And you're not having any . . . any sort of *relations* with the enemy."

I wrinkle my nose.

"Relations! Heavens no, Chloe. Why would you think that all of a sudden?"

"A friend of mine. She found out her sister went on a date with one of them. It made me worry. . . ."

"You don't have to worry, Chloe."

I force a laugh in an attempt to defuse the tension. Chloe joins in, but it doesn't sound altogether natural, and there's a funny expression on her face. It's hard to tell if she truly believes me—and the fact that I must continue to lie to her eats at me like a monster with razor-sharp teeth. All I can hope is that someday this war will be over, and she will know the truth.

Before I get ready for the salon, there is a visit I must pay to an address Geronte gave me at our last meeting. "I need you to help me with something," he said to me on the park bench. He disclosed no further details except where and when I had to meet him. I nodded, and the plan was set.

Telling the family I'm going in search of more coal, for they won't be suspicious when I come back empty-handed, I bundle up in my warmest layers and head out into the cold for the safe house nearby. I'm relieved that the address is in the Ninth, but my face and hands are still red and numb by the time I reach the building on the rue d'Astorg.

I tap out the code on the apartment door, and Geronte opens it. He greets me in his usual fashion—a sniff of the nose and an upward jerk of the head, like a hound.

"Follow me," he says.

Geronte leads me down an ordinary-looking corridor to a windowless bedroom, and inside, on the twin-sized bed, sits a tall man with broad shoulders and a pronounced jaw. He jumps to his feet when we enter the room.

"Bon-joor," he says.

Oh! His accent is funny. He must be an American.

"His plane was shot down about a month ago," Gerard explains. "Friend of mine found him hiding on his property. Asked if I could help get him out of France so he can fly again. I said I had no idea, but we'd try."

I shake the airman's hand.

"It's a pleasure to meet you," I say.

He flashes an apologetic sort of grin.

"Doesn't speak a lick of French," Geronte adds.

I turn to Geronte. I'm flattered he chose me to help.

"What can I do?"

"This man needs a guide to ride the train with him to Chartres," he says. "Somebody else will take him from there to Vendôme, and then he's on his way to Spain."

Geronte runs through the details of the assignment to me, and then to the airman in broken English. This is how it will go: I will walk ahead of the airman and show him the way. We will not speak—not that we could if we wanted to. We will act as though we do not know each other, as though we are just two random strangers on the same train. If anyone asks the airman any questions, he will show them a note explaining he is deaf and dumb. He can't let his accent give him away.

"When will we do this?" I ask Geronte.

"Tomorrow," he says.

I walk home in a daze. I spend the rest of the afternoon running through the plan in my head, and each time, I get more nervous.

But I must try to push the fear from my mind, because first, there is the party at the Hotel Belmont. Clutching our overcoats tightly about our bodies, Maman and I step out into the frigid air, which is colder than it was on my earlier outing, because the sun has gone down.

Ulrich is waiting for me by the fire. He even has two glasses of cognac ready to go on the small table in between our chairs. He leaps to his feet as I approach. "It is always a pleasure to see you walk through the doors," he says.

We exchange pleasantries, and then I slip into my usual

conversation style, asking seemingly innocent questions about which trains he'll be dealing with tomorrow. At this point in my work, I've mapped out a rough understanding of the general frequency with which German arms are coming into Paris through the Gare de l'Est. I try to think only of relaying this latest information to Geronte, and not of Chloe's worried face wondering if I'm having *relations* with any Germans.

Late in the evening, as the party winds down, Madame LaRoche's voice echoes from the adjacent room.

"One more drink before you leave, Odette! Come, now!"

I look through the doorway in time to see a tipsy Madame LaRoche leading an even tipsier Maman through the thinning crowd. The two of them must have had a grand old time tonight. Just before they disappear from view, Maman stumbles on a rug and grabs hold of a waiter to steady herself.

"I should probably leave soon," I tell Ulrich, who nods.

"Before you go . . . ," he says, his voice trailing off. He reaches into the breast pocket of his jacket and produces a brown paper package, along with a note.

"Oh, Ulrich—what is this?"

"Something for you. It is small."

Oh no. I don't want any sort of gift from a German, but what choice do I have? This is the role I must play.

I open the note first. It says:

My most dear Adalyn,

  I give thanks for the many evenings I have spent by your side. Your beautiful eyes and your wonderful stories make better the pain of being so far from home. If I cannot be in Berlin, I am glad to be here in Paris with you. I give you this gift in the hope it will keep you warm during the winter.

  Yours truly, Hauptmann Ulrich Becker III

I smile at him graciously. The note might have warmed my heart if it hadn't been written by someone in Ulrich's uniform. I stow it in my pocket.

Next, the package. I pull back the paper and my fingertips graze something smooth and soft.

"It is leather," Ulrich says. "From Germany."

He's given me a very handsome pair of gloves, the kind you'd be hard-pressed to find in Paris these days. It *is* very cold outside, and we haven't any heat half the time, and I suppose if I must accept a gift from Ulrich, at least it is something useful.

"These are lovely," I tell him. "Thank you."

"You are very welcome," he replies.

That final glass of champagne did not do Maman any good. She slips and slides on the icy roads all the way home, and I do my best to keep her upright. The five flights of stairs are something of an ordeal, but at last I guide her over the threshold of the apartment.

At the sound of the door, Chloe wanders into the foyer wearing a blanket like a cape. She didn't go out with her friends tonight, and she must be hungry for human interaction.

"You're home," she says.

"We had a *marvelous* night," Maman gushes in a much-too-loud voice. She's slurring her words.

"Yes," Chloe says, "I can see that."

And then my sister's eyes narrow. It's not Maman she's looking at, but me. Too late, I realize my mistake. I should have taken them off before I got home, but I was preoccupied with taking care of Maman.

In a voice as quiet and deadly as poison, Chloe asks: "Whose gloves are those?"

Quick, Adalyn.

I could say I borrowed them from the twins.

Or that I found them in my closet, a forgotten gift from before the war.

Just when I'm about to feed her a lie, Maman, oblivious to my plight, blurts out an answer at full volume:

"They were a gift from her German!"

Not even *a* German—*her* German. Her, as in belonging to me.

Chloe and I both freeze. Her blanket slides to the floor. It feels like everything is shrinking: the floor, the walls, the air in the room. My own heart—I think my chest is closing in on my own heart. Is that possible? Chloe is seething. Her jaw juts forward; her lips curl. I want to defend myself, but I can't. I have to stand here while the person I love most in the world decides that I'm her worst possible nightmare.

Papa comes shuffling down the hall, his housecoat swallowing his thin body. He's usually in bed by now, but he must have been drawn out by Maman's loud voice.

"Is everything okay?" he asks tentatively.

Chloe stares me down, almost daring me to speak first.

Maman beats both of us to it. Flinging her arms around Papa's neck, she cries, "Everything is wonderful!"

She needs to stop shrieking like that. Immediately. Everything is *not* wonderful. The fabric of my life is unraveling too fast for me to hold it together.

"Adalyn," Chloe says, and her voice is quiet, pleading, as though she's desperate to get through to me. "Tell me it isn't true. Tell me Maman isn't serious, Adalyn."

I wish she'd exploded. I wish she had screamed at me or thrown something at me. It still would hurt, but not as much as seeing my sister's bottom lip tremble at the very sight of me. Not as much as seeing the hope in her eyes still glimmering right before I speak the worst two words imaginable:

"It's true."

She clings to my gaze for one final moment. One fleeting chance to take back what I said. As I stand there, gloved hands hanging helplessly, I remember what Papa made me promise him as soon as I was old enough to understand: *Protect your little sister, Adalyn. Keep her from pain. I wish I could have done the same for my little brother.*

Right now, I can't keep Chloe from pain.

No, it's worse than that.

Right now, I am the *source* of my sister's pain. I am the worst pain she's ever felt in her life. I can see it in her face.

"But you can't do this," she begs. "You can't fraternize with the Germans . . . not while the rest of the world dies at their hands. . . ."

"The Germans could be here forever, Chloe!" cries Maman. "You *have* to calm down."

"I will *not* calm down," Chloe snaps at her. Then she turns to our father, tears welling in her eyes. "Papa—please—Papa," she says, "tell me I'm not making this up. Tell them that what they're doing is wrong."

Papa stuffs his hands into the pockets of his housecoat. Maman still hangs on to him, her head resting on his shoulder.

"I don't want to get in the middle of this," he mumbles.

Chloe looks at each of us in turn, and I know she's giving us one last chance to explain ourselves. First Papa, who avoids eye contact. Then Maman, who's off in her own dream world. Finally me.

"This is really who you want to be, Adalyn?"

I could fix this in an instant. I could spill all my secrets from the last two years right here, right now. It would feel so good.

I hear Luc's voice in my head.

You can't tell a soul what you're doing—do you understand that? Not a soul. Not your family.

I knew it would be hard, but not like this.

"I'm sorry," I say to Chloe. "I really am."

Chloe takes a deep breath. She picks her blanket up off the floor. When she speaks again, her voice is eerily calm.

"I am done with you all," she says. "I am done being a part of this sick, collaborationist family. If I could live somewhere else, I would, but I don't want to have to *explain* you to any of my friends. Someday, though . . . someday, I hope I never see any of you again."

Chloe marches off to her bedroom, and shell-shocked, I go to mine. The first thing I do is tear off the gloves. As I undress myself with shaky hands, I come upon Ulrich's note tucked inside my pocket.

I want to burn it right this instant.

However, walking to the kitchen would mean passing Chloe's bedroom, and I can't risk another confrontation. I don't feel like seeing my parents either, and I think they're in the drawing room. I should just go to sleep. I can forget what happened tonight, at least for a little while.

Instead of feeding it to the flames, I shove Ulrich's note into the bottom drawer of my desk, the one I never use, and slam it shut as hard as I possibly can.

I board the train to Chartres. *Do not think about Chloe.* I pause in the aisle and pretend to look for something in my valise so I can make sure the airman gets on. *Do not imagine what Chloe is thinking right now.* I find a carriage with two empty seats side by side. *Focus on what you have to do, Adalyn.*

I can tell the airman is nervous. His forehead is sweating, even though it's December, and he keeps having to mop it with a handkerchief. He has a long and treacherous road ahead of him; this trip to Chartres and then on to Vendôme is just the beginning. Once he makes his way down the whole of France, he will have to cross the Pyrenees into Spain, and from there, it's on to Britain by air or sea. *I would cross the Pyrenees in the dead of winter if it meant Chloe would somehow forgive me.*

I'm beginning to worry this airman's nerves will give him away. On top of the sweating, he keeps fidgeting in his seat and checking his pockets to make sure his papers are still there. When the conductor comes by to collect our tickets, his gaze lingers on the airman in his mismatched clothes for a second or two longer than normal. Is the suspicion in his eyes real, or am I imagining it out of fear?

I spend most of the trip staring out the window, thinking about last night and watching town after town fly past. This is how I notice when our train rolls to an unexpected halt about an hour into our journey. This isn't a planned stop. We're in between stations.

"What's going on?" asks an elderly man in our carriage.

My heart pounding, I slip into the aisle to try and catch a glimpse of what's happening. Following my lead, the airman comes out, too. There are footsteps behind us, followed by a small cough.

It's the same conductor from earlier.

"The Germans are coming on board for an inspection," he says in a very low voice, so both of us can hear. "They never check the lavatories."

Then he steps around me and proceeds down the aisle.

He doesn't stop to talk to anyone else.

Is it a trap, or is he trying to help us? If one thing's certain, it's that I don't want to see what happens when my nervous airman comes face-to-face with an armed German soldier. I lead him wordlessly toward the lavatory, and when I'm certain nobody is looking, I grab him by the sleeve and pull him in with me, wrenching the door closed and locking it tight.

It's a tiny space—cramped for one passenger, and certainly not enough room for two. His clothes are moist to the touch, and I can smell his sweat. He's as frightened as I am.

"The Germans are here," I whisper, and he seems to understand.

It's hard to say how much time has passed. Ten minutes . . . twenty . . . thirty . . . all I want is for the train to start moving again. I hear something—oh no. There are heavy thuds coming from the other side of the door, which can only be one thing: German boots. And they're coming closer. *Thunk, thunk, thunk.* Now they're right outside the door.

I feel the American's heartbeat against my cheek.

The doorknob jiggles.

This is it. It's over.

But then I hear the conductor's voice: "Out of order, I am afraid."

The jiggling stops. A German grumbles something about inferior French manufacturing. *Thunk, thunk, thunk.* The footsteps disappear out of earshot, and my whole body relaxes. The airman lets out a sigh of relief.

That conductor just saved our lives.

When at last we get off at the Gare de Chartres, I am grateful to be done with this assignment. I show the airman to the platform where he will start the next leg of his journey, and then without so much as a wave goodbye—which feels odd, given everything we've been through—I make my way to a different platform to catch the next train back to Paris.

At least this part of the plan worked out. The next train

is coming in a couple of minutes. Across the tracks, I can see the airman. He takes a seat on an empty bench and scans the platform for his next contact, who's meant to be a woman in a long brown coat and matching hat.

That must be her, climbing up the steps. Why is she moving so fast? For some reason, she darts across the platform like a hunted rabbit. She goes right up to the airman and speaks into his ear, like she's trying to warn him of something.

This is not right.

I watch from afar as the sickening scene plays out. The airman leaps to his feet and tries to run, but he doesn't get far. German soldiers appear at the tops of two staircases, pinning the airman and the woman in the brown coat between them. They brandish their pistols. They bark orders. The airman and the woman sink to their knees, their hands in the air.

Two soldiers rush forward to grab them—and then the train to Paris screams into the station, severing my view.

I climb aboard, shaking from head to toe. I stumble into an empty compartment and slam the door closed behind me.

I burst into tears.

The trip back to Paris is agony, as I fight to keep from crying any more. Panic riddles my body like gunfire, and I have nowhere to turn. Luc is off in hiding. Arnaud is gone. My own family doesn't know who I really am, and my sister despises me for reasons that aren't true. I'm stranded on a battlefield without any allies.

What good are we resisters really doing, scurrying around with our stupid papers and fragments of information? We didn't stop the Germans from taking the whole of France. We can't change the tide of the war. Innocent people are risking their lives for no good reason. The airman was young, no more than twenty-five years old, and now he may never see home again—and I can't escape the notion that I had something to do with it.

It's all too real. The weight of it is suffocating me. I cannot keep going on like this.

By the time I get off the train at the Gare Saint-Lazare, I am empty inside. I drift toward the exit, but along the way, I find my path blocked by a procession of sorts.

There are two red-faced porters in front, struggling to hold up the stack of trunks balanced precariously between them. Why aren't they using one of the carts?

"Schneller! Schneller!"

There's a group of German soldiers following the porters, laughing as they shout at the Frenchmen to carry their luggage faster. It's a parade of cruelty. When the older of the two porters has to stop and catch his breath, a German yells at him for being weak; another suggests that this is why the French were defeated so easily. More laughter ensues.

A moment ago I thought I was empty inside, but I was

wrong. The fire was in me all along. It just needed to be stoked.

As I watch the Germans go by, the flames swell to a roaring blaze. How could I have thought about giving up? I roll back my shoulders and step out into the frosty evening.

I hardly feel the cold.

CHAPTER 11

Alice

I feel terrible.

The morning after the party, I wake up with a splitting headache. When I sit up in bed, the nausea kicks in, and I sprint to the bathroom just in time to vomit a burgundy stream of last night's wine into the toilet bowl. It's half an hour of agony on the tile floor. Finally, I strip out of my pajamas and climb into the shower. I'm never drinking again for as long as I live.

The warm water feels good. I imagine it lifting away all the memories of Versailles and washing them down the drain. Whenever I remember another detail of the fight, I scrub my body harder with the rough brown bar of soap. My skin is red and raw by the time I turn off the faucet. I wrap myself in a towel and brush my teeth. I already feel better than I did fifteen minutes ago.

I'm changing into a fresh pair of pajamas when my phone lights up with an incoming text message. It's Paul.

"Hi Alice. I am very sorry for what happened last night. I wanted to help you through a hard time, but I see that I only made things worse. I would like to talk about it, if you want. Let me know."

And just like that, the nausea creeps back in. No, Paul, I don't want to talk about it. I want to forget it ever happened.

I squeeze my eyes shut and rub my temples, but I can't stem the latest stream of memories. It's not the details of Paul's speech that I remember most, but the way I felt listening to it. I was frustrated over Mom's text messages; furious that Paul thought he knew what was best for my family. And something else—something I can't put my finger on, but it was the worst feeling of all.

I'm just going to ignore the text message for now.

Three days later, it's still sitting there without an answer. I'm not mad anymore; I just want us to go back to normal. Lying in bed and staring at my phone, I try to open Instagram to distract myself, but instead, I accidentally tap my photo library. A wave of sadness crashes over me when I see the blurry picture of Paul lunging for my coffee cup on the bridge. The determination on his face—it made me laugh hysterically in the moment. Now it makes me miss him so badly, I can't even look at it.

Being around Paul was the best. Our conversation was

easy, like muscle memory. He listened intently and asked all the right questions when I talked about my family. He volunteered to help me without asking for anything in return. And then there were the little things, like how he smiled whenever I walked through the doors of the bookstore, and how he held my hand as we walked up the path at Versailles. I've never had a guy do those kinds of things.

Why did I have to get so angry?

You know why, says the voice in the back of my head.

It's true. I've had three days to think about what happened out on the balcony, and now I know exactly which feeling I couldn't put my finger on.

Shame.

I knew Paul was right, that we should sit down and talk to Mom instead of dancing around the problem.

I mean, I barely understand what Mom's problem *is*. I know she gets into these funks when she's sad all the time and she doesn't want to go out and do anything. And I know she went through a really rough patch back when I was in the first grade, and I had to spend all that time at Gram's. Outside of that, I'm basically in the dark, because my family has no idea how to talk to each other. It's embarrassing. To make matters worse, instead of admitting this all to Paul, who was only trying to help, I lashed out at him. But I wasn't really angry at him. I was angry at us.

Oh god, I'm such an idiot.

I stare at Paul's three-day-old text message on the screen. What am I supposed to say to him to make this better? Why am I so bad at this?

There's a knock at the bedroom door.

"Come in," I say.

Dad carefully opens the door. Once again, he slides into the room like a secret agent and closes it behind him.

"Dad, what are you doing?"

"I had an idea," he whispers, tiptoeing across the room to sit on the edge of the bed. "Another idea to help cheer her up." There's this light glimmering behind his eyes, like he's just found the magic solution to whatever Mom's going through. Here we go again, dancing around the problem.

"What is it?" I ask cautiously.

"So I was thinking," Dad says, "we're in *Paris*. Culinary capital of the world. Maybe she'd like it if instead of making dinner tonight, we surprise her and take her out to a really nice dinner. Someplace she'd really like."

"Dad—"

"I did some poking around on Yelp, and I think I found some great-looking places where we wouldn't need a reservation. The one I'm leaning toward is an oyster bar in the Marais—you know Mom loves oysters—and it has these great rustic brick walls, and a wooden ceiling, and—"

"Dad." I say it louder this time. "I don't know if that's what we should do."

He looks taken aback.

"Really? Does she not like oysters anymore? I can find somewhere else."

"No, it's not that." I roll a piece of comforter between my fingers, searching for the right way to put this. I'm about to venture into uncharted territory for anyone in the Prewitt family. With a deep breath, I say, "I'm worried Mom might be doing worse than we think. I'm wondering if maybe, instead of trying to cheer her up, we should do something a little more direct. . . . Do you know what I mean?"

Dad looks confused. It's like I asked him a question in a foreign language. "I don't know that I'm following, honey."

Well, here goes nothing.

"Do you think maybe . . . instead of a big fancy dinner . . . we should sit down with Mom and talk to her? We could tell her we've noticed she's been kind of down, and . . . um . . . that we want to help her fix whatever's wrong."

He winces. I seem to have touched a nerve.

"I don't think that's such a good idea," he says, shaking his head. "Mom obviously isn't ready to talk about it, and I'm worried that if we push too hard, we're going to upset her even more. We definitely don't want to risk that."

The look on his face is very serious. I didn't think of that, but he makes a good point. The last thing I want to do is put Mom in an even *worse* mood than she's already in.

Dad says firmly, "The safest course of action is sitting

back and letting her come to us when she's ready. Then maybe we can have that talk you mentioned. And in the meantime, you and I will just try to make this trip as special as we can for her. Okay?"

"Yeah, that sounds good."

"Great," he says, his face relaxing. He pats my knee from on top of the covers. "So what do you say we go to that oyster place?"

As far as restaurants go, Dad made a good choice. The dishes that keep going by our table look and smell incredible. The place is packed, and everyone seems happy to be here—everyone except Mom, that is, who's holding a menu but staring at a groove in the wooden table instead. Getting her here was a challenge. Dad practically had to beg her to get off the couch and change into clothes that weren't her same old stale pajamas.

"So—what looks good, ladies?" Dad asks.

"I'm not really that hungry," Mom mumbles.

Dad's expression falters for a second, but he picks right back up again in his real estate voice.

"Come on, Diane, you love oysters. Remember that place we went on Cape Cod last summer? Remember how big and juicy they were?"

Cape Cod couldn't have been a more different vacation— we were all so happy. We rented a house in Wellfleet, and every day Mom and I hit tennis balls on the red clay courts that were impossible to get used to. We ended up laughing more than we actually rallied. How could the Mom of last summer be the same person sitting across from me, putting down her menu and gazing out the window?

"I don't feel great," she says to Dad.

"Would a seafood tower change your mind?"

"Mark," she snaps. "Just order whatever you guys want."

While we wait for the food, Mom continues to stare out the window as Dad bombards her with more and more questions. It's like he's showing a house and thinks he's really close to making the sale. I get that he's trying to put a smile on her face—I've been there, too—but even I can see that this dinner isn't what Mom wants. She snaps at each of his conversation starters, and she gets increasingly irritable the longer his routine goes on. At one point she disappears to the bathroom for ten minutes, and when she returns, I think I can see red splotches under her eyes, although it's hard to tell for sure in the dim light.

And then the food arrives: a three-tiered arrangement of oysters and clams and spiky red crab legs. It would be a lot for a table of six, and it's absolutely obscene for just the three of us. I'm embarrassed to even look at the thing. Dad digs in right away. Mom doesn't. Dad asks, "Do you want me to crack one of the crab legs open for you, Di?"

"I don't want crab," Mom says.

Dad flags down a waiter. Mom looks mortified as the man

starts weaving his way toward the table.

"Look at the menu," Dad says. "You can order whatever you want."

"I said I'm not hungry," Mom hisses.

"Can I bring you something else?" asks the waiter.

"Diane?"

"I'm not hungry."

"Another glass of wine?"

"I'm fine."

"He's right here, Di. He can bring you whatever you—"

"ARE YOU LISTENING? I SAID I'M FINE, MARK."

The tables around us go quiet as everyone cranes their necks to see where all the commotion is coming from. Mom snatches up her purse and marches for the door. Dad looks shell-shocked. He's still holding the metal seafood cracker.

"I'm going to find her," I tell him.

"I can bring you the check," the waiter says pointedly.

Mom is sitting on a bench outside the restaurant with her arms crossed. This time I see for certain that she's crying. I sit down beside her and rub her back. I don't know exactly what to say to her, but I do know we can't just keep trying to cheer her up. It isn't enough. Dad got me all worried that a serious talk would make Mom feel worse, but look at her now, blowing her nose into a soggy tissue on a Paris street corner while Dad settles the bill for our uneaten meal. If this isn't rock bottom, we must be close. What if the risk is worth it?

On the cab ride home, I finally text Paul back.

"You were right about everything," I write. "Don't apologize. I'm the one who should be sorry." And then, because I want to be open with him, "I miss you, Paul."

I press send.

I keep my eyes on my phone the rest of the evening, as Mom and I watch some French news station in silence, but there's no response. There's still nothing by the time I get into bed. I'm starting to get a little nervous, but then again, maybe he's busy tonight. I'm sure I'll have a message from him when I wake up.

Except the next morning, I don't. Now I'm really starting to panic that I've messed things up for good.

"Just want to make sure you saw this," I type frantically.

An hour later, he still hasn't responded. I toggle the Wi-Fi and airplane mode settings to make sure my phone isn't broken, but everything seems to be working properly. Come noon, I can't take it anymore. I throw on my sneakers and hail a taxi to the first of two possible places Paul could be on a weekday afternoon.

I sprint to the bookstore, but there's a different clerk on duty today. She shoots me the evil eye for bursting through the door so loudly, but I don't care. I turn on my heel and run back out to the street.

Well, if he isn't at work . . . The bakery is just around the corner. I yank open the door and look around, and my heart sinks. The communal table is empty. Paul isn't here.

"Puis-je vous—" Vivi stops midsentence when she sees that it's me. "Oh, hello."

I don't know how to read the look on her face, but this isn't the same Vivi who greeted us at the door in Versailles.

"Hi, Vivi." My voice trembles. "I'm looking for Paul. Can you help me? I really want to talk to him."

"I don't know if that's a good idea," she replies, crossing her arms.

I guess she knows about the fight, then.

"Vivi, please," I say, moving toward the counter. "I have to tell him I'm sorry."

She shakes her head. She looks like she might cry.

"My brother had a difficult year," she says, her voice wavering. "This is why I was happy when he met you. But if you are going to push him away when he tries to open up, and then not speak to him for three days—"

"Vivi, I—"

"I just don't think it is best for him, Alice."

After all that she did for Paul, I can see why she's so protective. I need her to trust me. I take a deep breath.

"Vivi, I know it seems like I was mean to him for no reason, but you have to understand, I'm so new at this. I have all these feelings inside me, and I never know how to talk about them. My whole family's the same way, and we're a mess. I know Paul was just trying to help me. I think I knew it in the moment, too, but I didn't know how to express it. I'm ready to learn how to do it better. And I'm sorry."

Vivi's face softens.

All of a sudden, I hear footsteps from the kitchen, and a familiar pair of tortoiseshell glasses appears in the doorway. My heart skips a beat, just like it did when I saw him here for the very first time.

"Hey, Paul."

"Hey, Alice."

"You didn't happen to hear all that, did you?"

"Maybe a little bit," he says with a smile.

Vivi looks back and forth between the two of us, assessing the situation. Finally, with a small smirk, she adjusts her ponytail. "Well, I think I will go and check on the croissants," she says before disappearing into the kitchen.

"I really am sorry," I say to him.

"It's okay," he replies. "I am just happy to see you again."

"I missed you," I whisper.

"I missed you, too."

I'm not sure why, but at the exact same time, Paul and I look around at the rest of the bakery. There's still nobody here, and Vivi is off checking on the croissants. He steps out from behind the counter, and once again, like that afternoon on the rue de Marquis, there's nothing between us. We stare at each other fiercely. Without saying anything, we close the gap in two long strides. Then his hands are in my hair, and mine are on his waist, and the next thing I know our lips are colliding, and everything I should have said in Versailles is wrapped up into this one perfect kiss. His fingertips travel lightly down my back. His mouth is soft and tastes like warm tea. This is the way a kiss should be—not messy and rushed, but slow and sweet and gentle. Things with Mom may be a disaster, and I have no idea what'll happen with the apartment, but in this moment, everything feels like it's going to be okay.

We break apart at the sound of the bell tinkling over the door. It's a customer. Paul laughs, pulling me in close, and I rest my forehead against the soft cotton of his T-shirt. Eventually, he guides me over to the table to sit and talk over our *cafés américains*. I can't stop smiling.

"Well, I am happy you came by the bakery," he says.

"I am, too."

"I was thinking about doing that for a long time."

"You were?"

He nods, blushing. My cheeks feel warm, too. What did I do to find a guy like Paul? I know one thing for certain: I can't mess this up again.

"Paul, I should probably tell you about my mom."

"Okay."

"I think there's more to it than my grandmother dying."

With a steady voice, I tell him about Mom's dark phases that happen once every few years, because after what happened at the restaurant, I'm certain Mom's dealing with more than just grief. Paul is a good listener; he holds my hand and squeezes it when I get to the difficult parts. Finally, I talk about Dad's idea to sell the apartment.

"What do *you* think I should do with it?" I ask Paul.

"*Me?* I don't know. . . . It is for you to decide. . . ."

"But what if I can't?"

Paul exhales slowly, thinking. "Well, we have two weeks to figure it out, right?"

It makes me happy to hear him use the word "we," like we're on the same team again. "It's more like a week and a half at this point," I say.

He nods. "Right. Okay. Well . . . I think we should try to find out as much as we can about your grandmother and Adalyn in the time that we have, and then we will see how you feel. Yes?"

"Yes. That sounds good."

"Did you finish the diary?"

"I had to stop reading for a bit after the gross Ulrich stuff."

"Let's keep reading," Paul says. "I'll help you."

"Okay. That would be great," I reply. "I guess we should reach out to Ulrich, too. I haven't done it yet."

"Let's do it now."

We huddle over my phone and manage to come up with the least creepy Facebook message possible:

Hello Mr. Becker,

My name is Alice Prewitt, and I'm 16 years old. I know I'm a complete stranger, and I hope you'll forgive me for this strange message.

My grandmother passed away recently, leaving me her childhood apartment in Paris. In going through it, I came across an old letter addressed to her sister, Adalyn Bon-homme, from a man named Ulrich Becker III. I never knew my great-aunt Adalyn, and I'm trying to find some more information on her. I realize how unlikely this is, but I hap-pened to see your Facebook page and the photo of your father, and I'm wondering if there's a chance he might have known her. The letter was written during World War II, on stationery from the Hotel Belmont in Paris.

If you have any information about Adalyn, I would greatly appreciate it. (I can send along a photo of the letter, if it would help.) If you have no idea what I'm talking about, I'm sorry to bother you! Thank you very much for your time.

Sincerely,
Alice Prewitt

First, we translate it into German. Then, together—
because I don't want to do it alone—we hit send.

Oh my god, we just messaged the son of a possible Nazi.

I feel gross. Like I need to climb out of my skin. Then, out
of nowhere, the idea comes to me.

"You know, I basically ruined *le quatorze juillet,* and I still
feel like I should make it up to you," I say to Paul.

He glances over at the spot where we kissed.

"I think you did it right over there," he points out.

"I'm serious!" I playfully poke his shoulder. "I want to plan
a fun day for us."

"Oh yes? What do you have in mind?"

"It's a surprise."

I half expect him to protest, but he doesn't.

"Okay," Paul says, "I trust you."

CHAPTER 12

Adalyn

Shortly before midnight, on a chilly March evening without any moonlight, four Frenchmen crouched by the side of the train tracks in a village near Limoges. While two of them kept watch, and another pressed his ear to the ice-cold rails, the fourth secured the explosive in its place. When the train was just a few kilometers away, which they knew by the vibrations in the tracks, the men backed away into the trees.

They heard the train coming. *Chugga chugga chugga chugga.* Then they saw it, slithering around the corner like a great black snake. The Frenchmen knew exactly what the train was carrying: tons upon tons of guns and ammunition on its way to supply the German war effort in North Africa. They waited for the perfect moment, when the freight cars were over the explosive.

Then they cranked the detonator.

A few of the cars were blown clean off the tracks in a burst of flame. A dozen more were knocked over onto their sides, their contents spilling out onto the rail bed. The Frenchmen didn't have time to sit around and revel in their achievement; they grabbed what they could of the weapons and took off into the night.

What happened that night near Limoges was the result of Geronte's intelligence network passing information to a group of guerrilla fighters in the south. And it happened because a German officer named Ulrich Becker III was fooled into sharing his train schedules with a nineteen-year-old Parisian girl.

Clacking down the street in my annoying wooden clogs, I make my way to the latest safe house Geronte has been using for meetings. He told me to come as soon as I could, whenever I finished collecting rations for the day. The four Frenchmen who carried out the attack are in town for a few days before they have to go back to the countryside, and apparently, they want to meet the girl who procured the pivotal scheduling information.

Along the way, I try to shake off the run-in I just had with Chloe. As I descended the last flight of stairs to the lobby, she was shouldering her way through the front door and carrying a shopping basket. *Food*—it was a safe enough topic. I halted on the bottom step so she would have to face me to get by.

"What were you able to get at the market?" I asked her.

Even a single word would have been something. We'd never gone so long without speaking to each other. But Chloe didn't say anything—she didn't even look up.

"Chloe?" I asked.

With her eyes fixed on the floor, she shouldered past me the same way she pushed through the door. I had the sensation of being winded, even though I wasn't, and had to reach out and steady myself on the banister. Behind me, Chloe marched up the stairs, and every pounding footstep felt like a brutal beating.

But I mustn't think about it any longer, at least not in this moment. Right now, I should feel proud of myself for helping pull off the attack. All the evenings spent by the fire at Madame Marbot's parties actually led to something important in the fight against Germany.

It's impossible not to think about it, though.

When Geronte opens the door of the ground-floor apartment, I immediately sense that something is different about him. He doesn't sniff me like a hound; his weathered face seems softer somehow.

"Come in, come in," he says. "It's excellent to see you."

It's almost as if he's welcoming me into a dinner party. Who is this Geronte?

"You seem to be in a good mood," I point out.

"Well, I've decided to allow myself a little time to rejoice at our success," he says in an uncharacteristically upbeat voice. "Come, now, I have four young Frenchmen hiding out in the study who've been awfully eager to pass along their thanks."

I follow him through the apartment to a door at the back of the dusty drawing room. He taps out a series of knocks, then steps back to give me space. There's rustling on the other side of the door. Oh, I am excited to meet these valiant strangers!

"Remember to keep the noise down," Geronte warns.

The noise? What kind of noise does he think I'll be making?

The knob twists, and the door opens. I can hardly believe my eyes. The man standing in the doorway isn't a stranger at all.

It's Luc.

I run to him. I throw my arms around his shoulders and he lifts me into the air and spins me around again and again. Am I imagining this? No, it's real. He's here—he's real—he's alive.

"Luc, it's been so long!"

His lips are next to my ear, and only I can hear his reply.

"It's been too long. . . . I think about you every day, Adalyn."

When he sets me back down on the ground, it still feels like I'm flying. I step back so I can take a good look at him— the first time I've seen him in six months, since our goodbye in September. The schoolboy I met in the fall of 1940 is nowhere to be found in the man standing in front of me. He's dressed in a black beret and a grubby wool blazer that doesn't seem warm enough for the weather. His messy black hair is even longer, reaching his chin, and there's dark stubble cropping up on his perfect jawline, which is more pronounced now. He's lost weight. But underneath it all, I still see him, and I still see the fire behind his eyes. My Luc.

I glance at Geronte, who's plopped himself down in an armchair with stuffing poking out at the seams. For the first time in all the months I've known him, I see the old man smile.

I turn back to Luc.

"You derailed the supply train," I say in amazement.

"Well, it was all thanks to you," he says. "And, actually, it was the four of us."

In the excitement of seeing Luc, I completely forgot there are three more men waiting to come out. Now that I know who the first one is, I have a sneaking suspicion as to who two of the others might be.

Sure enough, Marcel and Pierre-Henri emerge from the study, joined by a thin-faced blond boy who I've never seen before. I embrace Pierre-Henri first; then Marcel, who must be six inches taller now. He introduces me to the blond boy, Raphael, who greets me with a firm handshake.

"Pleasure to meet you," Raphael says in a voice smooth as

honey. "I've heard all about you from the others."

"Good things, I hope."

"The very best."

My sister would certainly beg to differ, but for now, I'm not going to think about that. It will only mar the pleasure of seeing my dear friends again. We sit down at the kitchen table, and Geronte brings out six dusty glasses and a bottle of red wine he's been saving for a special occasion. He gives the glasses a perfunctory wipe-down with the end of his shirt, which isn't especially clean to begin with, and fills each one halfway.

We raise our drinks in a toast.

"To a job well done," Geronte says.

We spend time catching up on the last six months of each other's lives. Shortly after Luc and I said our goodbyes, he, Marcel, and Pierre-Henri went south to join a rural band of resistance fighters in Limousin. These groups are known as the *maquis*, and Luc says they're growing across the southern part of the country—mostly made up of other young people avoiding forced labor in Germany.

It was in Limousin that the boys met Raphael, who'd left Paris shortly before them.

"I showed them the ropes around camp," Raphael says. "Taught them everything they know!"

Luc and Pierre-Henri laugh and roll their eyes, but Marcel nods enthusiastically. "It's true!" he insists. "You showed me how to aim the Sten properly. My shots were going straight into the ground before."

"It's been so long—I want to know everything about . . . *everything*," I tell them. "Even the little things, like where you sleep!"

"Well, we sleep in tents . . . or in abandoned barns . . . or sometimes just outside," Luc says.

"That must be uncomfortable."

"It isn't too bad," he says with a shrug. I know he would never complain about the conditions, even if they were absolutely unbearable.

"And what do you *maquisards* eat?" I ask, eyeing the boys' thin frames. They all look to be wearing clothes that are two sizes too big for them; Luc's cheekbones are more pronounced than ever before.

"We eat whatever we can find," Pierre-Henri says. "Sometimes we get rations from people in the villages nearby, if they're feeling generous."

"And I can hunt," Raphael adds.

Still looking at Pierre-Henri, I notice something different about him. "Where is your camera?" I ask. It's strange to see him without it hanging about his neck.

"I had to leave it with my baby sister," he replies. "That camera wasn't meant for *maquisard* life."

The boys answer everything I want to know about life in the *maquis*, until there's only one question left for me to ask.

I've been putting it off for as long as possible, but I'll have to find out at some point, and it might as well be now.

"When do you all go back?"

"Tomorrow," Luc says, sounding sad. We lock eyes.

But then it's my turn to tell stories. I paint a picture of the stressful journey to Chartres with the American airman, and the disastrous way it ended on the train platform. I tell them all about Madame Marbot's salons at the Hotel Belmont, and how I spent night after night pulling details out of Ulrich and filing them away in my mind. It's a relief to at last be able to express just how much I despise these parties and nearly everybody who attends them.

Geronte drains his glass and sets it down with a thud. He clears his throat. Just like that, the mood in the room shifts. The lively conversation peters out. It's time to get down to the first order of business, and he's looking at me.

"Since you were so successful this first time around, I have a new German target for you," Geronte says.

I sit up taller in my chair. "Who is it?"

"Walther von Groth. SS lieutenant-colonel and newly appointed chief of Gestapo in Paris. They promoted him because he . . . went above and beyond, shall we say."

A chill goes down my spine. "What does that mean, exactly?"

Geronte pauses before he speaks again.

"There is torture, and then there is what von Groth does

to his prisoners," he says. "If you die early on, you are lucky, they say. . . . And then there's the retaliation. Von Groth has ordered the massacres of entire French villages as punishment for resistance activity. Six months ago, in one town, he ordered the women and children to assemble in the church, and then he locked the doors and lit the place on fire. When three people managed to escape, his men shot them. Nobody survived. Von Groth is the worst of the worst of them. It is impossible to say how many hundreds or thousands of people have died at his hands."

"And you want me to . . . to get information out of him?"

"Yes," Geronte says plainly. "If you are willing."

My heart is pounding. I picture the atrocities this man, von Groth, has already committed, and what more he might do if he ever found me out. Across the table, Luc looks frightened, but he doesn't say anything that might sway my decision one way or the other. This is up to me, and I know my answer.

"I am willing," I tell Geronte.

"Good," he says. "I'm getting information on where he spends the majority of his time. I will update you as soon as I have a clearer picture." And then, as if nothing terrifying has just transpired, he picks up the wine bottle and squints into the opening. "There's enough in here for a few more sips. Who wants them?"

Nobody objects when I hold out my glass.

For the next little while, Geronte and the boys meticulously compare the Sten submachine gun, the weapon of choice among the *maquis*, to the MP40 guns they stole from the train bound for North Africa. I lose track of the conversation, thinking of nothing but my new mission, and sipping my wine to keep my nerves at bay.

Suddenly, I notice Luc standing next to my chair. The others are yawning and stretching in the late-afternoon light coming through the window. Raphael has his feet up on the table.

"Would you like to go for a walk?" Luc asks.

"A walk?" I ask him.

"Yes, along the river."

"Is there someone we have to meet down there? Or something we need to drop off?"

Luc laughs sheepishly and looks at his feet. "I just thought it might be nice to spend some time alone."

It takes a moment before I can make sense of his request. For two and a half years I've been living this secret life where nothing is as it seems. I'm so entrenched that when a fellow resistance fighter asks if I'd like to go for a walk, it doesn't occur to me that that's all it is—a walk.

Together.

Me and Luc.

"Yes—yes, of course," I stammer. "Although, isn't it dangerous? If the Germans see you?"

"The sun is setting soon," he says. "We'll stay hidden."

He holds out his hand, and I take it.

We go down to the Right Bank of the Seine, keeping in the shadows. The city around us is dark and gray, but the sky is a deep pink that reminds me of the cherry blossoms on our street. After another frigid winter, I think I finally smell spring in the air.

Down by the water's edge, in the dark space under the Pont de la Concorde, Luc interlaces his fingers with mine. It sounds so silly, but I'm overwhelmed with emotion as I try to take in these simple pleasures: the brilliant sunset; seeing Luc again; the way our hands joined together so effortlessly, as though they were always meant to be that way. A memory comes to me with startling clarity, of lying in bed with Chloe and listing every single thing we wanted to do when the war was over. Isn't this one of the activities we named that day?

"Are you crying, Adalyn?"

We stop walking. I don't know what's come over me. Tears spill down my cheeks and collect in my scarf. Perhaps I didn't realize what a toll my work has taken. Hiding and pretending are all I know these days. But walking with Luc, I suddenly remember what *real* life is like—life without the Nazis forcing us all into the ground.

"It's just that I'm happy," I say feebly.

We both laugh at the ridiculousness of it all—oh, how

wonderful that feels, too! It isn't the fabricated trill of dinner party laughter but true, pure joy.

Luc wipes away my tears with his free hand.

"I'm happy, too," he says.

I pull him by the hand to a stone ledge underneath the bridge. Through the wide archway, we have a perfect view of the Eiffel Tower on the opposite bank, silhouetted against the sky.

"I was just remembering how my sister and I used to dream that one day we would stroll down the river with a boy and look out at the lights over Paris."

"I'm sorry we can't have the lights," Luc says.

"You know what?" I wiggle closer to him and rest my head on his shoulder so there aren't any gaps of air between us. "I don't think I need them."

His fingers find my chin. Gently, he guides my face toward his. I stare into his eyes, the eyes that pulled me in from the moment I met him. I could swim inside them and never need to come up for air. I could make them my home. It isn't fair that he's leaving again so soon.

His hand slides to the back of my head, and he pulls me in until our lips meet. My whole body turns to liquid and melts into his. I have never kissed anybody before, but somehow, I seem to know what to do. I brush my tongue against his lips, and he opens them for me. He knots his fingers deep into my hair, like he's holding on for dear life. Maybe he is. Maybe we both are.

I pull away and kiss him along his jaw, that beautiful line that looked so pronounced in the dim light of his parents' shoe store. How I used to think about caressing it! When my lips reach his ear, I brush his hair to the side and make my way down his neck. Luc moans with pleasure. At his collar-bone, I switch directions and make the same glorious trip in reverse. Soon, I'm back to his mouth.

"Wait," Luc says. He takes my face in his hands. "I just want to see you."

We stare into each other's eyes for a few moments, sharing things that neither of us can express in words. Then he kisses me again. And so we pass the next hour, although it feels like a matter of minutes.

It isn't until an elderly woman shuffles by and warns us about getting home before curfew that we break apart and find that the sun has gone down. If the Germans discover us out here, there could be trouble.

"I suppose we should get going," Luc says as he tucks a strand of hair behind my ear.

"I wish we didn't have to."

"I want to walk you home, but we mustn't be seen together."

"Walk me until we get close."

He takes me by the hand and leads me away from the

river, onto a street that takes us north toward my home and Geronte's safe house. As we traipse down the dark and empty sidewalk, our senses on high alert for the presence of Germans, Luc asks, "How are you feeling about the new assignment?"

"Scared," I admit. "But I know I can do it."

He squeezes my hand. "I know you can, too."

"You know, the hardest part isn't having to trick *les boches*. That part is almost easy, if you can believe it. They never suspect me, not even for a second."

"What's the hardest part, then?"

I think back to yesterday morning, when I brewed a pot of wretched chicory coffee and carried a cup to Chloe, who was reading by herself in Papa's study, away from the rest of the family. She didn't look up from her book when I entered the room, and she didn't say a word when I set the drink down on the table beside her. It felt like being invisible.

"It's having to trick everybody else," I tell Luc. "Like my sister. She thinks I'm a true collaborator. She hasn't spoken to me since December. She won't even make eye contact if we're in the same room." I can still feel the spot where her shoulder collided with mine earlier today, can still hear her feet stomping up the stairs. "And there's nothing I can do to fix it, because I can't tell anyone the truth."

"I'm sorry, Adalyn. That must be so painful."

I let out a sigh. "It's the most painful thing in the world, Luc. . . . Sometimes I feel so alone, because nobody knows who I really am. Not even my own family. Oh—this is my block, by the way. That's my building over there. You shouldn't come any further, in case someone sees."

We stop on the corner, under a streetlamp that hasn't been lit since 1940. Not too far from here, Chloe is most likely stewing in her bedroom—if she isn't spending the night at one of her friends' houses. Maman and Papa are probably reading in the drawing room, both pushing down any troubling thoughts of the world outside the apartment.

Luc steps in front of me and takes hold of my other hand. He pulls me in close, so my cheek rests upon his chest.

"Don't go," I murmur into the fabric of his jacket.

"I must," he says, smoothing my hair. "But I want you to know, when you're doing your work, and you feel like you're all alone . . . I know who you really are, Adalyn. And no matter where I may be, know that if I am breathing, then I am thinking of you."

We kiss one last time. It is soft and slow and sad. I am the one to break it off. If I keep going, I'll never be able to stop.

"You go," I beg him. "I can't bear to walk away from you."

Luc releases my hands and pulls his jacket tighter around his body, even though it's not particularly cold out. With a final nod, he turns and walks away down the block. As his shadowy form disappears around the corner, a fresh wave of tears cascades down my cheeks. Why did it take us so long to admit that we had feelings for each other? We could have done this a year ago. We would have had so much more time.

I allow myself another minute or so, and then I dry my eyes with my scarf. Enough. Nobody can know that I've been crying, or else they might ask questions that I can't answer. I straighten my clothes, fix my hair, and walk the rest of the way home on my own.

CHAPTER 13

Alice

I meet Paul on a busy street corner, the kind of place where stopping means getting jostled by passersby from all directions. I triple-check Google Maps to make sure we get on the right train, while simultaneously trying to shield my screen from Paul's prying eyes.

"Alice, do you need me to help you?"

"No! I want it to be a surprise." I stare at my phone for another minute. This Paris transit map really is confusing.

"What if you just tell me the general area?" Paul offers.

"Champigny-sur-Marne."

I see it dawn on his face. His jaw drops, and his eyes light up behind his glasses. "We're going to the French resistance museum!"

"Oh no, I knew that would give it away!"

"I don't care! I'm so excited," he says. "How did you know

I've always wanted to go?"

"You told me when I took you to see the apartment! It was after we found the letter from Ulrich."

Paul takes me by the hand and leads me down the steps to the station. "I cannot believe you remembered that."

"Speaking of Ulrich . . . I got a response from his son this morning."

Paul stops walking so abruptly, a businessman bumps into him and nearly drops his cup of coffee. After apologizing profusely to the man, Paul asks, "What did he say?"

"Let's get on the train first, and then I'll show you."

He leads me to get our tickets and board the correct line, which turns out to be on the RER A. It's probably a good thing I ended up letting him help me—I would have had us taking a route that was twice as long. As soon as we sit down, I take out my phone and show him the Facebook message I got from Ulrich Becker IV at 9:42 a.m. The English is choppy, but the takeaway is clear.

Alice—I bring your message to my father. First, he must say he is ashamed of the events of the war. As a young man, my father fights for love of his country, not for Hitler, and he does not ever support the Nazi party.

My father recalls Adalyn. He sees her many nights in Paris in 1942 and beginning of 1943, but not again after he has transfer to Belgium in the summer 1943. They did talk together, but no romance. She is just a friend to my father at that time, as he misses home. Thank you for your message. I hope I am helpful.

Paul pushes his glasses back up his nose; they slid down while he was reading. "They never ended up together," he says.

"They were never together at all—not in a romantic way, at least."

"This is good news."

"I know. Well, except that we aren't any closer to figuring out what happened to her."

Paul furrows his brow. "Who do you think she was *actually* writing about in the diary?" he asks.

"I have no idea," I say. "But . . . it definitely makes me wonder about Adalyn again. Like, think about those very first diary entries I showed you. And now this. Half of the evidence says she *wasn't* a Nazi sympathizer. But then there's the photo—and the Hotel Belmont. I just keep asking myself, like, who *was* she?"

"Hmmm," says Paul, leaning back in his seat.

We lapse into contemplative silence. It feels different riding next to Paul than it did on our way out to Versailles—good different. I keep looking over at him and thinking, *We kissed.* Sitting next to him, with his hand casually resting on my knee, I can't help but feel like we're a couple—like I'm actually in a real relationship for the first time in my life. Like Camila and Peter. Of course, I have to keep reminding myself I'm only here for a little while longer; then it's back to Jersey to get ready for another school year. I guess I should just enjoy this while I can.

The train pulls into the station, and we gather up our things. We exit onto a suburban street lined with unremarkable stores and cafés, and we follow the sidewalk as it crosses over a slow-moving greenish river. It's a bit of a walk from here to the museum, so we stop at a bakery for a quick coffee and a croissant along the way.

"So what makes you like the French resistance?" I ask as I pop the to-go lids onto our cups.

"Good question," Paul mumbles through a mouthful of pastry. He takes a second to swallow. "I think I have always been fascinated by how young some of them were. We learned about the resistance in school when I was little, and I remember thinking, Oh my goodness, these people were only a few years older than me, and they were rescuing Allied pilots and blowing up buildings!"

"They blew up buildings?"

"I think so, yes. They did all sorts of things. There wasn't really one official 'resistance' group, although Charles de Gaulle did send this one man, Jean Moulin, to try to bring together some of the networks. He was arrested by the

Gestapo, and they tortured him to death. They tortured a *lot* of people to death."

I grimace.

"Anyway," Paul says, "the point is the 'resistance' was basically a bunch of people doing different things in different places. Some of them delivered messages, some of them spied on the Germans, some of them gave shelter to Allied pilots when their planes were shot down . . ."

"I guess I always pictured a little group of guys in berets running around and sabotaging trains," I confess.

Paul laughs. "It makes sense. That's the only stuff they put in the movies."

The Museum of National Resistance looks like an old manor house on a sparse residential street, with a wrought-iron gate at the entrance. We go inside and I pay for our tickets, then follow Paul to a wall of glass cases showing all sorts of documents from the early days of the Occupation.

"They were so brave," I murmur, peering at a newspaper called *Résistance*. It was published by a group of people connected to the Musée de l'Homme in Paris, many of whom were later arrested by the Gestapo and either executed or deported.

We stroll from exhibit to exhibit, past the rusty old roneo machine and the replica of the explosive strapped to the railway tracks. I try not to think about Adalyn, because it only makes me frustrated. Paul and I are contemplating the collection of scary-looking submachine guns, when suddenly I realize I really have to pee after that cup of coffee on the way here.

"I'll just be a minute," I say, pointing to the bathroom sign up ahead. I leave Paul standing at the gun wall and hurry for the toilets.

When I'm done, I go back the way I came, past exhibits we haven't seen yet. As I skim the glass cases, something catches my eye—a series of black-and-white photographs. They all depict the same group of people in slightly different poses, and even though I'm sure I've never seen the pictures before, something about them seems familiar.

I go closer to the glass to get a better look. It's the girl—the girl sitting there in the grass. It's—

"PAUL!" I scream, startling a family nearby. "PAUL, COME HERE QUICK!"

As Paul races over, I blink a few times to make sure I'm not seeing things, but apparently, I'm not. It's definitely who I think it is.

"Alice," he says, breathing heavily. "What is it?"

My whole arm shakes as I point at the photos. I can't even remember how to speak. Paul looks into the glass case. Then he takes off his glasses, wipes them on his shirt, and puts them back on again. He looks into the glass case again.

"Oh my god," he says.

I can't believe what I'm seeing. Truly, it doesn't make

sense. She can't be here, in a French resistance museum . . . but somehow, she is. It's the same group of teenagers in each of the photographs—three boys, and one girl.

The girl is Adalyn.

Her piercing stare drew me in from across the room. It couldn't possibly be anyone else. That's her in each of the photos, sitting in the grass with the same three boys. The camera captured them midconversation, and someone must have been telling a funny story, because everybody's smiling and laughing. One of the boys is staring in awe at a butterfly perched on his finger, and I notice with a sickening jolt that he also has a Star of David pinned to his breast pocket. Could this be the friend Adalyn wrote about in her diary—the one who was rounded up? And who are the others?

"Look, there's a description," Paul says, pointing.

The paragraph is typed in English and French, so Paul and I read it simultaneously:

THESE PHOTOS WERE TAKEN IN THE LUXEM-
BOURG GARDENS BY PIERRE-HENRI BOUCHARD, A
YOUNG PHOTOGRAPHY STUDENT AND RESISTANCE
FIGHTER. IN 1944, BOUCHARD WAS ARRESTED
AND SENT TO THE BUCHENWALD CONCENTRATION
CAMP, WHERE HE WAS MURDERED. HIS YOUNGER
SISTER DISCOVERED THESE PHOTOGRAPHS AFTER
HIS DEATH. THE SUBJECTS REMAIN UNIDENTIFIED,

BUT THEY ARE BELIEVED TO HAVE WORKED WITH
BOUCHARD ON RESISTANCE EFFORTS PRIOR TO HIS
CAPTURE.

The part about the concentration camp is too horrible to read more than once, but I stare at that last sentence for a good long time with my mouth hanging open.

Paul seems equally dumbfounded. "So . . . after all this . . . she *was* doing resistance work?"

I dig my fingertips into my temples. "I mean . . . maybe? But it still doesn't explain the Nazi photo . . . and the Hotel Belmont . . . and also, if Adalyn was this great resistance fighter, then why would my Gram never mention her? That's the kind of thing Gram would have been proud of!" I sweep my hair into a bun as I search the photos for answers that I know aren't there. Why is it that the more I learn about Gram's past, the further I get from any concrete explanations? Now I'm starting to panic. I'm only in Paris for another week and a half, and I owe Dad an answer on whether I'm okay with selling the apartment. What if I need more time?

"Paul, what should we do?"

"I think we should tell the museum we know this person in the photo," he says. I can barely think straight, and it sounds like a smart thing to do, so I let him lead me back to the desk where we bought our tickets. Without a moment's hesitation, he goes to the woman and speaks to her in French, pointing first to me, and then in the direction of the photos. The woman listens patiently and nods her head. Then she picks up the phone and speaks to someone in a hushed voice.

"She's calling the museum curator," Paul tells me.

It only takes a few minutes for a woman with a shiny silver bob to come meet us in the lobby.

"Antoinette Richard," she says with a warm smile, shaking both of our hands. After Paul and I introduce ourselves— and we learn that Antoinette Richard speaks very good English—the curator leads us back to her office, a small room with bookshelves covering every wall.

"I hear that you have possibly identified a person in one of our photographs," she says when we're all seated.

"Yes," I reply. "It's my great-aunt Adalyn. It looks exactly like her."

"Do you have a photograph?"

"No—not on me, at least. They're all in her old apartment, which hasn't been touched since the war."

Ms. Richard's eyebrows shoot up so high, they disappear under her bangs. "Pardon me?"

I glance over at Paul, and he gives me a little nod of encouragement. With a deep breath, I launch into the story of Gram's apartment and everything I know about Adalyn, the good and the bad and the question marks in between. Ms. Richard is riveted, especially when I show her the photos I have of the apartment on my phone. This must be like

Christmas for a museum curator.

By the time I'm finished explaining things, I feel like I've run a marathon. "What do you think?" I ask helplessly. "Could she have been in the resistance, or was she definitely a Nazi sympathizer?"

Ms. Richard, who was leaning in to listen to my story, sits back and crosses her arms. "As a historian, I don't like to draw conclusions before doing the proper research," she says flatly. "Without seeing any of the documents myself, I'm afraid it is impossible for me to make a determination one way or the other."

"If we bring in more photos, would you take a look at them?" Paul asks.

"Most certainly," she replies.

"We'll bring you everything," I promise. But there's something I still want to ask her. "Ms. Richard, do you have any idea how I could go about tracking down my great-aunt? We don't even know if she's still alive, but if she is, I'd like to find her."

To my surprise, Ms. Richard says, "I have an idea." She pulls open the bottom drawer of her filing cabinet and riffles through it until she finds a red-white-and-blue flyer, which she slides across the desk. I read the title at the top.

"Project Geronte?"

"It was started by an acquaintance of mine, Corinne, whose grandfather ran an intelligence network based in

Paris. Because of the secrecy it required, it can be hard to know who exactly was involved. I mean, look at the situation you're dealing with here. The purpose of Project Geronte is to bring all these people together, with their families, in a sort of community. They get to meet each other and share their stories after all these years, and we as historians get to write it all down."

"You think someone there would know Adalyn?"

"I don't know. But I bring it up because they meet on the third Wednesday of every month, so the next one is a week from now. I'm not able to attend—tomorrow I leave for Canada to give a series of lectures, and I'll be gone for a week and a half—but I would be happy to put you in touch with Corinne. I think she's almost eighty, but she'll get back to you on email no problem. And I'll give you copies of the photos to take with you."

Paul and I look at each other, then back at Ms. Richard.

"That would be awesome," I tell her. "Thank you so much."

"It's my pleasure," she says, picking up the phone. "If your great-aunt is still alive, and she was in the resistance, then we must learn her story before it's too late."

I keep fumbling with the bottom button on my jacket. I just can't get it to go through the hole. Every time I think I have it, the damned thing slides out again. It must be due to the fact that my hands are shaking.

Finally, I get it done. I step in front of the hall mirror and study my reflection—my hair gathered on top and curling softly around my face, my lips painted bright red, a matching red ruby glittering at the base of my neck. I ask myself, *If I were one of the most evil men in the world, would I want to buy me a drink?*

I don't know. I haven't any idea how his mind works. But I hope so.

The wooden floor creaks. I hear footsteps coming from down the hall. Chloe. I would say goodbye to her, but I know she wouldn't answer. Instead, I watch in the mirror as she passes right behind me on her way to the drawing room, so close than I can feel the air move. This is the way we are now: two ships passing in the night. That's it. I'd better go.

The restaurant von Groth and his men frequent is called Au Coq Blanc—or it used to be, before it was changed to German. It's situated on the corner of rue des Saussaies and rue Montalivet in the Eighth Arrondissement . . . not far from Madame LaRoche's apartment, and opposite Gestapo head-quarters. Normally, I wouldn't dare walk down this street. I must try to stay focused on the task at hand, and not on the French prisoners who are currently trapped behind the doors of 11, rue des Saussaies, suffering from god knows what evil things von Groth has subjected them to. What if I become the next to join them? What if I, too, end up wishing I would die quickly rather than endure more of his torture?

My hands are shaking again. I need them to stop. Von Groth is smart. If he sees that I am nervous, he will know right away.

With a deep breath, I step into the restaurant. It's a splendid place, with dizzyingly high ceilings, mirrors as tall as three grown men standing on top of one another, and a massive chandelier. When my eyes travel down to the area beneath it, my breath catches in my throat—even after three years of Occupation, it still disturbs me—a half dozen Germans reclining with their polished black boots on the tablecloth.

Geronte showed me a photo of von Groth in the newspaper,

next to an article about his promotion. The man has a face like a shark, with a heavy brow and cold slits for eyes. His cheeks are hollow, and his lips are thin as a knife blade. It doesn't take me long to spot him, cutting himself a slab of meat with surgeon-like precision and transferring it onto his plate.

A waiter in a white shirt and black bow tie strides over to greet me. He is bald, with a skinny mustache that curls at either end. This must be the man they call Boivin, another one of Geronte's many contacts. With his job, he can conveniently observe the comings and goings at 11, rue des Saussaies. He also happens to know that von Groth, when he is done eating, has a habit of approaching single women seated at the bar.

"May I offer you a table, miss?"

"No thank you," I reply, following our script. "A seat at the bar will do just fine."

Boivin leads me past the Germans' table. On the way, he drops a menu, and I bend over to pick it up for him. One of the Germans wolf-whistles. Another bangs his glass on the table. I feel sick, but at least the plan is working so far. With the menu back in his possession, Boivin shows me to a barstool that's right in von Groth's line of sight.

That idiot German is still wolf-whistling, but at least it helps my cause. I smile coyly in his direction, as though his boorishness appeals to me. Some of the others look my way,

and I smile at them, too. I want the whole table to know that
I'm here—men are competitive that way.

Notice me, von Groth. I'm right over here.

As if the man just heard my thoughts, von Groth sets
down his fork, wipes the corners of his mouth with a cloth
napkin, and looks to see what his comrades are still whistling
about.

His ice-cold gaze makes it feel like I'm sitting in the cross-
hairs of a rifle. My gut tells me to flee for my life, but that
is not what I came here to do. So I gather up my courage. I
remind myself of the train attack in Limoges, which wouldn't
have happened without the details I gleaned from Ulrich.

And I lock eyes with von Groth. I smile at him. I even
wave, which I didn't do for anyone else at the table.

Von Groth holds our eye contact. He nods his head, almost
like a greeting. Then he turns back to his previous conversation.

I take small sips of my cognac, conversing with the bartender about nothing of any importance. As my glass gets
emptier and emptier, I start to wonder if my efforts with von
Groth were enough. He still hasn't come over here . . . and yet
every now and then, the hairs on the back of my neck bristle,
and I peer over to find von Groth gazing in my direction
again.

Just as I take the last sip of my drink, there's movement
over at the table. Von Groth stands up from his chair and cuts

a straight line to the bar, as though he were timing it. His boots click across the tile with purpose.

"The young lady will have another. And one for me, as well," he says to the bartender. His voice is as sharp as a needle. Without asking if I am expecting anybody, von Groth puts his foot up on the stool next to me and leans against the bar with his elbow. I find it hard to look away from the glare of his many medals, and from the blued steel of the pistol at his right hip. After he delivers our drinks, the bartender, so chatty just a few minutes ago, scurries away like a mouse.

"Your eyes caught my attention," von Groth says. "They are quite remarkable."

"You flatter me, Colonel."

"Lieutenant-Colonel, I'm afraid."

"Oh no, that's my mistake. I saw your photo in *Les Nouveaux Temps*. Congratulations on your new position. It is very impressive."

"I appreciate the praise, coming from a French girl like yourself. Too many of your people don't show us the proper respect." His eyes flit in the direction of the street—toward number 11. "Will you enjoy this drink with me?"

"I would be glad to."

Von Groth clinks his glass against mine. "I am Obersturmbannführer Walther von Groth. What is your name, miss?"

"Adalyn Bonhomme."

It's terrifying to give Walther von Groth my real name. I feel naked. But Adalyn Bonhomme is the girl with her picture in the society pages—the girl who hangs around the Hotel Belmont all the time—which means Adalyn Bonhomme is, once again, my best disguise.

"And what brings you to this restaurant all by yourself, Miss Bonhomme?"

I force a bashful smile. "Should the war prevent a young woman from trying to meet a nice man?"

Von Groth chuckles. "Do you speak German?"

"Unfortunately, no," I lie.

"No matter," he says, puffing out his chest, "I am fluent in French, among other languages."

"Teach me to say something in German, Lieutenant-Colonel."

"Okay. What would you like to learn?"

"Teach me how to say . . . 'The lieutenant-colonel looks very nice in his uniform.'"

"Der Obersturmbannführer sieht gut aus in seiner Uniform."

"Oh my! I will need your help to say that properly." I put on the worst accent I can muster, channeling all my former classmates who struggled during German lessons. *"Dare oh-burr-shturrm-bun-fü-rurr . . ."*

"Sieht gut aus . . ."

"Zeet goot owss . . ."

"In seiner . . ."

"In zy-nur . . ."

"Uniform."

"Oo-nee-form."

Von Groth raises his glass. "Spoken like a true German." I hate that when he smiles, his sharp little teeth poke down beneath his lip.

"I will teach you to say something else now, Miss Bon-homme." Von Groth touches my wrist, and I fight the over-whelming instinct to pull away. I try not to look at his hands, because I don't want to think about what they've done.

"Du bist wunderschön," he says to me.

"Ooh, what does that mean?" I ask as if I didn't already know.

"You are very beautiful," Von Groth answers, stroking my forearm now.

"Thank you."

"I think you mean to say *'danke,'*" he says with a wink.

Just then, one of the men who were sitting at von Groth's table marches over and stops about five feet away from us, his hands behind his back. He clears his throat. "Obersturm-bannführer, your car is waiting outside."

"I will be there shortly," von Groth says brusquely.

This is it, my last chance to make sure we meet again. Now I graze my fingers along *his* wrist.

"I do hope this is not the last time we see each other," I tell him.

"The Saturday after next, there is a luncheon happening at this restaurant to celebrate my new position. I would have you come as my guest, if you are available."

"It would be an honor."

"It is a plan, then. I look forward to seeing you here at noon."

Von Groth drains what's left of his glass and kisses the back of my hand with those terrible thin lips of his. Then he exits the restaurant, his German companions in tow. Oh my god, what did I just do?

"Another drink, miss?" asks the bartender, who magically reappears as soon as von Groth leaves.

"No thank you," I reply, holding on to the bar to make sure I don't faint.

Geronte is impressed with my work. I am, too, I must admit, once I recover from the shock of it all. Von Groth suspected nothing. He believed me when I fawned over his new title and his uniform. What can I get him to tell me when I have more time with him?

It's the night before von Groth's luncheon. I practice piano in the drawing room while Maman and Papa read in the armchairs by the window, its curtains drawn tight to keep in the lamplight. As I come to the end of a piece, Maman looks up from her book and asks, "Shall you and I go to the market tomorrow, Adalyn?"

I bite my lip. I've been putting off telling my parents about the luncheon until now, as it pains me to have them think I *wanted* to accept the invitation. But I have to do it. I chose this life of resistance, and when it comes to my spying, I must remember that the ends justify the means. The one thing making this easier is that Chloe isn't in the room to hear me. She's sequestered herself in Papa's study again, to keep away from us.

"I can't tomorrow," I tell Maman. "I've been invited to a luncheon."

"Oh! By whom, darling?"

"By . . . the new chief of Gestapo in Paris. I met him at a restaurant with some friends from university."

I keep my eyes on the score in front of me, but I hear the soft *thump* of a book closing.

"The Gestapo?" Maman asks hesitantly. I can guess at what she's thinking. Until now, she's found a way to rationalize being around the Germans at Madame Marbot and Madame LaRoche's parties. But the Gestapo, Hitler's secret police, have never been present at any of them.

I finally turn to face her, and sure enough, there's a look of concern on her face. Her eyes keep flitting over to Papa, searching for guidance, but his continued focus on his book makes it clear that he doesn't want to get into it.

"It's okay, Maman," I insist. "I'm going to try to bring back some food for us. And anyhow, I . . . I reason it can't hurt to have the Gestapo look upon our family favorably. The stories you hear . . ."

Maman sighs. "Yes . . . the stories you hear, indeed . . ."

A heavy silence fills the air.

"Very well, then," she says at last. "If you come to my room in the morning, I can help you pick out something to wear. We can go through the photos in my drawer and get some inspiration."

"That would be lovely, Maman." My own duplicitousness is making me queasy. "I think I shall go get some rest now, if you'll excuse me."

I say good night to my parents and make for the comfort of my bedroom, where I can shut the door and bury my face in a pillow. But when I get to the hallway, I see a triangle of light on the floor, emanating from Papa's study. Oh no. Chloe must not have closed the door all the way, in which case, there's a chance she overheard the conversation in the drawing room.

I hold my breath as I approach the study. Perhaps I'm being overly cautious. It appears as though the door to the study is *mostly* closed—how much sound would even pass through there? And in any case, Maman and I were talking at a rather low volume.

But as I pass through the triangle of light, I hear Chloe shift in her seat. *It's nothing*, I tell myself. But then, clear as day, my sister's voice hisses at me through the tiny opening.

"What an embarrassment you are."

In the morning, Maman sends me off in a lemon-yellow dress and a pair of teardrop diamond earrings, holding one of her coveted Boucheron clutches.

"You look like a walking ray of sunshine," she assures me, but I hardly feel that way as I make my way to the luncheon. I'm wounded by Chloe's insult, terrified to be in the icy presence of Walther von Groth again, and frustrated that the only people who know who I really am are miles away in some unknown location. I long the most for Luc, whom I haven't seen since our afternoon by the river, and Geronte hasn't let slip any new details as to his whereabouts. As I round the bend on to the rue des Saussaies, I remind myself what Luc said before he kissed me goodbye:

"If I am breathing, then I am thinking of you."

Please be thinking of me now, Luc.

The restaurant is a sea of gray-green uniforms. An infestation of rats. The tables have been pushed to the edges of the room so the guests can mingle as they nibble at canapés passed around on silver trays. There's a photographer taking pictures of the whole affair. The waiter Boivin welcomes me with a sweep of his arm. "He's over to the left," he whispers as I walk past.

I find von Groth at the center of a ring of admirers. When he spies me through the crowd, he snaps at two of his men to step aside and let me through. Von Groth kisses the top of my hand with his cold, hard mouth.

"Miss Bonhomme. I am delighted you joined us today."

"It is an honor to be here."

"You look even more beautiful than the last time."

"Why, thank you."

Our conversation is cut short as more men approach to offer their congratulations, but I stay by von Groth's side for the entirety of the affair. What the lieutenant-colonel doesn't know is that whenever he has an exchange with another German official, I pick up on every word.

At first, it's just a flurry of formalities. "Nobody deserved it more"; "The administration is fortunate to have you"; "I look forward to working with you." But as the affair begins to wind down, and certain less important guests make their way toward the exit, von Groth and some of his close companions take their seats around one of the big tables.

"Join us for a drink before you leave, Miss Bonhomme."

"I would be delighted."

Really, I would be sick, if it wouldn't give me away. Every

man around the table has a Nazi armband. Still, I slip into the chair next to von Groth and accept a glass of cognac as it comes my way. Nobody seems concerned by my presence, as they believe there to be a language barrier between us. I am nothing but another medal for von Groth to wear on his chest.

"Obersturmbannführer von Groth," says one of the men, who seems very eager to make an impression, "you must tell us, how has the position been treating you so far?"

"Very well, Richter," replies von Groth. "You know, the people of Paris are despicable in many ways, but they certainly make the Gestapo's job easier when they denounce each other to us. Of course, much of it is nonsense, and one must separate the true from the false, but that is something I am capable of doing quite easily."

There's a murmur of laughter around the table.

"Tell us about some of the true ones," says the man called Richter.

"Last week," von Groth says, "we were informed by a concierge that a young couple in her building had been stockpiling weapons underneath the floorboards of their apartment. The other day, we raided their home, and indeed found many firearms. The man tried to say he was simply a collector."

"Where are they now?" asks another man.

"The woman is in Fresnes," von Groth says. "The man is dead."

More laughter.

"Tell us another," begs Richter.

"Well, there is the raid we have planned for tomorrow." Everyone around the table leans in except for me, for I'm pretending I have no idea what's going on. But my ears are tuned to every word that leaves von Groth's lips.

"A man who runs a bookstore over on the rue Chauveau Lagarde informed us that the woman in the first-floor apartment across the street is sheltering a group of Jewish vermin. Of course, it may all be a lie, but *that* is the sort of report we must take very seriously."

The other men nod in assent.

I am quietly trying to absorb this horrifying information when the newspaper photographer approaches the table. "A picture of the group before I leave?" he asks.

"Please," von Groth says.

The lieutenant-colonel puts his arm around my shoulders. I wish he wouldn't touch me, but to pull away would be to give up my position. And so, as the other men gather around us, I do the thing that I must.

I smile for the camera.

When it's time to go, I leave the restaurant with von Groth and his men. Out on the sidewalk, he pulls me off to one side.

"I regret that we did not have more time to talk," he says. "It was a very busy affair."

"It's no matter," I insist. "I was happy to have been invited at all."

"Regrettably," he says, "I shall be traveling for the next few months, but if you come by here in the autumn, you will certainly find me, and I would very much like to buy you another drink, Miss Bonhomme. We can continue our German lessons."

"I look forward to it. Safe travels, Lieutenant-Colonel."

I let him kiss me on the hand once more—a truly foul sensation—and then I depart down the block, glad to be away from him. I have to admit, it is both a disappointment and a relief that I won't be seeing von Groth for another few months. I am going to go home and wash the back of my hand thoroughly, though first, there is something else I must do.

The rue Chauveau Lagarde is not too far away. It's a very short street, and as far as I can see, there is only one bookstore. I go into the building directly across the street, where I tell the sleepy concierge that I'm a friend of the woman in the first-floor apartment. She waves me up the stairs without a second look.

I rap on the door quietly so the neighbors won't hear. A minute goes by. Then the door opens just a crack. A woman juts her head through the opening. She looks thin and exhausted, like a small forest creature constantly on the run from predators.

"How can I help you?" she asks curtly.

"They know," I tell her. "They're coming tomorrow."

I watch the woman's fear swim up to the surface. Her eyes go wide, until there's white all around her pupils.

"Who are you?" she whispers.

"It doesn't matter," I answer brusquely. "Just get somewhere safe. All of you."

We lock eyes for a few agonizing seconds, one frightened woman to another. We are all in this together, tiny flames fighting to stay alight in this crushing darkness. She doesn't say anything else. She nods at me and shuts the door. I hurry back down the stairs, praying they get away without any trouble.

CHAPTER 15

Alice

I'm so nervous and excited for the Project Geronte meeting, it seems unfair that we have to wait a whole week. To pass the time, Paul and I analyze the pages of Adalyn's diary like two archaeologists, reading and rereading, desperately hunting for clues in her small cursive writing.

One early afternoon, we're behind his desk at La Librairie. It's a sleepy day at the bookstore, not a customer in sight and no new shipments to catalogue, so I rest my head on Paul's shoulder as we pore over the diary once again. But the minute his shift is over, Paul closes the book and reaches for his bag.

"Let's go," he says.

"Is everything okay?"

"Yes. But I want to kiss you very badly, and I cannot do that here."

I pack up my things as fast as I can. Paul takes me by the hand and leads me on a short walk to the Luxembourg Gardens. We follow the path to the back of the Luxembourg Palace, past the pond with the fountain in the middle, and finally to a shady patch of grass between two rows of trees with their branches and leaves cut into perfect rectangles.

We fall into the grass and kiss each other immediately, deeply. I used to imagine what it was like to French kiss someone, and I always assumed it was kind of complicated, with all those moving parts. I never thought it would come so naturally, or that I'd actually end up doing it with a French person. I don't even care that there are people around as I let his tongue push past my teeth. It feels amazing. And I have so many pent-up feelings from everything that's been going on, I just want to lose myself in the steady rhythm of our lips.

Somehow, we go from seated to lying side by side, facing each other. His hand travels slowly down my side and comes to rest on the bare skin peeking out from underneath my T-shirt. It sends happy chills through my whole body.

Then our glasses clank against each other, and we both dissolve into a fit of giggles.

"I figured that might happen," Paul says.

"I can take mine off, if you want."

"No, it's okay." He shifts back an inch and fixes his eyes on me. "You look so beautiful right in this moment."

I feel like I might burst into a fireworks display.

We both sit up and brush the plant life from our clothes, blushing feverishly. I reach for my backpack and retrieve Adalyn's diary.

"I guess we should get back to work," he says.

"It was a good study break," I point out.

Before we left the bookstore, we had been going over an entry from December 1943. Adalyn was writing about another brutally cold winter, about not having enough coal to heat the apartment, about wishing the war would end. One section jumps out at me toward the end:

> *It is so cold in here, my fingers are numb—and I am under the covers. These frigid nights would be so much more bearable if I were sharing my bed with Chloe, as we used to do. But Chloe hasn't come to my room in a year now. She's hardly ever home. When she is, she doesn't speak to me. She doesn't look at me if we pass each other in the hall. It shatters my heart every time.*

Based on that, we reasoned that Gram and Adalyn stopped speaking at the end of 1942, but we still can't figure out why.

"If Adalyn *was* in the resistance, then why would Gram be so mad at her?" I ask. "They both would have been on the same side."

"I just thought of something," Paul says. "What if your grandmother didn't know?"

"Didn't know that Adalyn was doing resistance work?"

"Yes," he says, still mulling it over. "Maybe it was secret."

"That's a pretty big secret to keep from your family."

"It is."

"I mean, they were *best* friends."

I turn to the last entry in the book, dated May 30th, 1944. The rest of the pages in the diary are blank, and I've been trying not to let my brain jump to conclusions about why my great-aunt might have stopped writing. The entries are much less frequent in 1944; maybe she just got too busy. Still, it's hard not to worry, now that I know what the final entry says.

When Paul read it to me the other day, he furrowed his brow, and his glasses slid down his nose. "This is a strange message," he said.

"What do you mean?"

"It's mysterious," he murmured. "It's like she's talking in symbols." And then he translated the cryptic message for me:

May 30th, 1944

Nearly four years it has been. Four years since the flame was lit. And still, my flame burns.

Here is the thing that is true about fire: It creates power, but it also creates destruction. My fire has fueled many victories, but it has destroyed what I had with the person I love most in the world.

My fire has caused me such pain but I can't put it out.
I don't want to.

Tomorrow may be the most difficult day yet. I am
frightened. I am trembling as I write this. But my fear is
far less important than doing what must be done.

Whatever happens, I sleep tonight knowing the risk
will be worth it.

My heart pounds as I look at the words again, now that I know their meaning. I'm equal parts desperate and terrified to know what Adalyn had planned for May 31, 1944. It can't be good that she wrote about doing something dangerous the next day, and then stopped writing in the diary . . . but Paul keeps reminding me we don't know anything for certain yet.

"Well, it really does sound like she was doing resistance work," I point out again. *"And still, my flame burns.* Charles de Gaulle talked about 'the flame of French resistance.' Adalyn quoted it earlier on in the diary."

"And it would explain why the entry is written in that confusing way," Paul replies. "She wouldn't have wanted to speak openly about her plans, in case someone found the book."

"There's still one big question, though."

"What is that?"

"Why was she hanging out with Nazis?"

"Oh . . . right."

I let out a groan and flop down onto my back, my arms splayed out to either side. Paul lies down next to me. I curl into his body, resting my cheek on the soft spot just below his collarbone. It feels good here. Safe.

"I know the chances are slimmer than slim," I say, "but I really hope we find someone who recognizes her at the Project Geronte meeting."

"You never know," he replies. "Maybe Adalyn *herself* will be there."

I bury my face in the fabric of his shirt. "Now you're making me all nervous again!"

"Sorry," he says. "I can try to distract you, if you want."

"How?" I grumble.

There's a slight disruption as he takes off his glasses and tucks them into the side pocket of his backpack. Then he lies back down and pulls me in close. Just like that, my brain completely shifts gears. With butterflies beating their wings inside my chest, I lift up my face so Paul can kiss me again.

The Project Geronte meeting is at a hotel in the Ninth Arrondissement, not far from the rue de Marquis. I tell myself it's a good sign, even though it actually means nothing. I meet Paul outside on the sidewalk, the photos of Adalyn tucked under my arm in the envelope Ms. Richard gave me. I'm so nervous, I'm shaking. I feel like I did when I opened the door of apartment five for the first time, completely unaware of what I'd find inside.

Paul looks really good in his blazer and dark jeans. I've never seen him in anything other than a T-shirt.

"You dressed up," I point out.

"Well, what if Adalyn is here? I wanted to look good in case I end up meeting your family."

I smack him with the envelope. "She is so *not* going to be here." But even as I say it, my heart thuds. What if, by some absurd stroke of luck, she *is*?

Paul offers me his elbow, and I take it. Having him by my side makes me calmer.

"Hey, Paul?" We're riding up the escalator to the party room in the mezzanine.

"Yes?"

"I just want to say . . . thanks for coming with me. And for helping me out with everything. I never would have gotten this far without you."

Now we're standing outside the double doors with the Project Geronte signs taped to them. Before we go in, Paul takes my face in his hands and kisses me on the forehead. It's the most unexpectedly romantic thing that's ever happened to me. My knees wobble.

"It is my pleasure," he says. "I am just happy to be with you, Alice."

Three men—one very old, helped by two who must be in their seventies or eighties—shuffle past us and go into the room. This is incredible—some of the people on the other side of these doors were actually part of the French resistance! It's history in real life.

"Should we go in?" Paul asks.

"Yes."

We open the doors onto a carpeted conference hall with chairs lining the walls and people milling around in the middle, many of them as old as the men we saw come in. I hear faint forties-sounding music playing, which they probably have to keep low so the guests can hear each other okay. There's a long table with artifacts laid out—copies of old newspapers, posters, some rusty old weapons—and another table with a spread of wine, cheese, and bread.

A strong hand grabs my upper arm. "Alice? Paul?"

I spin around. If this is our host, she looks a lot younger than eighty. Sixty-five, maybe. She's styled her short white hair so that it spikes up in the front, and she's dressed in a tailored red pantsuit.

"Yes, that's us," I tell her. "Are you Corinne?"

"*Oui*. It is a pleasure to meet you." Her English is choppy. She greets us both with a firm handshake. "Antoinette told me all about your story. I am glad you came here tonight."

"I'm glad you let us come! So . . . your grandfather led a resistance network?"

"That is correct."

"I don't know if you would recognize photos of anyone he worked with, but . . ."

I slide out the black-and-white copies Ms. Richard gave us. Corinne inspects them close to her face, then hands them back, shaking her head. "My grandfather worked with many people during the war, some as young as these people here. I do not recognize them, but you are welcome to ask anybody in this room. I see a number of new faces here tonight. You never know."

"Here—meet my friend Micheline." Corinne touches the arm of a frail woman passing by on the way to the drinks table. The woman looks confused but smiles warmly at us. Corinne asks her a question in French, and she points at the photos in my hand. Micheline's eyebrows go up. She beckons for me to pass her the pictures. My heart racing with anticipation, I hand them over. She squints at them for a minute, the wrinkles in her forehead growing even deeper, and then says simply, *"Non."*

"Merci beaucoup," says Paul, as Micheline toddles away. Corinne goes off to greet another new arrival.

My heart sinks. "I wanted her to recognize them."

"She was the very first person we tried," Paul says, patting me on the back. "Come on—let's go try that couple over there. I can do the talking, in case they don't speak English."

We go up to the man and woman standing alone by the window.

"*Excusez-moi*," says Paul, "*pouvons-nous vous poser une question?*"

We go through the same routine as before, handing over the photos and watching with bated breath as they analyze them. And just like before, they shake their heads and say, "*Non, désolé.*"

Non, désolé—no, sorry—become the words of the evening. Nobody recognizes Adalyn or any of the boys. Some people take it as a jumping-off point to explain their own exploits during the war, and we get totally distracted by their incredible stories until one of us remembers we should probably keep circling the room.

After shaking her head at the picture of Adalyn, one old woman shows us a black-and-white photograph of herself in 1942. The first thing I notice is her hair, because it looks hilarious. It has this big bump in the front that must be a foot high. It's taller than her actual head. As we share a laugh about it, I glance back at the photo and realize there's a star on her dress. It has the word "zazou" in the middle of it.

"I think my grandmother wore the same star," I tell her, remembering the purple dress left behind on Gram's bed. "Her name was Chloe Bonhomme—you didn't know her, did you?"

She shakes her head again. "It was so many years ago,"

she replies in her raspy voice. "The memory works in funny ways. There are tiny things I shall never forget, like the taste of the ersatz coffee my mother used to make . . . or the smell of the iodine dye she would paint on her legs to make it look as though she was wearing silk stockings, which we could no longer afford. Other things, they are gone!" She jokingly raps her knuckles against her head.

"Why did you wear the word 'zazou'?"

The woman smirks. "That's what we called ourselves," she says. "We were little rebels! We did the opposite of whatever Pétain and his Vichy government told us to do. He wanted the girls to stay in the home and become mothers, so of course we dressed like this and went to all the jazz clubs. It was quite a time!"

Even after all these years, I can still see a spark behind her eyes.

As the woman hobbles off on her walker to say hello to Micheline, my heart swells with pride. Gram was a rebel! I wouldn't have expected anything less. She was like that until the end of her life, shunning Mom and Dad's repeated suggestions that she hire a full-time caregiver.

"So if Gram was one of these *zazous*," I say to Paul, "she probably wasn't too happy that her mom was going to the Hotel Belmont every other weekend. . . . And then, if she found out that Adalyn was doing whatever she was doing with those Nazis—"

"She would have been really mad," Paul says, finishing my thought. "Mad enough to stop speaking to her."

"And don't forget how close they used to be, from the beginning of the diary."

"It would be like if Vivi started hanging out with Nazis," he says. "I don't know how I'd speak to her again, either."

We migrate to the corner of the room so we can survey the scene. By this point, the photos of Adalyn are limp and creased from being held by so many different hands.

"Who next?" Paul asks.

I look around, but I don't see anybody new. "I feel like we've asked almost everyone," I say despairingly.

"How about that guy?"

I follow Paul's eyes to the opposite corner of the room. It's the very old man we saw when we came in—the one being helped by two other people. Truth be told, the guy kind of gives me the creeps. I've noticed him staring at me since the beginning of the night.

"He seems a little weird," I mumble. "Let's try the ladies by the pistols instead."

Paul agrees. But the ladies by the pistols end up being another strikeout. Same with the woman in the wheelchair with little French flags attached to the top, and the tiny old man in the black beret. Now people are starting to trickle toward the door. Out of the corner of my eye, I keep catching Corinne hugging people goodbye. My heart is hammering again. This is it—our last chance to find someone, *anyone*, who can tell us anything about my great-aunt.

That man is still over there in the corner, finishing a glass of red wine. Sure enough, he's also still staring at me.

But I have to do it.

I politely interrupt Paul's conversation with the man in the black beret. "People are starting to leave," I whisper. "We should try the guy in the corner."

Paul nods. We say goodbye to his new friend, who hurries off to snag the last slice of baguette. Then we approach the man, whose two companions sit on either side of him. The man has been staring the whole time, obviously, but now all three of them look up expectantly. Paul clears his throat.

"Pouvons-nous vous poser une question?"

There's a sense of urgency in the way the old man nods, his eyes never once leaving my face, even though it's Paul who's talking. They have a brief back-and-forth in French, in which I hear the word *appartement* come up—meaning apartment—and then Paul tells me I can hand over the pictures.

The man brings them up close to his face, just a few inches away from his nose. I guess the others will have to wait their turn. He holds them like that for a long time—maybe even a full minute. Paul and I exchange apprehensive looks. What's the man staring at? Is he searching for memories that are long gone?

Suddenly, something strange happens. The man's arms begin to quiver. He grips the papers so hard, I'm scared he's going to tear through them.

One of his younger companions puts his hand on the man's shoulder. *"Quel est le problème?"*

Finally, he lowers the photos, and I'm shocked to see that he has tears in his eyes. There's a collective intake of breath among the group. Then the man looks directly into my eyes and says something to me. Paul looks confused.

"I'm so sorry, I don't speak much French," I explain to him.

"I said that you look just like her," the man repeats in English, his voice wavering. "I saw it from the moment you came through those doors."

Now my voice is shaking, too. "Did you know my great-aunt?"

A single tear springs free and rolls down the man's cheek. He nods his head. With a trembling finger, he holds out the photograph and points to the shaggy-haired boy sitting in the grass next to Adalyn.

"This boy is me."

CHAPTER 16

Adalyn

I have learned how to turn myself off.

On the outside, you wouldn't know the difference. I still talk and laugh and smile like a nineteen-year-old girl who doesn't know any better. But on the inside, I'm empty. The real Adalyn simply vacates the premises. This way, when I look into his cold eyes, I am not consumed by white-hot rage. When he lays his hand on my leg, I do not even flinch.

This clever technique is how I make it through the autumn and winter of 1943–1944 when von Groth returns to Paris for a longer stretch of time. I visit him once every two weeks or so, in the same restaurant across from Gestapo headquarters. I make sure to arrive toward the end of his meal, then wait for him to join me at the bar. He always does.

On a turbulent evening in late January, the wind blowing particles of ice against the window, not even a minute goes

by before I hear the telltale sound of von Groth's boots clicking across the tile. The bartender brings us two glasses of
cognac without even asking; he knows our routine by now.

It's about to begin. I turn myself off.

"Miss Bonhomme," says von Groth, "have I ever told you
what joy it brings me to see your face at the end of a difficult
day?"

I giggle. "You tell me this every time, Walther!"

"Well, it is the truth. The worse my day is, the better it is
to see you." He takes a long sip of his drink.

"What made today so difficult?"

He presses his lips into a single, razor-sharp line. "People
not doing what I tell them to do."

Sometimes, the people who get dragged in for questioning
by the Gestapo miraculously get released, and through them,
we learn how von Groth treats prisoners who refuse to give
him information. Word travels among resistance networks of
vicious beatings, of ice-cold bathtubs and near drownings, of
bottles forced into people's mouths until their lips split from
the pressure. I pretend that I know none of this, suppressing
my fiery hatred of him, as I always do.

"I would never disrespect a lieutenant-colonel," I purr in
response.

"I know that," von Groth says. "But unfortunately, not all
the French are like you, Miss Bonhomme."

He places his hand on my thigh. I can handle this; I feel

nothing. Sometimes, if I'm wearing one of my divided skirts, he slides his fingers in between the buttons and massages my bare skin. This I can manage, too, for when von Groth lays his hands on me, he seems to calm down, and when von Groth is calm, he tends to let loose more details. If he gets information through cruelty, I get it through feeding his ego.

I rub his shoulder. "Will you have to deal with these misbehaving people again tomorrow?"

"No," he growls. "I've been dealing with them for weeks. I don't want to see them anymore. They'll go to Pithiviers the day after tomorrow."

So there's going to be a prisoner transport from Paris to the Pithiviers internment camp on Thursday. I make a mental note.

A man from von Groth's table approaches us and clears his throat. "I must be going," he informs the lieutenant-colonel in German. As usual, I listen in without them knowing.

"Ah, Goehr." Von Groth folds his hands and turns to the man. "Back to Toulouse so soon?"

"I am afraid so," says the man named Goehr. "The resistance is giving us more trouble than I would like. . . . Railway attacks have gone up, and it seems the Allies are dropping more and more weapons from their planes . . ."

"Then we must *shoot them down*," von Groth spits. "Snuff the resistance out."

Goehr nods curtly. "So I will see you back here for our

next dinner? It is scheduled for May, yes?"

"May 31," von Groth replies.

"I shall not miss it."

There's going to be a meeting on the thirty-first of May. I make another mental note. The two men shake hands, and Goehr leaves the restaurant. Von Groth and I chat for a little while longer—mostly about his family, whom I feel like I know by now. His wife, Erna, lives with her sister back in Berlin. The couple's only son, Klaus, was killed by the Allies in Belgium. Eventually, I tell von Groth that I must be getting home, for my parents are waiting up for me. Like always, he is sad to see me walk out the door, and like always, I am relieved.

Back at the apartment, Maman lays out sausage and cheese she purchased on the black market. Then she joins me at the table with a glass of water, which she cradles between her hands.

"Were you out with the lieutenant-colonel again?" she asks, her voice a little higher than normal. Even though she's trying to conceal it, I can tell that she's worried.

"Yes, Maman. And you don't have to be nervous. It was perfectly fine," I insist.

"I—I'm sure it was, darling. I just want to know that you're safe."

"I am, Maman. I promise."

I wolf down my dinner as fast as possible to avoid having to answer too many of Maman's questions. The less we have to talk about this, the less I have to lie to her. When I'm finished, I thank her for the food and head down the hall to bed, past Chloe's door, which happens to be open. Sitting on her bed, she looks up as I pass—the way an animal detects a sound—but when she sees that it's me, she scowls and returns to the book in her lap.

I crawl under the thick stack of blankets, wishing she were lying next to me and not hating me in the bedroom next door.

The next day, after I make the tedious rounds at the market, I bundle up to face the harsh winds again and rush to the safe house in my slippery wooden shoes. Geronte told me to come by this afternoon, so I told Maman and Papa I had schoolwork to do at the library.

Sure enough, his gnarled face appears in the doorway after I knock. When he opens the door all the way, I see there's somebody in the room with him: Luc. I haven't seen him since we said goodbye outside my building last spring. I run to him and throw myself into his arms, breathing in his scent of grass and earth and burying my face in his ragged clothes. Because Geronte is standing right behind us, I don't go to kiss him, even though every fiber of my being wants to feel the touch of his lips again.

"What are you doing here?" I ask incredulously. I run my

hands along the outline of his body, in complete disbelief that after all these months apart, Luc is standing in front of me again.

"I'm in Paris to drop off a few messages from contacts in the south," he says. "I can't stay too long, but I figured a night wouldn't hurt."

I notice dried blood and a cut above his left eye. "What is this?" I ask, touching it lightly with my fingers.

"Don't worry, looks worse than it is," he says. "We had a brutal run-in with the *milice*."

The *milice* are the Vichy militants whose job is to quash resistance efforts. "Are you sure you're okay? What happened?"

"I'm sure. Raphael jumped the gun and started firing before we got the all clear. Got himself hit in the shoulder. I had to drag him out of the way. Bullet grazed my forehead. I'm fine, and he's fine, but it was a close call. . . . Anyhow, I'm just so glad to see you."

I hold him close to me again, grateful he's alive. "I'm so glad to see *you*."

"Ahem." Geronte clears his throat in a very loud way. I almost forgot he was here. "Let's talk, because I have to be on my way sooner rather than later."

We sit around the same table where last spring, the three of us—along with Marcel, Pierre-Henri, and Raphael—celebrated the attack on the Limoges train. Geronte smacks the surface in front of me with the palm of his hand. "Okay, you," he grunts. "Tell us what you got out of him."

"They're transporting prisoners to Pithiviers tomorrow night."

Geronte nods. "Luc, you'll take that news south when you leave. See if your *maquis* can intercept it. Anything else?"

"Yes, there was one more thing," I reply. "Von Groth mentioned a dinner with other Gestapo men on the thirty-first of May, in the same restaurant where I've been meeting him all this time."

"Interesting," Geronte says. "You know anything else about it?"

Why is he being so impatient today? I think back to that brief conversation between von Groth and Goehr. They didn't give away many details . . . except for one more thing. "One of the guests is stationed in Toulouse," I remember. "If he is coming back to Paris for a dinner, then it must be a fairly significant gathering, no?"

"Interesting," Geronte says again.

". . . It shouldn't be any problem for me to get an invitation from von Groth, and then I can go and listen to their whole conversation. They still don't know that I understand them."

Just then, Luc mumbles something so softly, I can't make out a word. He's looking down, and his words go right into his chest.

"Speak up, boy," Geronte commands.

Luc seems surprised, as though perhaps he didn't realize he spoke out loud at all. He chews his lip. "I said . . . we should bomb it."

There's a moment when nobody speaks. It's complete silence, save for the blood pumping in my ears. How strange this all is. Four years ago, my life revolved around schoolwork and piano lessons and going to dinner parties with my friends. Now I'm contemplating plans to take people's lives.

What is even stranger is that I want to do it. I want to stage an attack, like with the train in Limoges. I know it would be dangerous—*extraordinarily* dangerous. Any kind of attack on the Germans is risky enough, but to do it right across the street from Gestapo headquarters seems like we're asking to be killed if anything goes awry. But if we pulled it off, we would kill Walther von Groth, and who knows how many of his men?

I can see Geronte mulling it over, his jaw muscles chewing on the information. "It'll most likely get you killed, but otherwise it's a good idea," he says eventually. "I'll need some time to think about how it would work. I can take care of logistics, but you'll have to handle the explosives."

"I'm sure we can do that," Luc says.

"Okay. I will speak about this to Boivin. Until you get my signal, you will mention this to no one else." Geronte's chair legs scrape across the floor, and he gets to his feet. "I have to leave now. There's something important I must attend to."

"Is it anything we can help with?" I offer.

"Afraid not. It has nothing to do with our work," he replies. Then his face softens, in a way I haven't seen before. "My daughter just gave birth," he says. "I'm on my way to meet my first grandchild."

I watch the old man leave, my heart bursting with happiness for him. And then I remember I don't even know his true name. As the door closes behind him, I suddenly feel like I might cry.

"Sometimes I forget that we're real people with real lives," I tell Luc.

"I know exactly what you mean," he says.

"You do?"

"Of course I do. I haven't seen my family in over a year now. I'm always in hiding. Every conversation is in some kind of code."

Luc and I are alone in the safe house now, just me and him in this barren apartment without any other furniture. He stands up and walks around to my side of the table. Then he takes me by the hands and pulls me to my feet. "Most of the time, I have no sense of who I really am," he whispers to me. He looks at me with the intensity of a lightning storm. "But then I see you again, and I remember."

I can't hold back any longer. I kiss him with every fiber of my being, like he's the oxygen I need to breathe. For the first time in what feels like forever, I don't turn myself off. I sink my fingers into his hair and let his hands explore my body, from my chest down to my hips. His touch doesn't make me flinch; in fact, I long for it. I want him to feel me everywhere, and myself to do the same to him.

I pause for a minute, so I can lead him down the hallway to a room where the setting sun casts its magenta rays through the window. There's nothing in here except for us and the fading light. Luc thankfully finds some blankets in a closet, and we spread them out across the floor. Once we undress each other, we wrap them around our two bodies like a cocoon. I've never been this close to another person before. At first, when it happens, I'm surprised by the fullness. I forget how to breathe and recall it again in the span of a single second. Then I want more. More of Luc; more of us; more of this real, beautiful life.

By the time it's over, the sky has gone from pink to black. It's after curfew—too late to go home now. Under the gray blankets in the empty apartment in this city infested by rats, Luc and I fall asleep wrapped in each other's arms, remembering who we are.

It's over a month until we see each other again. On a cool almost-spring morning, the five of us gather round the table in the safe house: me, Luc, Marcel, Pierre-Henri, and Raphael. As we wait for Geronte to come and lay out the plan for us, the room crackles with nervous energy. Luc keeps running his hands through his long hair, Raphael (his shoulder healed, but still stiff) drums his fingers on the tabletop, and Marcel makes empty observations about the weather, to which nobody responds. I imagine we're all thinking the same thing: that what we're doing is so dangerous and so powerful, it hardly seems real.

There's a precise series of taps on the door, and Pierre-Henri rushes over to open it for Geronte, who comes in like a strong gust of wind. Everybody looks up expectantly, and maybe even with some fear in their eyes.

"I've just been to see Boivin," he says. "The plan is set."

Underneath the table, I squeeze Luc's knee. He puts his hand over mine and squeezes back.

"First things first," Geronte continues, looking specifically at me. "Bonhomme, you're going to have to stay far away from this one."

"Why?" I demand. "I'm just as capable!"

"Nobody doubts that you're the most capable person here. But the explosive will be in a suitcase, and that suitcase will be placed in the dining room during von Groth's dinner. If you're there as his date, you're toast. And if you—"

"If I am the one to deliver it, he'll recognize me." I understand now. I'll have to keep my distance and pray that it goes according to plan.

Geronte spends the next half hour relaying the intricacies of the operation, and the four boys volunteer for their various roles. Raphael, who seems intent on proving his skills after his mishap against the *milice*, volunteers to deliver the bomb to Boivin inside the restaurant. Privately, I am relieved, because this means Luc will just be standing watch out back. Marcel and Pierre-Henri will be stationed at other points around the outside of the building.

By the time the meeting breaks up, I'm desperately impatient for May 31st to be here. I want von Groth to suffer; I want to punish him for what he's done to our people. But until then I need to keep up the ruse, so I must accompany him to another luncheon, this one in the nearby village of Auvers-sur-Oise.

I ride out with von Groth in the back seat of a German staff car. He seems different today: tense, but also distant. Normally, he'd want to reach over and touch me in order to relax, but today, he stares straight ahead with his hands folded neatly in his lap. His facial muscles protrude from his clenched jaw. He's even scarier when he's quiet.

"Berlin was bombed again the other night," von Groth says, breaking the heavy silence as the car trundles over the rocks and pebbles in the road. "I have received word that my house was destroyed—my house, which has been in my family for more than a hundred years."

I don't have a care in the world for von Groth's house, no matter how old it is, but nevertheless, I let him know that I'm devastated on his behalf. "That is terrible to hear, Walther. I hope your family is okay."

"My family is fine. But you French . . . you don't know how lucky you have it. We could have destroyed Paris if we wanted to, but we didn't."

Yes, you did. And soon you're going to pay for it.

"I am so sorry, Walther."

"The goddamn Allies won't rest," he says bitterly, as though he didn't even hear me. "They're bombing Pas-de-Calais, and we hear they might invade there in June. We also hear Norway."

My heart skips a beat at the thought of an Allied invasion of France. Geronte seems certain that it will happen eventually, although he hears the Allies are deceiving Germany about where exactly they'll attack.

"What do you think will happen, Lieutenant-Colonel?"

I expect him to champion Germany's military superiority, as he usually does in conversation with his men, but instead he sighs and gazes out at the horizon.

"I do not know, Miss Bonhomme."

He stares off to the side for a long time. A full minute, maybe.

Then he says, again, "I do not know."

"But you have always been so confident. I . . . I admire that about you."

He pauses. "I am going to confess something to you, Miss

Bonhomme." He speaks very softly, so that the sound of crunching stone all but completely obscures his voice. I have to lean over if I want to make out anything he is saying. Von Groth looks down at his lap. "I fear for the Fatherland," he mutters, almost imperceptibly.

A large bump in the road shakes von Groth from his spell. He rolls back his shoulders and straightens his spine, as though he's neutralizing the admission he just made.

"Ah," he says, "that must be the village there." He points to a cluster of medieval buildings off in the distance. "There had better be enough food to feed us all. I'm ravenous."

It's the end of April, nearing May, and the weather is warm enough that we can eat outside. A few of the Germans have brought French women with them, too. We sit at a group of tables arranged in the yard of what appears to be an ordinary cottage—not an official building, but a person's home. There's a vegetable garden just over there, and laundry hanging on a line round the back.

"You are staying here, Essig?" asks von Groth to a broad-shouldered man at our table.

"Yes, this is where they placed me," says the man named Essig, who didn't come with a date. "It is nothing to write home about, but it has its charms."

He jerks his head in the direction of the cottage, where a woman is struggling to make it through the front door with a large platter of meat and potatoes. Of the two dozen men, no one gets up to help her. I want to, but I can't. It's something the real Adalyn would do, but not the one I'm pretending to be.

She serves our table first. From farther away, she looked like she was Maman's age, but up close, she seems to be a young woman who has been aged by the last few years of war. She is very thin. Her dull gray clothes hang off her body as though they're two sizes too big, though I expect they fit her once. When she reaches out to drop a potato onto my plate, I see the space behind her collarbone is as deep as a well. I recognize the expression on her face. She is exhausted and angry but doing her best to push it all down.

"Come sit on my lap, darling," barks Essig in French. "I'll let you have some of the food."

"No thank you," she answers, her voice even. The men snicker as she goes off to serve the other tables.

I don't want a single bite of food that the Germans forced this woman to cook for us. I've eaten too well in this war, and it shows. I still have a figure. But there are so many families who must rely on the rationing system and nothing else, going days without a proper meal. I wish the woman would take my plate for herself, but if I gave it away, it would arouse too much suspicion. Racked with guilt, I cut into my round potato coated in precious butter.

Across the table sits a scrawny girl who accompanied one of von Groth's men to lunch. When we first sat down, I despised the way she fawned over her German date, remarking on how the sunlight made his medals sparkle, but I understand now. She shoveled the meat and potatoes into her mouth the second they touched her plate, and now she eyes the uneaten food sitting on mine. If she is starving, can I judge her for accepting the German's invitation? Where do you draw the line between doing what is right and doing what you must to survive?

One of the men tosses his leftover meat to a stray dog prowling the edge of the yard. The scrawny girl looks as though she might cry.

After half an hour of listening in on von Groth's conversations, I need to use the lavatory. I've held it as long as possible, not wanting to go inside the woman's home, where I am certainly not welcome, but now it's bordering on an emergency. I excuse myself and walk to the door of the cottage.

I step tentatively into the main room, which feels dark compared to the bright sunlight outside. There's a fireplace in here, but not much else; the Germans must have requisitioned her furniture. I feel sick at the thought of her living here alone with a man like Essig.

I find the woman in the kitchen doing dishes, her back to me. She scrubs a pot with unnecessary ferocity. Or perhaps it is necessary.

"Excuse me, I'm sorry to bother you, but may I use your lavatory?"

She stops scrubbing.

"It's down the hall on the right."

On my way to and from the toilet, I pass a framed photograph of the woman and her husband on their wedding day. Where is he now? Dead, possibly. Or suffering in a German prisoner-of-war camp, while another man makes himself at home in his house, with his wife.

I have to pass through the kitchen in order to leave the cottage, which means walking past the woman as she puts away her pots and pans. I keep my head down as I go by.

"Filthy German whore."

She spits out the words like machine-gun fire.

I don't stop. I careen toward the door, feeling like I've been shot through the heart. If only she knew the truth about me. . . . If only she knew what we have planned. . . .

Being in the presence of von Groth for the rest of the afternoon is nearly unbearable, but I keep up my smiling facade. Somewhere, a bomb is being built that will fit into a suitcase, which will pass into the hands of a seemingly innocuous waiter, who will plant it next to von Groth's table on the evening of May 31st. This is the thought that keeps me going, when all I want to do is rescue this woman from her miserable existence: that in a matter of weeks, Walther von Groth will be dead.

CHAPTER 17

Alice

"That's *you*?"

I can't believe what the man just said. He's the missing link to Adalyn. And to Gram. My heart's beating so hard, I think I'm going to pass out, and Paul brings over a chair just in time for me to collapse into it.

"Yes," the man whispers. "It's me." There's a jagged scar on his jaw that moves when he talks.

Where do I even start? What question do I ask first? I'm so overwhelmed, I start to giggle. What is wrong with me? Paul gives me a sideways look that politely suggests I might want to pull it together. Whew. Okay. This is really happening.

"What's your name?"

"Luc Pelletier."

"I'm Alice Prewitt."

I'm on the verge of exploding from excitement, but I can't tell how Luc is feeling. I don't know what I expected to happen, but it's not this. He doesn't reach out to shake my hand. In fact, he's not even looking at me—he can't take his eyes off the photo.

"I'm sorry," Luc says in a thick, raspy voice. His bottom lip trembles. "I just need to step outside for a moment."

"Do you need me to help you find the restroom?" asks one of the two men.

"No."

His face contorted in a strange expression, he gets to his feet and makes for the door a little unsteadily. The other man rushes over to make sure Luc can manage on his own, and Luc waves him away. The man walks back, frowning.

"I'm very sorry," he says. "We have never been to one of these gatherings before. Luc has never wanted to come. I don't know why not."

"So how do you two know Luc?" Paul asks.

The man picks up the photo Luc had left on the chair. He points to the boy with the star on his chest and the butterfly balanced on his finger. "This is our older brother, Arnaud."

"It *is*?" I feel like I've been knocked off my feet all over again.

"Yes," he says. "I am Eugene Michnik."

"I am Ruben," says the other.

I remember Adalyn's diary entry about her Jewish friend

sent to the Vel' d'Hiv. "Your brother . . . was he . . . ?"

"In 1942, our brother and our parents were rounded up with thirteen thousand other Jews," Ruben says solemnly. "They were taken to the old cycling arena, and then to Auschwitz. They did not survive."

"I'm so sorry," Paul and I say in unison.

"Things had been getting worse and worse for the Jews," Ruben continues. "Our father could not work anymore; we had no bank account; we were not allowed to be in certain public places; and of course, we were made to wear the yellow star. A doctor who knew our father offered to hide us in his apartment. He and his wife had a secret room concealed behind a wardrobe, big enough to hold two young boys, but no more. Our parents took us to their door, hugged us goodbye, and said they would see us again soon. Two days later, the roundup took place."

"We think they knew something terrible was going to happen," says Eugene, jumping in. "Otherwise, they never would have split up our family."

"About a month later, we were taken to a secret home for Jewish children in the Free Zone," Ruben continues. "They gave us forged documents so we could cross the demarcation line. We lived there for the rest of the war, with other children who had been smuggled out of the internment camps. There were people who taught us music and math and English, and sometimes, if it was safe, they let us play outside."

"Wow." It feels like such an insufficient word in response to the brothers' story, but I can't think of what else to say. I'm amazed.

"After the war, we were sent to live with a new family in Paris," says Ruben. "One day, I was at the market, and I saw Luc. He was very thin, and rather sickly, but I recognized him as a friend of Arnaud's . . . and we have been in each other's lives ever since. When I was eighteen, and Eugene was sixteen, we moved in with Luc. We lived with him until we each got married."

"Did Luc ever get married?"

"No," Ruben answers. "We are his family, for the most part."

"I wouldn't say that Luc has been unhappy his whole life," says Eugene, "but he is . . . haunted, in a way. What happened in the war never fully left him. For years, we've tried to get him to come to one of these meetings, but he always said no—he never wants to talk about the war. We had to drag him here tonight, and obviously, I am glad we did."

"Speaking of Luc," says Ruben, "where is he?"

We scan the room, but Luc is nowhere to be seen among the remaining Project Geronte people. The event is really winding down now; Corinne is stacking the empty plastic wine glasses and tossing them into a trash bag.

"I'll go check on him," Eugene offers. "He might need some help in the restroom."

With Eugene gone, the rest of us go to the table to help Corinne clean up. We tell her about the incredible connection we made, and her face lights up. She drops everything she's holding and pulls the three of us into a hug.

"Ruben!" Eugene rushes back into the room and grabs his brother by the shoulder, breaking up our celebration. There's concern written all over his face. *"Il est parti."*

"Quoi?"

"Il n'est pas aux toilettes."

Ruben's face falls. Corinne looks confused. I turn to Paul to give me the translation.

"Luc isn't in the bathroom," he says. "He's gone."

CHAPTER 18

Adalyn

One more night. That is all that stands between now and the thirty-first of May.

It may as well be an eternity. I cannot get to sleep, no matter how hard I try. Every time I try to close my eyelids, they flutter like the wings of a butterfly until I open them again. I'm too anxious to simply lie here and stare at the ceiling, so I grab my diary and climb onto the window ledge, where I sit with my knees tucked up under my nightgown.

I rest my forehead against the cool glass, remembering how I used to long to see the blanket of lights over Paris again. Now I can hardly picture it in my mind's eye. I suppose I've gotten used to the dark.

In the silver-blue light of the moon, I crack open the cover of my diary and read the first entry, from May 30th, 1940. Exactly four years ago, to the day. I forgot that I found this book while I was looking for bandages. Oh, how badly my feet hurt! And how shaken I was after our journey on the road. If only I'd known then how much worse things were going to get. The only bright spot is that I met Luc.

I read every entry from the past four years, the sentences coming to life like a movie. Every time I see Chloe's name, the lump in my throat gets bigger, and by the time I get to the roundup of 1942, my tears are splashing onto the paper. I blot them with my sleeve so the writing doesn't wash away. All the terrible memories in these pages. . . . Tomorrow, we will make certain that they did not happen in vain. I must remember this, for I am also desperately frightened.

With a hand I can't keep from shaking, I write another entry in the book. At last, I think I might be growing tired. When I'm finished, I tuck the diary into my desk drawer, among the pencils and coins and bobby pins. Then I crawl back into bed and fall asleep.

My plan is to leave for the safe house at five o'clock, so I can see the boys off before they go. All through the day, I am a jittery mess. Climbing off my bicycle, I lose my balance, and my shopping basket clatters onto the sidewalk. I drop to my hands and knees and pull back the checkered cloth to survey the damage. Oh no—I've managed to break the one egg I could find at the market. The yolk bleeds over everything, including my fingers.

Upstairs in the kitchen, Maman helps me wash off my things.

"I'm sorry I broke the egg," I tell her.

"It's okay, darling. It was just a mistake. We will make do."

Could the egg be an omen? No, I don't believe in such things. Still, there's this sense of foreboding I can't seem to shake, and it's getting worse by the second.

"Maman?" I try to keep my voice steady.

"Yes?"

"A friend from school has become rather close with a German officer, and he has offered to drive a group of us down to the Riviera to celebrate the end of the school year. I don't know exactly how long the trip would be, or when we would leave, but if I go, there's a chance I would be away for quite some time. Would that be okay with you and Papa?"

"Well, I would miss having you here with me," Maman says, "but it sounds like a lovely vacation, darling. You deserve it, what with all the hours you spent in the library this year."

"Thank you, Maman." I kiss her cheek. "Perhaps I will tag along, then. We'll see."

I probably didn't need to lie to Maman, but I did it as a precaution in case something goes awry, and we all have to go underground, into hiding. . . . But this will not happen. I'm dwelling on worst-case scenarios, things that are unlikely to happen. I must think positively.

I go to my room to lie down and calm my racing heart, but

lying down is no use. My thoughts go to terrifying places. What if the boys are caught before they plant the bomb? They won't be. They pulled off the attack in Limoges. What if the Gestapo get their hands on them? Even if they torture them, I know they will stand strong. What if the boys are killed? You mustn't think that way, Adalyn.

I know I don't believe in premonitions, but something about this one feels as real as black storm clouds gathering in the distance. There is something I must do before I leave. Something I must say, in case I never get another chance to do so. Chloe is hardly ever home these days—usually off with friends instead—but earlier this afternoon, as I was washing up, I heard her come in the door and stomp down the hall. She's here, right on the other side of my bedroom wall. My heart pounding so hard that I can feel it behind my eyes, I fly off the bed and into the corridor.

"Chloe." I bang on my sister's door. There's no response. "Chloe, open the door."

Still, there is silence, but I know that she's in there, because I heard her moving around before I knocked for the first time.

"Chloe, will you let me talk to you? It's important." More silence. I knock again, as though it will make a difference. "Chloe, please."

I try the doorknob. It's locked. And I only have a couple of minutes before I have to leave. What is she doing right now—waiting for me to go away and stop bothering her? Or is a part of her wondering if she should hear what I have to say?

"Chloe, if you just unlock the door, I can explain everything." I'm desperate now. I won't tell her any important details, but I need her to know that I've been on her side all along. I need her to know. Just in case. But she won't come to the door. She won't answer me at all. This is hopeless. I thump on the door as hard as I can, rattling the wooden frame. "Chloe, for god's sake, will you listen to me?!"

The clock in the hall chimes five times. If I want to see Luc, then I need to leave right this minute. "Chloe," I say one last time, my cheek pressed to the door, "everything you're upset about . . . it's not what you think. I swear."

I can't detect any movement from inside the bedroom. I just hope she heard me.

The bomb is death wrapped in a package you wouldn't look twice at. One of Luc's many contacts built it for us. It's a simple briefcase: black, leather, with silver clasps—the kind of thing a businessman would carry to work. Inside, there's an explosive powerful enough to take out a whole restaurant, and Walther von Groth with it. The six of us stand around the table, almost scared to get too close.

Beads of perspiration spring up on Raphael's forehead as he fastens his trench coat. Underneath, he wears a spare uniform provided by Boivin. With it on, he'll look exactly like any other waiter in the restaurant, except that he'll be carrying a deadly weapon.

"Better get going," Geronte says as he checks his pocket watch. There's a collective intake of breath from the group.

"Run through the plan for me one last time," I ask them, fear swirling around in my chest.

"We'll be standing watch to make sure nobody leaves the restaurant," says Pierre-Henri, gesturing to himself and Marcel, who flashes a confident smile.

"Boivin will let me in the back door, and I'll go into the dining room and place the briefcase," says Raphael.

"Better dry that sweat or you'll give yourself away instantly," Geronte growls at him. "Those men are like sharks. They can smell one part blood in a million parts water." Raphael mops his forehead.

"I'll be waiting at the end of the street in back of the restaurant to make sure he gets out safely," says Luc. "Once Raph links up with me, we'll come back here." He clasps my hand.

He stays holding it as we leave the safe house in waves: first Marcel and Pierre-Henri, then Raphael, with the briefcase; then me and Luc. I decide to walk three-quarters of the way to the restaurant—far enough away that I won't be seen, but close enough that I'll be able to hear the bomb when it goes off.

"Tell me something to take my mind off what we're about

to do," Luc says as we make our way toward the restaurant. With the insides of our wrists touching, I can feel his heartbeat. It's very fast.

"Remember the first time we met? I was so nervous to meet you, I was convinced I would forget the password."

"Of course, I remember. 'Did you make it here okay?'"

"'The trains ran smoothly.'"

We both laugh nervously.

"We're going to make history today," I tell him.

"Tell me more."

"And I think the war may be reaching its end."

"Keep going."

"Germany isn't as strong as it used to be. They're being bombed by the Allies. They're losing on the Eastern Front. An invasion of France could happen any day now. And the resistance groups are more organized than ever before under de Gaulle. Luc, von Groth admitted to me that he's worried."

"My god, I hope so," he says. "For France—of course—but for us, too. I just want to be with you, Adalyn. Like two normal people who don't have to hide all the time."

"I want that, too, Luc."

We come to a halt. We're already at the intersection where we agreed I would wait. There's a bench over there, and no Germans loitering around, at least for now.

We turn to each other. Even with our conversation, the black storm clouds feel like they're right over my head. Luc kisses me swiftly on the cheek. I need to tell him; I need to tell him what I've known since the night we spent on the floor of the empty bedroom. I know he must feel the same way about me.

"Luc, I—"

"Tell me when I'm back," he begs me. "I already can't bear to walk away from you."

I hold my tongue and return his kiss on the cheek. "Okay. Good luck, Luc. I'll see you soon."

"That's right. I'll see you soon."

Luc goes on down the road, and I go to the bench to wait. I feel so panicked that I can't tell if only a minute has passed or an hour. Has Boivin let Raphael into the restaurant yet? Has he planted the briefcase? The sun, my only measurement of time, has disappeared behind the tops of the buildings, and all that remains is hazy pink twilight. Paris settles in for another dark night.

A butterfly lands next to me on the bench, silent as air. Slowly, it opens and closes its orange-brown wings, revealing a magical bright blue around its body. Whenever I see butterflies, I think of Arnaud. He would want to be a part of this, today. This is for you, Arnaud. I inch my finger across the wood to see if the butterfly will climb aboard, but at the last moment, it flutters its wings and drifts off into the shadows.

And then I hear it.

The blast makes it feel like the Earth is splitting in two—a loud, low *boom* that rattles my ribs and has me gasping for breath. It's the sound of danger—no, worse. It's the sound of death itself. Glass shatters. Somebody screams. Then come the boots, as every German soldier in the vicinity rushes toward the explosion. Two of them sprint by so quickly, I feel the breeze left in their wake.

You're too late, boys.

My head spinning and my heart pounding, I hurry back to the safe house. The first part is done—von Groth and his men are dead. Now all I need is that my four friends get back safely. They'll be fine. I know they will. The hard part was getting the bomb into the restaurant and making it go off. The rest is smooth sailing.

Please, let them be fine.

A breathless Pierre-Henri opens the door for me, and there's a huge smile on his face.

"We killed Nazis," he says jubilantly as he pulls me into a bear hug. "You know I always wanted to do that."

Marcel and Geronte are sitting at the table. With a stab of panic, I notice Luc and Raphael aren't back yet.

"When are the others supposed to be here?" I ask.

"Should be any minute now," Geronte says. Marcel keeps his eyes fixed on his watch.

I can't stay in here, not with all this nervous energy. I need some space. I go down the hall to the empty bedroom and sit cross-legged on the blanket we left on the floor. *Come back, Luc. Please come back.*

I don't have a watch, but I know it's been longer than a few minutes. I hear the men murmuring out in the kitchen, and a wave of nausea crashes over me. Is something wrong? Did they get caught? My breathing becomes quick and shallow. He must be in trouble—either hurt or arrested, or both. If Luc is taken away, I will never forgive myself for not telling him how I feel—for not shouting it in the middle of the street when I had the chance, when I was holding his hand. . . . I lie on my back to keep from fainting. The worst has happened. I've now lost the *two* people closest to me in the world.

Was that the door? I spring to my feet, alert as a hunting dog. I could be hearing things. I don't know if my mind is working properly.

And then I hear his voice, asking, "Where is she?"

He's looking for me. He's back. Luc. My Luc. I race into the hall and skid to a stop, just in time to see him appear at the opposite end.

We race for each other and collide in the middle, a tangle of limbs and hair and breath. I feel as though I'm soaring above the city on newly sprouted wings and watching as all the lights in Paris turn on at the very same time. We did it! We did it! We did it!

And now I have to tell him the truth about how I've felt for a long time, since our afternoon by the river, or longer, even.

Maybe it happened the moment I met him.

"I love you, Luc."

He cradles my face in his hands and rests his forehead against mine. "I love you, too, Adalyn."

Nothing in this world is certain anymore, but I know for a fact that I've never been happier than I am in this very moment.

"Why were you so late getting back here? You gave me such a fright!"

Then Luc pulls away, and I get a good look at his face. He isn't grinning, like I am. My own smile fades.

"Luc, what's the matter?" I ask.

"I got held up because I was waiting for Raphael," he says. "He never made it to me."

"No."

Luc nods solemnly.

"Do we know for sure that he's . . . that he's . . ."

"Not for sure," Luc says, but his voice shakes. "I . . . I suppose he might have run the wrong way and gotten lost, but . . ."

He doesn't need to finish the grim sentence. We both know perfectly well that Raphael wouldn't have gotten lost—after all, Luc wasn't stationed *that* far from the restaurant. If he never made it to the meeting point, then it's likely he never made it out of the restaurant. I didn't know him as well as the others, but he was still a friend. This is terrible.

Luc takes me by the hand and leads me back to the kitchen, where the mood is tense. Pierre-Henri paces around the table with his hands clasped behind his head like a prisoner. Geronte sits at the head of the empty table, drumming his fingers on the tabletop and peering at his pocket watch. Only Marcel seems to have any shred of real optimism left in him; he stands by the door, and at every small sound outside in the hall, he presses his eye up to the peephole.

"I really don't think he's coming," Luc says to Marcel.

"He still might!" the boy replies. "You never know."

Luc and I join Geronte at the table. Pierre-Henri wanders over, too. Everybody seems unsure whether to celebrate our achievement or mourn the loss of Raphael.

"He knew what he was getting into," says Geronte. "You all knew the risk involved, and you decided it was worth it." He looks around at us one by one, and we all nod. "I think it goes without saying that this isn't how we wanted things to end up tonight, but we must not forget that we just achieved the impossible. Germany's grip on France was already weakening, and we just cut off one of their fingers."

Geronte is right. We signed up for this work because we'd give anything to defend our country from evil, including our lives. I'm still racked with sadness, but maybe in time, I'll be able to look back on this night with pride.

There's a sharp rap at the door. A pattern that doesn't sound anything like our code.

My stomach turns to stone. I see the blood disappear from Luc's face. Everybody freezes—everybody except for Marcel, who's been waiting desperately for Raphael to return. Marcel, ever the optimist, never quite as astute as the rest. At the sound of the knock, his face lights up with excitement, and he lunges for the doorknob.

"Marcel, *no!*" I shout.

But the door is already open, and a man throws Marcel into the wall. They tear into the room like wildfire, men in long black coats with their guns drawn.

It sucks the air from my lungs, except somehow, I'm still screaming. Luc—where is Luc? He's grabbing me by the wrist. We have to get to the hallway, Luc—to the hallway. We can escape through another room. The magenta sunset. The bedroom has a window. I try to yank him in that direction, but I can't go any farther. The men keep multiplying. They have us pinned against the wall.

I hear Luc's voice. It's like an echo.

"I've got you," it says. "I've got you, Adalyn."

A soldier slams the butt of his rifle into Geronte's mouth. There is blood. Blood everywhere. Then they seize Pierre-Henri. He screams.

They're closing in on us.

"Hold on to me, Adalyn."

And then a rifle butt comes for Luc, colliding with the side of his face. It smashes his jaw, that beautiful jaw forever imprinted in my memory, and I can't hold on to him any longer, because they're dragging him toward the door.

The hand on my wrist isn't Luc's anymore. I try to wrench myself free, but he twists my wrist and it feels like it's about to snap, and all I can do is follow him out to the hall and through the lobby, my screams reverberating off the walls. All that comes out is Luc's name over and over and over again. The man slaps me. I scream some more. He slaps me again.

And then Luc's voice.

"I'm here, Adalyn!"

They drag us through the front doors out onto the sidewalk. Through the darkness, two blue headlights swim toward us like the eyes of a shark. The car comes to a stop, and the passenger side door opens and closes with a slam. The man who steps out has blood on his face, but I would recognize him anywhere. His mouth is like a paper cut. But how? How is he here? How did he survive?

He barks orders at his men. Marcel, Pierre-Henri, and Geronte are shoved into the back seat of a car. I don't understand. The bomb—it went off. I heard it go off.

Von Groth turns around. He looks triumphant. And then his gaze meets mine. It's dark outside. Maybe he won't recognize me. But he does. I can see it—the fire rising up and licking the insides of his eyes—the triumph molting into fury.

"You," he growls.

There's a deafening noise. Not a boom, but a crack. Somebody shoves me hard in the chest. A blood-curdling cry pierces the night. Not me—Luc. Luc is screaming. Why? Now my torso feels hot. It's burning. Like a fire poker is wedged between my ribs.

"Adalyn!" Luc shouts. "Adalyn, are you okay?!"

Am I okay? I don't know. I have no idea what's happening. I feel wet, all of a sudden. I look down. That's when I see the blood.

Nobody shoved me. Von Groth shot me.

Blackness.

I come to on the ground. I taste blood.

"ADALYN!"

The stars look so beautiful tonight. Like lights. My blanket of lights over Paris.

"ADALYN, YOU'RE GOING TO BE OKAY!"

Okay?

Luc is asking if I'm okay.

Did you make it here okay?

That's what he asked me.

Did you make it here okay?

I was so nervous!

Did you make it here okay?

The trains ran smoothly, Luc.

The trains ran smoothly.

CHAPTER 19

Alice

He's vanished. Luc Pelletier, the only person in the world who can tell me about Adalyn, has vacated the premises.

"We'll help you look for him," I tell Eugene and Ruben.

"Thank you," Eugene says. "He can't have gone far."

I cram the photos into my backpack as the brothers explain their dilemma to a very concerned-looking Corinne, who happens to be standing in between us at the hors d'oeuvres table. Her jaw drops, and she immediately offers her assistance.

Paul and I make for the door with our three new companions. Corinne, Eugene, and Ruben are all surprisingly agile, and we canvass the mezzanine in a matter of minutes. There's no sign of Luc. We make for the escalators, squeezing in two to a stair.

"I guess he meant it when he said he didn't want to come," Eugene says.

We split up when we get to the lobby. Eugene and Ruben go to check the bathroom, Corinne goes to the sidewalk out front, and Paul and I, who are quicker on our feet, take the rest of the ground floor. Luc isn't in the café or the gift shop.

"Look, there's a back garden," says Paul, pointing to a sign hanging from the ceiling with an arrow on it.

We fly down the hallway, our shoes springing off the carpet, until we get to a set of glass double doors that look out on a grassy courtyard. I scan the area, and at last, I see him on a bench in the far corner, half concealed by a tall, flowering bush.

"You should go ahead," Paul whispers. "I will go find the others."

"I feel like I'm the one who made him angry," I whisper back.

"Maybe he's not angry, just a little anxious."

"Paul—"

But he's already going back down the hall, leaving me alone to approach Luc, who doesn't know I'm here yet. Okay. I can do this. For Gram and Adalyn. I push open the doors, walk across the grass, and announce myself as I step around the bush so I don't startle him.

"Luc? It's me, Alice."

I'm scared that if I look him in the eye, he'll get upset again, so instead, I stare at the scar on his jaw. It moves.

"Alice. I am sorry I left. It is not easy for me to speak about these things."

I work up the courage to make eye contact again. Paul, as usual, is right. There isn't any anger in Luc's thin face. Only sadness. But I think I see a willingness to talk with me. Even though I'm not any good at emotional conversations, I'm going to do my best here. What would Vivi say right now?

"Luc . . . I know you didn't want to come here tonight, but I'm really happy you did. And . . . um . . . even though it's hard, I would love to ask you a few questions about my great-aunt. I've been trying to figure out what happened to her."

His mouth twists into an uncomfortable-looking position. I think he's trying to stop his lip from trembling again. I sit down beside him, my denim shorts and Converse sneakers a sharp contrast to his brown loafers and pleated khakis. I put my hand on top of his. We sit in silence for a few seconds, until he takes a ragged breath.

"She died," Luc says.

I was prepared for that. Still, it's upsetting to hear it announced so . . . officially.

"When?" I ask.

"May 31, 1944."

The day after Adalyn's last diary entry. I open my mouth to ask another question, but close it again when Luc pulls his hand out from under mine. He covers his face and begins to sob.

I don't know what to do. How am I supposed to comfort him? I wish I had a pack of Kleenexes in my backpack.

"What happened that day?" I ask him gently.

"He shot her," Luc says between sobs. "She died on the street. Right in front of me. I could not help her."

"Who shot her?"

"A Nazi. He is not important."

"Why not?"

Luc's shoulders shake harder than ever when he answers me. "Because it was all my fault."

Just then, the double doors burst open, and Paul appears in the courtyard, followed by Eugene, Ruben, and Corinne. They look like they're about to race over, so I hold up my hand and motion for them to wait so Luc can have some time to collect himself. I wish Paul had taken a tiny bit longer to find everyone so that Luc could have kept on talking. *"All my fault"?* What did he mean by that?

When Luc spots the others waiting by the door, he wipes his eyes with the back of his hand. I give Paul a nod, and he collects chairs for everyone and positions them around our bench. By the time everyone is seated, Luc has dried his tears. He still looks devastated.

"Luc just told me what happened to Adalyn," I explain to the others. "She . . . um . . ." I glance at Luc for permission to repeat what happened, and he gives me a small nod. "She was shot and killed by a Nazi on May 31, 1944."

Everybody's eyes widen, but none can beat Corinne's. "That is the same day my grandfather was arrested," she says. "He was involved in bombing a restaurant full of Gestapo."

Next to me, Luc stirs. He turns to Corinne and draws another ragged breath. "So was I," he says quietly, "and so was Adalyn." A chill travels around the group. "Geronte was our leader," Luc continues. "He was an incredible man."

Ruben offers Corinne a tissue, and she dabs at the corners of her eyes. "He really was," Corinne replies, and she and Luc share a knowing look. To the rest of the group, she explains, "When my grandfather was arrested, he refused to give up any information, so they tortured him extensively. He was old, and his body couldn't manage it. He died in Gestapo custody, but he never betrayed his network."

"The other people from the photographs . . . were they involved, too?" I ask Luc.

"Yes. Pierre-Henri and Marcel and . . . and Raphael. He was the one who betrayed us."

I want to know all about what happened in the attack, including whatever this Raphael person did, but there's something else I need to ask first—the question that's been eating at me since the start of the summer. "Luc, do you know why there's a photo in Adalyn's apartment of her partying with a bunch of Nazis?"

"She was not partying with them," Luc says immediately. "She was spying."

"Spying?"

"Yes." His voice cracks. "She was the bravest person I ever knew."

I'm too dumbfounded to respond.

"Luc, maybe you should start at the beginning and tell us everything," Eugene suggests, and everybody in the circle nods in agreement.

But Luc shakes his head. "I can't do it," he confesses. "It is too painful."

I look into the old man's eyes, swollen from crying. It must be terrible for him to dredge up the memories he's kept locked away for so many decades. He's had an open wound since Adalyn died, and I want to help him heal it. I lay my hand next to his on the bench.

"Luc, you said Adalyn was the bravest person you ever knew, but without you, nobody will ever know her story. Her legacy won't live on."

Something shifts behind Luc's eyes, and he sits up straighter. He puts his hand on top of mine.

And then he begins.

It's late by the time Luc reaches the end of his story, and the fairy lights strung across the courtyard have turned on. Over the past hour, I've teared up so many times that the bottom of my T-shirt is wrinkled from being used to wipe off my glasses. Adalyn was doing resistance work from the very beginning of the Occupation. She started by spreading resistance tracts and other secret messages, and ended up spying on the Nazis, who didn't know she could understand what they were saying. She never told anyone in her family, including Gram.

I can't even imagine.

Luc just finished taking us through the night of the attack, and how it all fell apart. In a sick turn of events, he ended up piecing it together from von Groth himself, who bragged about it while he was torturing Luc for information.

What happened is this: Von Groth apparently thought Raphael looked suspicious the moment he entered the dining room. He was sweating profusely, and it wasn't especially hot outside. When Raphael dropped the briefcase, von Groth got up and followed him into the kitchen and out the back door. Raphael tried to get away, but von Groth seized him.

Then the bomb went off—with von Groth *outside* the restaurant.

Von Groth put his pistol to Raphael's head, and the boy divulged his secrets, including the address of the safe house.

"Raphael always talked highly of himself," muttered Luc, "but he collapsed under pressure."

When von Groth saw Adalyn and realized he'd been tricked, he was so furious, he shot her in the chest. He and his men arrested everyone else. Geronte died in a cell in Gestapo headquarters. Luc, Marcel, Pierre-Henri, and Raphael were tortured and eventually deported to a concentration camp in Germany called Buchenwald. By the time the Allies liberated it in April 1945, Luc was the only one of them still alive, and barely so.

When Luc chose to skip over the details of what happened in the camp, nobody pressed him.

"So the Gestapo never went for your families after the attack?" I ask him.

"No," he says. "Thankfully, they became distracted."

"By what?"

"D-Day. The Allies invaded France a week later."

Of course. I read somewhere that when our troops landed at Normandy, the Germans weren't as prepared as they could have been. They'd been led to believe that the Allies would invade somewhere else—a place in the north of France called Pas-de-Calais.

"Did you ever try to find Adalyn's family when you got back to Paris?" I ask Luc.

"As a matter of fact, I did," Luc says. He's more talkative now that he's gotten so much off his chest. "I remembered where they lived from the time that I walked her home. I went to the building, but a neighbor—a woman named Emmeline Blanchard—told me they didn't live there anymore."

Paul and I look at each other at the exact same time, and I know we're both thinking the same thing.

The apartment.

"Did Emmeline say what happened?" Paul asks.

Luc rubs his chin. "Yes, she said that shortly after D-Day, the parents left Paris to hide at a relative's in the south. This was when the tides had turned, and the French were hunting down any possible collaborators in their midst, including women who went to the sort of parties Adalyn and her mother attended. She had expected them to return to Paris eventually, but they were caught in an Allied bombing raid, and they didn't survive."

I feel sad for them, especially that they died without knowing the truth about their daughter.

"Did she say anything about Adalyn's sister? Chloe?"

"Yes. I found out I missed her, too. That summer of 1944, she met an Allied soldier and they fell in love. She disappeared to be with him."

So that's how the home became abandoned. Adalyn was killed by von Groth. . . . Maman and Papa slipped out of Paris with plans to come back at some point, only they never made it. . . . And Gram basically disowned her family, met a soldier—Gramps—and moved to America to start a new life with him. It all makes sense now. Except . . .

"Didn't Adalyn's parents wonder why their oldest daughter just disappeared?" I ask.

Luc chuckles wistfully. "The neighbor said something about Adalyn joining some school friends on a summer vacation," he recalls. "I knew it wasn't true. I suspect it was a lie

Adalyn told her parents in case something went wrong, and they believed her. She loved them. She wouldn't have wanted them to worry."

I take a second to absorb everything I've just learned. In my head, I run through everything I wanted to know about Adalyn and check off all the boxes, making sure nothing goes unanswered. It all adds up, but there's still one thing I want to ask Luc.

"Luc," I say as delicately as possible, "you said earlier that you felt like Adalyn's death was your fault. Why do you think that?"

He lets out a long, slow sigh and hangs his head. "Because the attack was my idea in the first place," Luc says miserably. "If I'd never brought it up, she would have lived."

"You don't know that," Corinne points out. "It could have happened some other way. She was doing dangerous work, Luc. You all were. You can't blame yourself for that."

"I do," he says, blowing his nose.

And then I have an idea. I unzip my backpack and dig past the photos and a sweatshirt, down to the very bottom, where I find the book. "I think you should read what she wrote the night before the attack," I say as I pull out Adalyn's diary.

The writing is too small for Luc to manage, so Paul reads it out loud to the group. I ask him to repeat the last line with extra emphasis: *Whatever happens, I sleep tonight knowing the risk will be worth it.*

"You see?" I say to Luc. "You're not responsible for anything. Adalyn knew the risk involved, *and she wanted to take it*. She said that whatever happened, it would be worth it."

Everyone chimes in with words of encouragement and pats Luc on the knee. I want him to accept the truth so badly. He's been carrying around this guilt with him for so long, and it doesn't have to be this way.

Luc asks, "May I hold it?"

He's pointing at the diary.

"Of course," I answer.

I hand it to him.

He holds it against his heart.

And finally, he smiles.

CHAPTER 20

Alice

"Mom! Dad!"

I burst through the door of the Airbnb with my hair flying in every direction, my backpack sliding off my shoulders, and at least one of my shoelaces untied.

After Paul and I exchanged information with our new friends and said our goodbyes, promising to speak again soon, I sprinted home so I could tell Mom and Dad everything I'd learned before they went to bed.

"Are you okay?" Dad asks from the couch, where he and Mom are watching some Netflix comedy special.

"Yes, yes, I'm fine. I'm great, actually." I drop my backpack on the floor and stand on the living room rug, in between my parents and the TV. "I have so much to tell you, I don't even know where to start."

"Breathe, Alice," Dad says.

I tie my hair up to let the heat off the back of my neck. Then I take a deep breath. "I know what happened to Gram's family. I know why the apartment ended up abandoned! And Gram's sister, Adalyn—you're not going to believe this. She was a spy for the French resistance!"

Mom is stone-faced. I know she doesn't like apartment talk, but there's no way I'm keeping this a secret. Dad fumbles for the remote so he can turn the volume down.

"Sorry, just a second," he says.

I can't wait. I'm talking at a mile a minute and I can't slow down. "I finally found somebody who knew Adalyn. He told me everything. Her story is incredible. She started off distributing these anti-Nazi flyers, and then she—"

"Hang on, I'm just going to pause this," Dad says. Why are they acting like I'm inconveniencing them with this information?

When the show has been paused, and Mom has spent a sufficient amount of time arranging the blanket over her lap, Dad motions for me to proceed. I realize, for everything to make sense, I need to start further back; I need to talk about all the research I did. All this time, they probably assumed that Paul and I were running all over Paris doing normal teenager things, not reading about life under the Nazi Occupation. So I tell them the full story, from finding the diary and learning about Gram's family fleeing Paris, and seeing the newspaper clipping that made me think Adalyn was a

Nazi sympathizer, to learning the truth about her relationship with Ulrich Becker III. Next, I launch into everything I just learned from Luc. I show them the photos from the Museum of National Resistance and name each one of Adalyn's friends. I tell them about the attack on the Gestapo and how it all went wrong. I go through every single detail, right up through the explanation of how the apartment essentially became a time capsule.

By the end of it, I'm wiping my fogged-up glasses on my T-shirt *again*, but my parents aren't having the same reaction. Mom has merely pulled the blanket up closer and closer to her chin, and Dad just looks tense, his eyes darting from me to Mom.

They're *really* not going to like what I have to say next.

". . . I've thought about it, and I don't want to list the apartment," I say at last. "I want to keep it. It's a part of my history—of *our* history."

Dad exhales through pursed lips. That's not a good sign.

"Alice, Mom and I appreciate all the research you've put into this," he says, even though he and Mom haven't said a word to each other. "That being said . . . all those things happened a long, long time ago, and I think there's value *now*, today, in the three of us moving on from this difficult period and starting fresh."

I open and close my mouth like a goldfish, searching for words, but finding none. I can't believe what I'm hearing.

Except no, maybe I can, because this is the way my family is. This is the way we've always been, for as long as I can remember. We don't deal with any of our actual problems. We just cover them up however we think is easiest. But look at Mom, hiding under a blanket right now. What we're doing isn't making anything easier.

"It's not going to work!" I shout. "We're not just going to be able to start fresh! How are we going to move forward if we have this big—this big—this *weight* tied to our ankles?"

"Alice, what are you talking about?" Dad asks impatiently. "What 'weight'?"

"I'M TALKING ABOUT MOM!"

Both of them look horrified. There's nothing but dead silence in the living room, followed by the sounds of laughter and applause coming from the TV.

"Sorry," Dad mumbles. "It does that if you leave it paused for thirty minutes. . . . Let me just pause it a—"

"WILL YOU JUST TURN IT OFF, DAD?"

He inhales sharply, then lets the air out through his nose. He presses the power button, and the light from the TV goes off. We're in the dark.

"Okay, Alice." He's pulling out his rarely used Don't Test Me voice. "What were you just saying about your mother?"

"I'm saying that, Mom, you're clearly not okay, and I don't think we're doing a good job at helping you!"

At that, Mom pulls the blanket up over her face, and we

can hear her whimpering underneath. Dad looks panicked. He throws his hands up in frustration. "Alice, this obviously isn't helping either!" he cries.

He wants me to give up. He wants to go back to our polite pretend-life. But I won't. I climb into the space between them on the couch and put my arm around the soft bundle that is Mom. I can feel her crying. Her body goes stiff for a moment, and I prepare for her to try and wriggle free, but then, to my surprise, she allows herself to melt into my side. The lump of her head comes to a rest on my shoulder.

"Mom," I ask gently, "can you hear me?"

The lump nods. Now is the time. As soon as we got home from that awful night at the seafood restaurant, I started doing research on how I should talk to Mom, since I didn't have any clue how to go about it. I typed in her symptoms— everything I could remember since I was little—and all of the websites came back with the same answer: depression. They completely explained Mom's dark phases; apparently, some people go years feeling fine and then suddenly experience symptoms again—sometimes randomly, and sometimes because of a specific situation. The death of a family member, for instance.

I read about how to talk to someone with depression, all the things you should and shouldn't say. The latter sections sounded a lot like me and Dad. This time, instead of writing a poem and stuffing it into a drawer, I wrote out a speech to say to Mom, and I've been practicing it in my head ever since.

I say it loud and clear so Dad can hear it, too:

"Mom, I love you so much, and I hate to see you in pain. I want to understand how you're feeling, and then I want to help you get through it. Whatever it is, it's normal. And I want you to know you're not alone . . . okay?"

Please let this get through to her. Mom's shoulders gradually stop shaking, and she pulls the blanket off her face. She tilts her head and looks at me with bloodshot eyes, and I mean *really* looks at me. She isn't inside her glass box anymore. For the first time in months, I see the Mom that I know.

She wipes her eyes.

"Okay," she says back.

My family's first language is small talk. It isn't easy to learn a new language when you've been speaking one way your whole life, but it's something we're working on. I'm over the moon that we're finally opening up to each other, even if it's hard to do. The only time I've regretted it, though, is right this very minute, in the back seat of the cramped rental car, as Dad bombards Paul with question after question through the rearview mirror.

"So I'm curious to know, how do you kids define your relationship? Are you 'official,' as they say these days?"

Oh my god. Can't we just go back to meaningless pleasantries? Ask him about sports or something! I wish I had an eject button to launch myself out of the car right now, except then I'd be stranded in a random French suburb in the middle of December, wearing a cocktail dress. Not ideal.

"Yes, Mr. Prewitt, we are official," Paul says with a laugh. He's been handling the conversation so well. "I feel very lucky to be Alice's boyfriend."

My god, this is mortifying. Very sweet, but mortifying. As I dig my nails into the leather, Mom peeks into the back seat and mouths, to both of us, *I'm so sorry.* Everyone but Dad dissolves into a fit of giggles, but pretty soon, even he's laughing, too.

In August, when we got home from Paris, I took the lead on signing us up for family therapy. On top of that, Mom started seeing a therapist of her own again. I say "again," because it came up in one of our sessions that when I was in the first grade, Mom attempted suicide. After all this time, I never knew, but it explained all the doctor's appointments and the time I spent at Gram's. For a while, she was getting help, but then she stopped going, because she was too ashamed— and she was feeling a lot better, anyway. Dad didn't press. He figured it was a one-off.

Whenever Mom's depression returned, Dad avoided talking about it because he didn't want to upset her more, and I took my cues from him. That's the way things stayed in our family. Until last summer, when Gram's death sent Mom into the worst bout of depression she'd had in a long time, and I realized we couldn't keep tiptoeing around the truth. Mom needed help. She still does. We all do.

Snow-covered trees whip past the window in a black-and-white blur. Every so often, there's a gap where you can see the icy Marne River running along the side of the highway. The last time we made the trip out here, Paul and I had no idea what we were going to find. This time around, I have a much better idea of what we're walking into. We talked about it with Ms. Richard for months, and this past week, we brought her some of the key items to put on display. Tonight, we're going to see the new exhibit for the first time.

Dad parks the car, and we follow the shoveled walkway to the front of the Musée de la Résistance Nationale in Champigny-sur-Marne. There's a sign on the door that says *"Fermé pour un événement privé."* "Closed for a private event." I signed up for French club this past semester, and I think I'm getting better.

We go inside.

Ms. Richard greets us in the lobby with a tray of champagne, which she sets down on the front desk. Then she hugs each of us one by one. "You're the first ones to arrive," she says. "Would you like to see it?"

"Yes please," we say in unison—even Mom.

We follow her through the empty halls to the spot in the museum where Pierre-Henri's photos are on display. They're still there, but now, they're just one part of a big display dedicated to Adalyn and her resistance group. The pages of

Adalyn's diary are reprinted and hung chronologically, along with photographs and other artifacts to show what was happening at the time. There's the picture of Adalyn surrounded by Nazis—one of whom, I now know, is Walther von Groth. When I discovered it back in June, the photo made me sick. Now I look at it and beam with pride.

Ms. Richard has done an incredible job putting this together—better than I ever could have imagined. At my request, she even agreed to put Gram's purple *zazou* dress on display. I'm not sure if I believe in an afterlife, but if there *is* one, I hope Gram and Adalyn are looking down and seeing they were on the same side all along.

As I stare at Gram's dress, Paul wanders over to my side. I take his hand, and we appreciate the relic together.

"I think she had a feeling," I say.

"Who?"

"Gram. I think a part of her always wondered about Adalyn. That's why she hung on to the apartment until the day she died but never said anything about it. She didn't want to go digging up the past, because it was too painful . . . but she didn't want to close the door completely, either. Just in case."

"I'm glad she never let go."

"Me too."

As we marvel at the exhibit, the guests start to trickle in. Vivi nearly bowls us over, followed by Theo, Claudette, and Lucie moving at a slightly more relaxed pace. Paul's parents, who I met the other night when they drove in from Lyon, arrive next; his mom presents me with a bouquet of flowers, and then the two of them get to talking to my parents. There's Eugene and his wife, Sylvie, and Ruben and his wife, Isabelle. Luc brings up the rear, sporting an off-kilter black beret and holding on to the crook of Corinne's arm for support.

Once he takes it all in, Luc simply says, *"C'est parfait."* It's perfect.

And sure enough, it's a perfect evening. When everyone's finished enjoying the exhibit, we move to an upstairs room for dinner overlooking the river. It's beautiful to see the golden lights snaking along the water's edge. During the meal, as everyone talks about Adalyn, I'm relieved to see that Luc seems to be at peace. He's quiet, and somewhat serious, but I think that might just be his personality. As we finish our desserts, Ms. Richard asks him if he'd be interested in becoming a periodic speaker at the museum. After a brief hesitation—and some encouragement from the rest of the table—he agrees.

Just when I thought things couldn't get any better, they do. Once the plates are all cleared, and some of the others are indulging in an after-dinner drink, I wander over to the window to get a better look at the lights along the Marne.

After a few seconds, a hand comes to rest on my lower back. It's Paul.

He kisses me on the cheek. "I have an early Christmas present for you," he says as he reaches into the breast pocket of his blazer.

I poke him playfully in the arm. "I thought we agreed we were just going to go out for dinner."

He pulls out a folded piece of paper and hands it to me. Opening it up, I find a printed copy of an email from New York University. Oh my god. My heart leaps.

"Paul, what is this?" I demand, even though I know exactly what it is. I'm just too excited to form coherent sentences.

"I got accepted to a visiting student program at NYU," he says, rubbing my back. "I will be there from January to May, with the option to extend it through the summer if I want."

"Oh my god. I'm so excited, I think I might cry."

Paul laughs, and pulls me in for a hug. I missed his smell, being away for so long. Relying on FaceTime these past few months has been manageable, but we still miss each other constantly. Starting next month, he'll only be an hour's car ride away—maybe less, depending on the traffic. We'll be able to see each other on the weekends.

With my head resting against his chest, we gaze out the window together. I'm probably getting ahead of myself, but maybe Paul could come stay with us over spring break. We can stay in separate rooms, if it would make Mom and Dad more comfortable.

I'll talk about it with them, because that's what we do now, or we're trying to. For years, we lingered on the bank of the river, scared to dip our toes in the water—but how do you cross to the other side that way? There's only one way to do it, and we've finally figured it out. We have to hold each other's hands and wade into the deep.

ACKNOWLEDGMENTS

A huge thank-you to all the people who worked on this book and supported me throughout the process:

My editor, Catherine Wallace, who waded into the deep with me to explore the murky waters between good and evil. You are brilliant, and it was a joy to bring this book to life with you.

My agent, Danielle Burby: I am lucky to have you as an agent, and even luckier to have you as a friend. Thank you for writing dates, *Bachelor* nights, and helping make my book dream come true.

The team at HarperCollins who produced, designed, and spread the word about this book: Renée Cafiero; Mark Rifkin; Jessie Gang; Shannon Cox; Aubrey Churchward; and Erin Wallace, I am so grateful for your hard work.

My parents, Lisa and David; my brother, Russell; and my in-laws, Carol, Bob, and Hilary. Your excitement and encouragement have meant everything to me. I love you!

Finally, my husband, Tim. My love. Thank you for exploring Paris with me; for your boundless knowledge of military history; for reading and listening to this book a thousand times; and for being by my side, always.

READ ON FOR A SNEAK PEEK OF

ONE

Eva, present day

I swear to god, sometimes the harder I try to do the right thing, the more spectacularly I end up failing. I was right on time for French, but when I get to the classroom and open the door, the desks are completely empty.

Time to pull out the trusty ol' schedule and see where I messed up—again. On Monday, I sat in the wrong room and gradually realized the teacher was speaking Spanish, not French, which I probably should have deduced earlier from the red-and-yellow flag tacked to the wall. When her back was turned, I seized the opportunity to stand up, whisper "*lo siento*" to my confused classmates, and tiptoe to the door.

Strangely enough, I seem to be in the right place. Maybe I'm just the first one here.

Oh, shoot.

It's Friday, which means there's an assembly in between first and second periods. I swing my open backpack onto my shoulder and run full speed down the hall, which is

1

empty—*obviously*. That should have been my first clue. Breath-less, I burst onto the quad, and to my relief, there's still a small crowd of navy-blue blazers shuffling up the steps of the auditorium next door. I join the back of the line all casually, as if sprinting is my go-to mode of transportation. I feel beads of sweat poking out beneath my thick, dark curls.

I'd love to snag a seat next to someone I can introduce myself to. Even as an outgoing person, it's been harder than expected to meet people. Well, let me clarify: I *technically* meet people all the time—group discussions in class; meals in the dining hall where I plop myself down in whatever open seat I can find; the line for the communal showers that inevitably stretches down the third-floor hallway in the half-hour before curfew—but it's hard to *actually* meet people. Like, in a "let's hang out and not talk about school stuff" way.

Most students at Hardwick are "lifers," meaning they start in the fifth grade and go all the way through; by eleventh grade, social groups are calcified like bone. Despite being the same Eva Storm who could strike up a conversation with literally anyone in New York City—a talent that came in handy when my friends and I had to get past bouncers at the college bars near NYU—I've felt more or less invisible since Mom and Caleb dropped me off here last weekend. At Tuesday's assembly, I sat down beside a girl from my English class who'd seemed kinda nice when we'd gotten into groups to read scenes from *Macbeth*. I said, "Howdy, 'tis me, Banquo"—my delivery was funny, I swear—and she said, "Sorry, do you mind going over there? I'm saving a spot for someone else."

Shocked at her dismissal, not to mention her failure to appreciate high comedy, I had to move across the aisle to a seat beside my math teacher, Mr. Richterman, who smelled like a blend of coffee and chalk and didn't seem to recognize me.

At the top of the stairs to the auditorium, an exasperated teacher in a no-nonsense pantsuit shouts at people to tighten their ties and fold down their collars. "Margot and Cassidy, *please* unroll your skirts," she calls to a pair of girls with their arms linked. They giggle and cry, "Sorry, Ms. Pell!" as their fingers fly to the fabric at their waists.

"You there, with the curls! Stop!"

Oh no. My foot is on the final step, and Ms. Pell's laser-beam gaze is pointed at me. The other boys and girls weave around me, rubbernecking like they're rolling by a car crash.

"You can't go in there dressed like that."

Is this a prank? Some kind of Hardwick initiation? I'm wearing the same black loafers, same white knee socks, and same gray kilt as every other girl who's walked through those doors. But then she reaches out, pinches the corner of my cardigan, and holds it up like the tail of a dead mouse.

"Friday is formal assembly," she snaps. "You need your blazer."

Ah. I figure this rule is printed somewhere in the student handbook I got on my first day, but there are a *lot* of rules at

Hardwick (like, sixty-something pages of them), and it isn't exactly easy to keep track of them all. I know the biggies—like the aggressive nine o'clock curfew every night except Saturday—but I'm hardly an expert in formal assembly regulations. Right now, my blazer is hanging off the chair in my dorm room, conveniently located on the opposite end of campus.

"I, um, don't suppose you'll take pity on the tragic new kid?" I venture. *You know, the only new student in the whole eleventh grade—the one whose mom and terrible stepdad sent her away to boarding school like a character in some depressing fairy tale.*

Ms. Pell's mouth forms a thin, wrinkled line. "I don't take pity on students for things they can control, such as remembering a mandatory clothing item. This is how we've done things for over a century, and I'm afraid you won't be the exception. You'll have to sit out on the steps today."

"But—"

"*Sit*, please."

There doesn't seem to be any other option, so I sit on the steps, facing the last few arrivals like a fool in a dunce cap. Finally, I hear the door shut, and I'm alone: one tiny speck on a quad surrounded by the ancient stone buildings of Hardwick Preparatory Academy. I picture my loneliness multiplying, like cell division. What I could really use right now, besides a blazer, is a friend.

Maybe my problem is that I just can't summon the Hardwick spirit that everyone else seems to have. You've got the eager beavers, who dash to the front row of every class; the student council members, who make enthusiastic announcements about upcoming social and charity events; the athletes, who strut around campus in their special team jackets; the ultra-rich kids, whose last names sound familiar during attendance because they're also the names of buildings around campus. They all have their own deep, meaningful connection to this place—not like where I used to go in Manhattan, where everyone had their own shit going on outside school. At Hardwick, it's like they're one big happy family, and I'm an intruder barging into the living room with mud on my shoes.

Well, wouldn't be the first time.

Okay, positive thoughts, please! I won't always be an outsider. I'll find someone to hang out with eventually—right? Like . . . uh . . . that redheaded girl in math class, maybe. Jenny something.

Jenny actually seems kind of promising.

I don't have anything to go on, really. It's just a hunch. But compared to the other people I've encountered in my first week at Hardwick, the girl with the pin-straight, waist-length red hair who sits behind me in math doesn't seem quite so—I don't know—*indoctrinated* by this historic boarding school of ours. The other day, as Mr. Richterman went on about the point of intersection of something or other, I was staring out the window directly beside my desk when I caught her gaze in the reflection of the glass. At first, I wasn't sure if she could see me too, but then she jerked her head in the direction of the whiteboard and rolled her eyes. The moment the bell rang, she gathered her things and marched out of class, but I'm certain we had a connection of some kind. Maybe I'll see if I can talk to her today.

When I walk into the room for third-period math, Jenny's sitting in the same seat as last time. I get a better chance to look at her now: pale porcelain skin; long, lanky limbs; fuchsia lipstick that clashes horribly with her hair, but somehow—maybe it's how she leans back confidently in her chair, arm resting on the windowsill—she makes it all look so cool. Even the blazer and kilt. She looks at me without any expression on her face.

"Hey," she says.

"Hey."

She acknowledged my existence. After a week of invisibility, it feels like a drug. I slide into the empty desk in front of her.

Mr. Richterman takes his position at the front of the room. His voice is dry and robotic, like he's been teaching this stuff since the school's founding in 1906. "Okay, class, let's start by reviewing quadratic equations . . ."

Across the room, two dozen mechanical pencils click into action. I try my best to follow along and take notes, but twenty minutes in, I'm having a hard time keeping my grip on the lecture.

Finally, Mr. Richterman puts down the chalk and wipes his fingers on a handkerchief he plucks from his breast pocket. "Now, for the next few minutes, I'd like you to break off into pairs and work through the questions on page forty-nine. If you finish early, feel free to test your knowledge with . . ."

There's already chatter brewing as people lay claim to their partners, so I twist around, ready to shoot my shot with Jenny. Sweet—she hasn't paired off with anyone. Better yet, she nods at me.

"You wanna do this, or what?" Her voice is deep. A little husky.

I drag my binder into my lap and flip my chair to face her desk. "Okay, but I feel like I should warn you: I haven't fully grasped anything math related since, like, *Sesame Street*."

She cocks her head and purses her fuchsia lips, like she's analyzing me. There's an awkward pause where I'm certain I just Banquo'd myself again.

Then she laughs—loudly. It's a full-on cackle.

"Quiet, please!" Mr. Richterman shouts.

Jenny downgrades to a giggle and leans over the desk. "Guess what?"

"What?"

"You could put a gun to my head, and I would not be able to confidently tell you what a parabola is."

We both snort and try to hold in our laughs, which is always next to impossible when you're not supposed to be laughing. Jenny and I do our best to focus on the math problems, but they're also next to impossible, so we end up playing tic-tac-toe in the margin of the textbook. She beats me in the first two rounds, but in the third, I draw a triumphant line through my three diagonal Os.

7

Putting down her pencil, Jenny abandons the game and peers out the window. "It's so nice out," she says longingly, twirling a lock of coppery hair around her finger. I didn't notice it before, but her nails are painted the palest of pinks, even though nail polish is expressly forbidden (according to a page of the student handbook I actually remember).

I follow her gaze out the window, down to the main quad, where two groundskeepers snip at a highly manicured garden. Inside the rectangular edges, yellow flowers are arranged on a green background to spell out "HPA," for Hardwick Preparatory Academy. A bronze plaque at the front notes which wealthy alum donated funds for such a thing. There are a *lot* of those plaques around Hardwick, dating from the early 1900s to now. Again: people really love it here.

"I wanna be *outside*," Jenny whispers. "Don't you?"

She stares at me with those huge gray eyes flecked with gold, a smirk playing on her lips. She isn't like the other people at Hardwick. She *sees* me. Maybe I'm not thinking straight, but her last question almost sounds like . . . a challenge. My heart thumps like I'm boarding a roller coaster.

"Okay, back to your desks so we can go through the answers as a class!" Mr. Richterman calls out.

Damn. I turn back to my desk, but my pulse still pounds as I consider my next move. I have an idea—something that worked one time at my old school, when my friends made a pact to skip class and go lie out in the sun on Randall's Island. But do I dare?

I find Jenny's reflection in the window.

8

She's looking right back me.

That's it. I'm doing it. I scribble three words in the corner of a piece of paper, tear it off, and crumple it into a ball. I flick the ball along the windowsill with just the right amount of force, so that it rolls to a stop near Jenny's shoulder.

Through the window, I watch her notice it. Then she looks at me. I give her a small nod. She grabs the ball of paper and unfolds it in her lap, reading my simple message:

COME WITH ME.

Once again, our eyes find each other's in the glass. Baby, we are *doing this!* The next part is up to me. I close my eyes and steel myself for pain. Three . . . Two . . . One . . .

Smack.

I fling my upper body onto my desk, letting my chair legs scrape against the floor for added effect. People gasp. Mr. Richterman stops talking, and everyone turns to the source of the noise. Slowly, I push myself up, blinking and looking around like I'm in a daze.

"Miss Storm, are you okay?"

I pretend to sway dangerously in my seat. "I-I don't know," I reply. "Low b-blood sugar, maybe . . ."

Mr. Richterman pinches the bridge of his nose and scans the room. "Can someone please accompany Miss Storm to the infirmary? I don't know if I want her walking there on her own in this state."

9

Yes. This is exactly what I was banking on—but will Jenny get the message?

Before anyone else can volunteer, her gravelly voice comes to the rescue. "I'll take her, Mr. Richterman."

"Thank you, Miss Price."

"It's no problem at all."

"All right. Off you two go."

The next thing I know, Jenny is helping me from my seat and shepherding my fake-stumbling body out the door. We keep up the act as we descend the wide wooden staircase and step outside onto the quad. I'm delirious with excitement that we pulled this off. Hopefully I don't *actually* faint now.

"This way," Jenny whispers, because we're still in earshot of classrooms with open windows. She turns sharply to the right, down a shady path that snakes behind the library. I follow her across an empty parking lot, because she seems to know what she's doing and where she's going. She leads me into the sprawling glen that surrounds the campus, home to a network of twisting trails that ramble for miles through the trees.

I'm no stranger to this part of campus: every morning, I've been sneaking out the back door of Ainsley House to go jogging through the woods. I'm actually a pretty strong runner; I did cross-country all throughout middle school, back when I still wanted to prove I was good at stuff. I was definitely one of the best on the team, but still, Mom and Caleb never came to my meets, which were often in Jersey or Connecticut. In high school, I gave it up—gave it all up, really. But running still makes me feel happy, especially this past week, when I've been stressed about not fitting in here.

When we're deep enough in the trees that I can't see any school through the gaps between trunks, Jenny finally speaks.

"Nice performance in there, lady. I'm impressed."

"Hey, you gave a nice performance, too. You seemed *very* concerned."

"But your final stumble into the door frame!" She mimes a chef's kiss. "Brava."

I laugh. "Why thank you."

"Seriously, you were so smooth."

"I tried my best."

Jenny tosses her hair over her shoulder, then takes off her blazer and ties it around her waist. For some reason, I'm hyper-aware of the way I'm walking, my body just behind her left shoulder. Should I stay in back and let her lead? Or should I move to her side, like we're friends? My solution is to stay at a perfect diagonal, tracking my position in relation to hers with every step.

"So. You're new, right?" Jenny asks bluntly.

Oh, great. I can feel myself deflating faster by the second. Do we really have to focus on what an outsider I am? "Yes, ma'am. How long have you been here?"

"I started last year," she says, "so I know what it's like. Everyone's friends already, and you're basically this invisible blob drifting around campus. Like, *Hello?! Does anybody want to talk to me?*"

11

Wait. Jenny was new last year? Jenny actually *gets it*? Oh my god, I want to hug her. "Yeah, that's exactly how I feel."

"You managing okay?"

"It's a little lonely." An understatement. "But I go for these long runs every morning to try and clear my head. That helps."

"Oh, cool. You're a runner?"

"Yeah. Just for fun. Not, like, marathons or anything."

"I *hate* working out. Did you try out for cross-country?"

"Nah—I didn't even know there had been tryouts until they emailed out the sports schedules the other day."

"Damn. Sorry, dude."

I shrug. "It's whatever." In reality, I'd been a little disappointed.

Jenny suddenly stops in the middle of the path, tilting up her face to catch a narrow ray of sunshine that somehow made it through the crisscrossing branches. "Hold up. The lighting here is really great." She pulls out her phone and opens the camera app with the fastest thumbs I've ever seen. "Just a quick pic. This might be feed-worthy." She slips her backpack off her shoulders and holds it out to me. "Do you mind?"

I take it from her immediately. "No. Of course not."

"Thanks." She shakes out her hair so it hangs all over the place—but in a cool way—and ever so slightly purses her lips. She takes about twenty rapid-fire selfies, swipes through them, and hearts a few. Others make her recoil in disgust.

"For Instagram?" I ask.

"Yeah. I'm getting five hundred bucks to post a photo with this lipstick on, so . . ."

"Whoa. Did I just witness you . . . *influencing?*"

"Oh my god, stop. That word is horrifying." But she smiles to herself as she puts her phone away, and we start walking again. She forgets to reclaim her backpack, and for some reason, I don't say anything. I just keep on carrying it.

"So, how did you end up here anyway?" Jenny asks.

Oh, good. A chance to revisit the memory of the night they told me I was enrolled—the four of us sitting around the table in our Upper West Side apartment eating takeout sushi. The way Mom leaned over and squeezed my shoulder with her polished talons, like she was telling me something good; that smug look on Caleb's face that made me want to hurl my dinner at him. When I found out my half sister Ella, who's in ninth grade, wasn't going to boarding school—it was just me, the *other* daughter, being sent away—I really *did* pick up a cucumber roll and throw it at Caleb's chest, which unfortunately only bolstered their argument that I needed a stricter academic environment.

But I give Jenny the sanitized version—the one that doesn't hurt as much: "My mom and her husband want me to get my grades up before college applications. I was kind of slacking off, I guess. But they didn't tell me I was going to Hardwick until, like, right before we left. So . . . surprise! I'm here."

"Jeez. That is *seriously* harsh."

"It wasn't amazing! How'd you end up here?"

"Well, I'm from Philly, but my parents bought this major brewery in Albany, so we moved up there. Hardwick's like two hours away, but it's by *far* the best private school upstate, so I was like, 'Yes. Let's do this.'"

"Ah. Less harsh."

"Yeah. Your story is rough, dude. And I take it you weren't at another boarding school before?"

"Nah, it was a small public school in Manhattan. It's, um, super weird having my *school* tell me when I need to be in bed with the lights out. I'm surprised they don't supervise teeth brushing."

Jenny laughs again. Every time it happens, I feel like Mario collecting coins in a Nintendo game. "Yeah, the curfew was hard to get used to," she admits. "And the Saturday classes—super rough." She pauses and then her voice changes. It's softer and sharper at the same time, like she's telling me a secret. "Eva, I know everything feels like absolute garbage right now. But I promise, Hardwick is a great place. And it gets better as soon as you find the right people to hang out with. Listen . . . I know we like, *just* met, but you seem really fucking cool."

Oh my god.

I was right.

Jenny and I were destined to be friends.